CJ Rivera

THE FINAL ORCHARD

ANGRY
ROBOT

ANGRY ROBOT
An imprint of Watkins Media Ltd

Unit 11, Shepperton House
89 Shepperton Road
London N1 3DF
UK

angryrobotbooks.com
twitter.com/angryrobotbooks
No Happily Ever After

An Angry Robot paperback original, 2024

Cover by Mark Ecob
Edited by Gemma Creffield and Dan Hanks
Set in Meridien

ISBN 978 1 91599 826 2
Ebook ISBN 978 1 91599 827 9

Printed and bound in the United Kingdom by CPI Group (UK) Ltd, Croydon CR0 4YY.

9 8 7 6 5 4 3 2 1

MIX
Paper | Supporting responsible forestry
FSC
www.fsc.org
FSC® C171272

To my dad, for every wild story that ignited my imagination.
To Amy, for always being there to spark new ideas.
To Jonathan and Ma, for your unwavering support.
And to my girls, for their endless inspiration.

Ever has it been that love knows not its own depth until the hour of separation.

— *Kahlil Gibran*, The Prophet

CHAPTER 1
RO

And it was there, inching towards the intersection of Third and Lake, that life as I knew it ended.

I was stuck behind an elderly driver, my hand on the car horn and my patience depleted, as the windshield projected an aggressive "LATE" reminder.

I had been trailing this woman for several single-lane blocks, and for someone in a state-of-the-art autonomous car, she was moving impossibly slowly. Either she refused to engage the self-drive mode or was too proud to admit she didn't know how. That tended to be the case with a lot of these "Second Lifers." Extended lifespans just meant they had more time to horde wealth and spend money on shiny status symbols that they couldn't engage with.

I caught a glimpse of her reflection in a storefront window on Main Street; she didn't look a day over 40, although most people didn't these days if they could afford it. Considering the sheer number of metallic casings she wore on her hands, forearms, neck and ears, she was most likely pushing 135. Of course, it was hard to know that for sure – Adornments were used to combat age or illness, as well as vanity. Sometimes all three.

This woman touted a glimmering gold-plated neck cuff engraved with floral vines growing towards a blossom of emerald jewels over her entire left ear. It was one of the most extravagant and ostentatious customizations on the market. Clearly it was safe to say her Adornments were elective, not essential. She had chosen to continue living way past her time, and to display that privilege lavishly. Just another entitled old lady worthy of my stewing resentment, which grew closer to boiling over with every flash of her brake lights.

I don't know what infuriated me more, her continued existence or the reality that my own parents never had the opportunity to live their full age potential. As they matured, their bodies grew weaker, less capable, frail. When physicians finally signed off on their Adornments for emergency medical intervention, our insurance company wouldn't cover the installation. What little my parents had was gained through hard work and sacrifice, crossing the Outlands and spending tireless years laboring in the factories of the Refinery Lands. All to build a better future for their family here in the Burg, aka the City of Burgeoning Industry. They spent their lives off grid, with no synthetic aid, to spare their children from crippling debt.

They never had the chance to fully enjoy the fruits of their labor and, worst of all, they never knew how it would all pay off. In mere moments, their daughter was going to pitch her life's work to the founders of NuBio Technologies.

It was a formality, really, given their open interest in my work with Rapid Maturity Gene Manipulation protocols. The process suggested that by splicing an RMG – specifically a reprogramed GATA6 protein, which plays an important role in organ development – into suggestible stem cells and up-regulating its expression, one could assign the cell's specialization and grow any tissue or organ in record speed, making it viable for transplant sooner.

Tissue could be generated from a single cell and was inexpensive to scale, making it an ideal therapy for the sick and elderly members of the underserved communities, largely ignored by Adornment providers. These products would level the playing field and give people a chance to perform to the utmost of their abilities and compete with the bionically enhanced Elites.

A fully organic alternative to Adornments. Organix.

It was going to be a game changer.

If I could get there in time for the meeting.

"Come on lady! Move it!" I shouted and slammed the horn a few more times. Why had I let her pass me two miles back? Being the better person was never worth it.

The bridge to Ingenuity Row was right across the intersection, opening up to two lanes as it extended over the lake. My windshield projection flashed another appointment reminder and started a five-minute countdown, while the console display silently mocked me with an advertisement for some newfangled Adornment. *"You, only better,"* the caption read as an ageless model caressed her platinum chest. *"Book your appointment today at BodyMOD."*

The commercial was followed by a short news bulletin of yet another protest from radical groups opposing Second-Lifers and their strain on remaining resources. I agreed with their message but knew better than to think that only protesting would change anything.

"You have the right of way!"

I thrust my head and arm as far out of my window as possible, hoping she'd spot my extended middle finger in her rearview mirror and take the hint. My face sizzled in the rising sunlight, there were only a couple of sun safe hours left to the morning. The woman's windows were retracted all the way up and I could hear her radio blasting.

"Another smog warning is in effect. Increasing temperatures and atmospheric conditions are expected to be favorable for producing high levels of ozone pollution in the Bridgewater, Bunker and surrounding areas this afternoon."

Was she deaf? Maybe if she hadn't engulfed her ears in jewels, she could hear the abrasive medley of her radio and the honking horns of the cars lined up behind her.

The woman didn't budge, and the other cars at the intersection ahead continued to pass.

"Move your damn car!"

"Mommy, what are you doing?"

The small voice from behind startled me. I had almost forgotten she was there. Rune had been quietly engrossed in her new Index since we got into the car. I was never one to buy the latest gadgets, especially not for a four-year-old, but it was secondhand, and we were on the precipice of immeasurable success. It was about time we celebrated our efforts.

After long nights spent in the lab, the hours focused on research rather than her, Rune never complained. She was my rock, my North Star. We were all we had, and I wanted her with me for the most important meeting of my life. I wanted her to see that hard work and determination breeds success. An Index wouldn't make up for the moments lost, but she deserved something for her patience.

Rune had been so excited unwrapping it. She pulled out the device the size of an adult index finger and rapidly unfolded it over and over into a seamless expanding screen. As it powered on with neon lights flying across the display, she looked up at me gleefully.

"Mommy!" she squealed with joy. "Now I'll be as smart as you."

She was already ten times brighter than I was at her age; she knew what she held in her hands wasn't just a game, but was access to all the indexed information the world had to offer. With all that knowledge at her fingertips, this kid would be unstoppable.

The car behind us honked its horn.

"What's going on?" Rune asked, pausing briefly from her exploration to look out the window.

"Nothing baby, just another Second-Lifer who can't drive."

I slid my head back into the car and the seat belt suddenly hugged me tightly into the chair. The safety sensor was severely overdue for repair, it was always deploying at the wrong times. I apprehensively checked my shirt hoping the freshly minted wrinkles didn't cause it to look as old as it actually was.

Could I drive around her instead? I craned to look over at each side of the woman's car; there were no pedestrians on the narrow sidewalk, it was entirely possible to pass her. In the rearview mirror I could see a few cars in the distance behind us attempting the same thing.

I carefully turned towards the right and for a moment considered hitting the back of her car, but decided the cost would far outweigh the satisfaction. I continued to drive up onto the sidewalk and slowly pulled around her, my car settling into a steep slant by the stop sign. Half of it was on a flat cement walkway, the other half was on a hill that led up to the corner building. I never did spring for those upgraded boosters; they would have come in handy now to level out my car.

"Mommy we're sliding," Rune assessed accurately.

"Mhmm."

As I approached the woman's passenger side, I arranged my face into the most disdainful look I could muster. From my elevated angle I could see the full interior of her car through its wide-open windows and it enraged me even more. The pure excess of it all! The rotating cushy white pod seats set in a chrome half-shell complimenting the car's sloping exterior, the retractable coffee table, and a six-foot console display extending the length of the dashboard for entertainment viewing pleasure. Ad-free, I noted. It was too much.

And there sat the owner, with full femoral and tibial Adornments down her legs, plated in gold to match the top half of her body. Airconditioning fanning her short platinum blonde curtain bangs. She was stoic, with both hands on the wheel, staring straight ahead, missing the full glory that was my look of absolute contempt.

I should spit on her car. But this new model car would self-clean and that would piss me off even more.

"Mommy, I dropped my Index! It slipped." Rune kicked the back of my seat. "Get it for me."

"Hang on, mommy's driving, I'll pick it up when we park."

I proceeded to gradually move forward towards the intersection, glaring at the driver of the car next to me.

"Mommy, please!" She kicked again, beginning to wind herself up.

"Just a minute," I said in a perky tone belied to the expression on my face.

"Mommy!"

If I had looked back at Rune, even just for a moment, then maybe I wouldn't have noticed the woman's eyes. Maybe I wouldn't have seen her petrified irises shifting furiously in every possible direction, as if locked inside her own head.

If I had only looked back, I wouldn't have glimpsed the woman's parted lips, frozen, and the indiscernible guttural noises surely coming from within.

If I had just looked back instead of staring bewildered at the woman's state, then maybe I would have seen the car coming up full speed behind us.

I didn't feel the crumpling metal as the car crashed into us; the shards of glass digging into my skin as the windows shattered; the crack of my skull when my head slammed against the door frame; the burns of the airbag as it pounded me into my seat. I didn't hear the squealing of tires; the honking horns of oncoming traffic. Or Rune's screams from the back seat.

We were suspended, all sense of direction simply vanished. We seemingly rotated in place, and all I could hear was the sound of that woman's radio.

"You can help decrease ozone pollution by sharing a ride, driving a covered transporter, taking your lunch to work, conserving energy,

and keeping your vehicle properly tuned. Thank you, this has been an Air Quality Alert."

Then we broke the surface of the lake. The weight of the car pulled us deeper into the water, the seat belts tugged us in tighter, bracing for impact.

CHAPTER 2
EVER

I am buried alive.

I inhale struggling to satiate my lungs, each breath shallower than that last. Is this how it ends?

Stay calm Ever, I command silently into the darkness as I float underground in my sterile glass box. They say anxiety is like a virus, it multiplies, infecting every cell, taking control until its host is fully incapacitated. If I give in to mine, I may never make it out of here.

I remind myself that I wanted to be placed in this coffin, that I needed to prove myself, and that he would finally see how special I really am. I volunteered for a second drawing. For another chance to sacrifice my body for the greater good. It's been nearly 16 years, and I will not be overlooked, not again, not this time. Tomorrow I'm getting out. Tomorrow, I begin.

I try to find serenity in absence.

In the melody of silence.

In the darkness.

In my lightness.

My breath billows out to coat the thick ceiling of glass each time I exhale. Tiny hairs rise to attention on my goose-pimpled arms, while the two thin slices of white cloth covering my chest and hips serve no purpose other than modesty. There is one glass panel positioned two inches above my head; another glass panel set just beneath my toes. Suffice it to say,

I've reached my limit with being cramped and confined. This would be the last time.

Absolute numbness is the only way to survive.

Don't think, I tell myself. Don't feel. Don't be disappointed.

Easier said than done. A person could go crazy down here waiting for the clock to run out. Time can't be trusted. It lengthens and constricts, breaking its own rules by our mere perception of it.

Most notably when there is something to look forward to.

My anxiety, a mixture of eagerness and trepidation, is rising and permeating through the container. My breathing speeds up, but I can't afford it to. What if I use up all the oxygen? What if it doesn't replenish quickly enough?

I begin to itch.

The soft circles I trace relieve the pinch of the needle, leaving white rings on my brown skin. The sudden motion and shift in venous pressure cause a surge of blood to rush up the attached tube. Blood is one of the most important contributions here in Helix Colony.

Contributions are not optional.

I take another controlled breath to settle myself, then clench my fists rapidly, increasing my output, and sending blood up through the needles and tubes tethered to me. The more I give, the more I should be rewarded. Blood slithers through catheters, feeding the glass walls of this vessel. Crimson pours down the inner surfaces of the overhead panels.

I watch, unsettled, as my own insides spill around me like an encapsulated waterfall.

The seconds creep by at their leisure. Despite all efforts, I find myself tracking every breath and counting every drum of my heart. I've been trapped in the Helix my entire life, and as much as I hate to admit it, I thought I would be used to captivity by now. The same routine. Days blurring into one another. Wake, eat, train, give – my energy, my devotion, my very essence – to the cause. All in the hope of proving myself worthy of liberation.

An icy sensation crawls up my spine and at once, my attempted concentration is pierced by a red light flooding my periphery. It forms a thin graphic line that extends towards the center of my vision, shooting upward then sharply downward and back up again in rapid motion to the rhythm of my elevating heart rate. It's the vitals tracer in my Bright-i lenses. Scratching the injection site must have accidentally triggered the application. When I move my hand back, blue text blinks in the lower left quadrant of my vision.

06:47:00. It's early morning.

I like to imagine that it's springtime on the Surface. The sun is just peeking its head over the blankets of horizon, stretching out its soft amber arms. Enveloping a drowsy earth, sweat dewed on its grass lashes.

I saw that image in a book once, before they became contraband. They say that world doesn't exist anymore, that the sunlight was replaced by shadows long ago.

A slight twinge in my shoulder reminds me disconcertingly of my confinement. The air is thinning, or am I imagining it? I'm beginning to feel dizzy, and my hollow stomach berates me with deep growls and protests. I have to shift all my focus towards staying conscious. The little drive I have left is quickly slipping away, as if being drawn and collected in the series of tubes penetrating my container.

What if it's gone too far this time? What if I can't sustain another blood drawing? My heart is now rocketing in my chest, panicked, and the glass panels seem to be inching inward.

It's all in my head.

I wanted this; there is no room or time for silly fears.

I touch the palm of my hand to the glass panel alongside me; its frigid surface shocks my mind into increased clarity. I look out at the row of glass coffins beside me; there are twelve of us, each levitating in the magnetic field of darkness, barely illuminated by a dim exam light. The other Subjects look so calm, so confident in the process.

They told us we are all special. We are the future. We will save the species. They are our Keepers, protectors of Helix Colony, and our shepherds to the Surface.

I can hear the blood pounding in my ears and pulsing in my neck. Blood that is so crucial for the welfare and survival of those on the Surface. I'm acutely aware of the frothing sound it makes as it rushes between the glass panels, yellow plasma separating from the deeper red and spiraling through catheters. My head is foggy, and an involuntary swallow quickly turns into painful lock jaw. I realize I can't breathe. Am I running out of air?

My arm jerks without my permission, followed by another twitch in my neck. I panic again and try to reach for the ports in my arms, but I'm no longer in control of my body. My chin juts upward and my head spasms. A previously subdued and rhythmic audio tone now rises erratically from the vitals tracer.

Between convulsions I force my eyes towards my feet, and through sheets of blood sliding down the glass panel I see her. Behind the rows of white coats taking notes in the gallery across from us stands Sio, my Keeper, wearing a foreign expression I can't quite place, mouthing words I can't quite grasp.

A single high-pitched note rings out as vials continue collecting blood. I slip into darkness, grasping the message written in the lines of her face.

Fear.

CHAPTER 3
RO

There was only nothingness, a void, and I was swimming in it. Not a single particle of light, no smell, no sensation of feeling. How long had it been? Was I sinking deeper? Or was I ascending? There was no sound to guide my senses, save for a distant ring trudging through the dense air to reach me.

At first, I wasn't sure if I even heard it at all, just a brief hiss in my ear that steadily grew louder, swelling as it approached. Unrelenting, until it became a sharp pounding behind my brows, forcing my eyes open. At once my vision was flooded with a painful red light, hot, nearly scorching my pupils, and I gasped as if breathing for the very first time.

"Rune!" I shouted into the red, my voice cracking. "Rune baby, where are you?!"

My vision seemed unable to adjust to the light, the heat had dissipated but I still couldn't see. Immersed in a thick impenetrable red glow, something heavy weighed me down. This must be what it's like inside a womb. Did we not make it? Was this reincarnation? If so, why rather than peace and calm, was I feeling a terrible sense of dread?

"Rune!" I continued to shout, panicked and trying to refrain from sobbing. I didn't want to scare her; she must have already been terrified. I needed to convey strength and fearlessness in the face of not knowing where the hell we were.

"Rune, please say something and Mommy will find you!" My voice didn't echo like I expected it to in the vast redness, but rather bounced off seemingly nearby walls, returning in a muffled state. Wherever *here* was, it was small, which meant Rune was near, most likely too shaken up to speak.

"Don't be scared baby, I'm coming to get you," I said, unsure how to follow through.

I tried shifting my shoulders, kicking out my legs and arms, twisting my neck, but to my horror, I couldn't move, it was as if I was restrained. No response came from Rune.

"We're gonna be okay, just hang on," I said, hoping to reassure us both, but the familiar fingers of panic encircled my throat. I was utterly helpless. I couldn't move, I couldn't see, I couldn't find my daughter.

"Help! Somebody, please help!" I shouted. It was the only thing I could do. I was at the mercy of anyone who could hear me, if anyone was even there. I shouted and sobbed and called out for Rune until my throat was raw, but I remained alone.

The moment I accepted there was nobody coming, that I was doomed to limbo, the red world around me peeled away. Someone yanked my head backwards, pulling an LED sleeve off my head. I recognized it immediately – I had seen similar cranial sleeves, albeit low budget versions, used on research patients of colleagues. They were portable computed tomography (CT) scanners which produced images of cross sections of organs, bones, and tissues. Newer models had an added light emitting functionality, red light that targeted the body's main structural protein and collagen, to support healing. It also served to recharge the mitochondria in the eyes to improve vision.

How bad a shape was I in?

"Sorry for the wait Dr. Arata," said a male nurse wearing red scrubs.

This must be a corporate-owned facility – a standard hospital color-coding system would never assign such an alarming and disquieting color to their staff. He was probably an imaging specialist, which would make sense considering the CT scanning sleeve.

"You sustained serious injuries, we wanted to ensure full and accurate head scans were completed," he continued.

The stark overhead fluorescent lights washed out my vision slightly, but I could see that the room was small with a large screen the length of the wall in front of me. In one quadrant I could see what I assumed was a live feed of my doctor in her office. She wasn't engaging with me, so I figured she was observing multiple other patient feeds on her end.

Extending from the top to bottom left of the screen was a life-sized outline of my body with areas highlighted in various colors. Shades of orange filled the head, bright red filled one leg, and hues of yellows, greens, and blues filled out the rest. Wave forms and other units of measurement populated the remaining areas of the screen, continuously moving and updating as if alive themselves.

To my right was a floor-to-ceiling window, in tinted mode to keep out the sweltering sunlight. I assumed it was late afternoon – the fever hours. Most people would be indoors in sun-safety lockdown now. I could see the tops of buildings nearby, wavy from the heat, so I knew we were high up. In the distance, trees encircled bone white buildings with bifurcating bottoms that made the structures look like they were melting into the ground from the heat, while creating wide welcoming entrances for its luxury occupants. Spanning the plaza, vegetation grew up the sides of a sprawling complex in the Financial District. The vertical gardens were an eleventh-hour attempt to combat the effects of greed-induced environmental degradation. Across the way was the bridge to Ingenuity Row. We never made it over.

Rune.

I snapped my neck to the left, but there was no other bed in the recovery room.

"My daughter! Where's my daughter?" I shouted. "She's only four, she was in the car with me, where is she?!"

The nurse waved and a supply cart rolled across the room to his side.

"It's okay Dr. Arata, you just need to relax and stay still." He pulled open a small drawer within the cart.

Without answering my question, he placed a vial of silver liquid, followed by a clear vial, cotton swab, and syringe on top of the cart. Then he reached over to fold down the blanket covering my body, revealing what had been holding me in place.

A mesh body cast encased me from the shoulders down. The woven material was the color and rigidity of bone; peeking out through the gaps was my severely bruised red and purple skin. The sight reminded my brain of just how much pain I was in, and a heat began to reverberate throughout my body.

The nurse slid a needle through one of the holes in the mesh and plunged the contents of the vial into my right shoulder.

"You need to stay still," he said in an irritatingly calm tone. "Your chest and legs were crushed in the accident; you must allow the nanites to do their job." He said it as if the knowledge that tiny robots coursing through my veins and repairing damaged cells would put me at ease, when all it did was increase my agitation.

"Please, just tell me, is she okay? Where is she?"

Ignoring me, he moved down towards my legs still covered by the blanket and folded it upward creating a pile above my knees.

"Is she in surgery? When can I see her?" I pleaded. "She must be so scared. Please just let me out of this thing."

He peeked his head over the blanket pile, giving a look that meant there was no way I was getting out of here, then went back to tinkering with my legs. I thrashed against the mesh cast, which proved to be more of a cage than a stabilizing mold.

"Why aren't you listening to me? I need to see her and make sure she's okay. Afterwards, I'll cooperate."

"I'm afraid we can't do that at the moment," he said, removing the blanket from my thighs. The mesh body cast continued down my legs, but just below my right knee, instead of the cast was a long chrome casing extending to my ankle. "The Adornment is still adhering. Your tibia was fractured in multiple places. Repair was not viable; installation of a full tibial synthetic was required for you to maintain mobility."

I was one of them now – the enhanced. No longer pure, not organic. No longer my parents' daughter.

"I did not consent to the procedure, or to any further procedures. Get me out of here now and take me to Rune."

He approached the supply cart and removed the cap from a clear liquid-filled vial.

"We cannot allow you to injure yourself, not while in our care. You have a lot of promising work ahead of you," he said with a smile that sent chills down my spine.

How would he know that? Who was funding this Adornment?

"Let me out, I do not consent!" I screamed, hoping the doctor watching my feed would intervene, but she just looked on unfazed as the nurse approached and the pain of my injuries began to echo throughout my body.

"I do not consent!"

Pain was washing over me in waves now, but I continued to fight against the cast as he pressed the needle to my neck.

"This is for your own safety, and it will help with the discomfort."

"Stop!"

Then looked at me with unfeeling eyes. "The girl... I'm sorry, but she didn't make it."

The flood of excruciating pain crested over me; every inch of my body and soul felt as if it was being stabbed simultaneously.

He injected, and then at once, it was all gone.

CHAPTER 4
EVER

Ever.

Someone is calling my name.

"Ever." The voice is deep, familiar, and close.

Right above me. Hushed, demanding.

"Vee, wake up."

Through two blurry slits, I see Reed, his broad shoulders hunched. He heaves a sigh as he leans into my face, stormy gray eyes studying me. His strong dark brows furrow as he tucks a hand under my neck. Reed is only a few weeks older than I am but is nearly twice my size. If I didn't hate him, I might find him somewhat attractive, rugged, with eyes full of surprises.

"Hey, ugly," he smiles. The scar from his cleft lip revision curls up slightly and tugs at his nose.

I frown as he shoots a quick glance over his shoulder. I am floating upward, slowly and gently, I realize that it's Reed, raising my head, neck, and torso to fluff a pillow underneath me on the bed in the MedLab.

How unusually kind of him. I must be dreaming. I try to shake the soreness from my upper body, and the sting from my bitten tongue.

There is a shuffle of movement at the other end of the room, just beyond Reed's shoulder. Vada, one of the younger Keepers, appears to be annotating her holo-projection over a supply cart. Beams of light emanating from a small rectangular device create a wide display in front of her. She glides a few fingers across the air and then rapidly extends the tips of those fingers in succession, leaving bright dots in their wake. Vada's short platinum blonde hair rests on her shoulders in a sharp line, heightening the angles of her gaunt face. Despite her severe appearance she is one of the kinder Keepers, mainly because she keeps her distance.

Rumor has it she was rescued from the Surface, just as we Subjects were. But unlike us she was a child with no abilities, already scarred by war. She was found emaciated and left for dead in a remote ditch on the Surface. Her family had been murdered by the Forms. If it wasn't for His Grace, the Chairman himself, she would have perished. After witnessing the annihilation of her entire village, she spent days crouched in the dirt, waiting for death, until the Chairman discovered her and pulled her from the rubble.

He brought her back to his underground sanctuary, the impenetrable labyrinth of titanium walls we call the Helix. He nursed her back to health and although she wasn't genetically special, and had no valuable skills, she was still human. One of *Us*. She deserved a fighting chance. In his infinite generosity, he extended resources to provide her with training and gave her a post and a life here.

I figure that she's just so grateful to be here, to be alive, that she's less strict, more willing to let things slide and look the other way. But some Subjects think she doesn't engage because she's afraid of us, of what we can do. I'm not sure either way.

What is she doing here in the MedLab? I'm certain my own Keeper wouldn't willingly give up an opportunity to document my failures.

Reed leans back, apparently done fussing with my pillow. I see through the ruse now; he's acting solicitous and considerate for Vada's benefit. Performing the role of the model MedLab tech.

"What's going on?" I manage to groan.

"You gave us quite a scare there," he says with irritating condescension. "It appears the sudden and rapid spike in blood loss sent your body into a seizure. Your levels were already low, and your body couldn't handle it. We had to reverse the filtration and give you a pint back."

Weak. I chide myself for losing control against my eagerness; I gave too much of myself too rapidly by taking on another drawing. It was meant to give me a slight edge over the competition, but now it could backfire. Blood is a critical contribution to the troops on the Surface. To miss a pledged blood quota represents a *non-fulfillment*, a failure, and not just a personal one. A failure to support the cause. It lowers a Subject's rankings, hurting the chances of being chosen to ascend and join the Saviors in the recolonization efforts.

Every few months, one of the luckiest among us, a top performing Subject who has proven their value and obedient devotion to Helix Colony, is chosen to join the Saviors and aid in the fight against the Forms for the Surface. It's a step towards freedom for the species, and a step towards our own freedom from the underground. I want more than anything for that to be me. It is my time.

But the additional blood drawing was a mistake.

As if reading my mind Reed says, "That was a stupid move. What did you think would happen?"

He pulls my arm towards him and proceeds to replace my IV before taking a seat next to the bed.

"I obviously didn't plan on a seizure," I strain. "Besides, everyone gets a little crazy before a Selection. I needed to solidify my position."

"Yeah, you went all-out didn't you?"

I cut my eyes at him, then slowly prop myself up on an elbow. The bed sheet slides down a bit and I yank the sheets upward trying to cover my body from Reed's view when I notice someone has taken the time to dress me. I'm wearing the usual Subject uniform, a sterile white tank and white drawstring pants. Heat rushes to my cheeks as I realize Reed had most likely completed the task himself.

"Don't flatter yourself," he says. "I've seen better."

"Oh yeah, who? This is what genetically pure looks like. I'm perfect."

"Can't be too sure about that. You're flawed, just like me. Only your flaws are on the inside." He winks at me, and I want to punch him. He's not just teasing me, there's an underlying threat in his comments.

Now sitting up, I tap my wrist and blink three times in rapid succession to call up the current Subject rankings to my field of view. But all I see is an error message requesting a system refresh. My Bright-i must have timed out when my heart rate took a dive; the enhanced corneal implants rely heavily on the body's own internal energy as a power source. Visual analytics are a huge part of our training. We rely on the lenses for so much of our information processing required on a daily basis, from our own internal biometrics to AI simulations and communication.

"How long was I offline?" I asked.

"A few hours."

Crap. I'm not only behind on my blood quota but now I'm low on my power share as well. The rest of the Subjects had certainly generated several hundred watts while I was out. Kinetics is another way we contribute to the infrastructure of Helix. For several hours a day, we pedal, we run, and we kick to generate the energy that powers this place. The more a Subject generates, the higher their ranking. Being this close to a Selection Ceremony, everyone is putting in overtime. My hold on first position is looking more and more tenuous.

Could I contribute more hair? I reach up and massage my closely cropped waves. Not enough.

"You definitely wouldn't be my pick to join the Saviors," Reed says.

I shoot him a dirty look, but he continues with a smirk. "You clearly don't have the stamina. You'd jeopardize the team and what's left of our species. We can't have that."

That stings. Not because I believe him, but because he sounds just like her, and he knows exactly how I feel about Sio. Sio is my personal Keeper. She monitors my every move and never lets a damn thing slide. She created this place, hand-in-hand with the Chairman, back when it all started. Although, I guess it would be more accurate to say when it all ended. Sio developed the ReGeneration Program and trained the other Keepers to enforce a strict observation regiment *"For the protection and safety of the new generation."*

Striking a fellow Subject is frowned upon, but Vada is updating my intake form and is too preoccupied with her recordings to engage with us. I close my hand into a fist, making sure to jut out my knuckle so it hurts, and punch Reed hard in the bicep. The cabinets behind him shake with the impact. I pull back my fist and see the indent my knuckle left in his arm, along with his bodily impression in the backrest of the chair behind him as he leans forward and cocks his head. He just smiles at me with pity as though he truly believes that I am weak, which further infuriates me. Although I have enhanced strength, he has heightened insensitivity coupled with rapid healing. It's a dance we've done since we were kids, and it never fails to irk me.

"It's a good thing Selections aren't up to you," I say. "Take a long hard look, because after today you'll never see me again."

The moment the words leave my lips, I feel a slight twinge of regret in the pit of my stomach for saying them. But when Reed nonchalantly reclines in his chair, extending his long legs and lifting his feet to my mattress, painfully tugging on my IV, I yelp and glare at him.

When we were kids, it was always me and Reed against the world. We had such grand plans for our future and spent more nights together than I can remember, hiding out past curfew in the Utility Room. More accurately referred to as the Disutility Room, where all items that had outgrown their usefulness were tossed. I guess our friendship was fated for the same.

We would spend hours dreaming up Surface missions with the Saviors, and in every foray, we successfully defeated an enemy skilled in body infiltration, exterminating the Forms from our lands, saving the world. But life is not that simple, and I sometimes find myself feeling embarrassed looking back at the delusions of our childhood.

Reed is my oldest friend, one of the first. Despite his physique and top ranks, he has never been selected to ascend. We've never really talked about it, but deep down we both know he will never leave Helix Colony.

Reed is a Flawed Subject, and there is zero tolerance for any impurity on the Surface. *"Perfection is Paramount."* The Keepers worry any defect could manifest itself in other ways, making the Flawed susceptible to being taken over by the Forms. The Chairman is extremely careful not to allow flawed characteristics into the remaining gene pool. An undeniably harsh fate for Reed who has such a minor physical variation, but who am I to question the Chairman?

As a Flawed, Reed had been assigned to a laborer position months earlier along with the other Flawed Subjects in our age group. That's when he ended our friendship. All his friendships, in fact. I think he secretly held out hope that he might still make the cut and rise to the Surface if he worked hard enough. Instead, he was placed on medical detail, which is a far better position than becoming a full-time Pedaler or a member of Security, who were sent to work on upper floors, never to be seen again. But he didn't see it that way. His mission from his first assignment onward would be to ensure the health and well-being of those preparing for above ground conditions.

Reed, rather than rise to the occasion and realize what a privilege it is to contribute to the cause in such an involved way, has decided to be an asshole. He acts as if it's his job to make everyone around him feel as miserable as he does, including his former best friend.

Although I clearly have not yet been selected to surface either – one could say I am prone to non-fulfillments – tomorrow is my birthday, I am turning 16, making me the eldest remaining genetically pure Subject, and automatically beefing up my position in the hierarchy. I have undergone the most training and testing, and I am biologically flawless, therefore I am the most resilient and equipped to survive on the Surface.

"You ever think that maybe you're just not Savior material?" Reed's voice pulls me out of my reverie. I am *not* in the mood for this.

"With your track record of screw ups throughout the years, you're not exactly a desirable new member. The Saviors are legendary. They are mighty champions of humanity, resilient, ruthless, and not to mention obedient. That's not you. I think it'd be best for everyone if you just admit that to yourself and sit back while someone better equipped for the role is selected."

Vada's ears perk up, but she says nothing and continues to document away.

"So, what, I'm just supposed to stay down here with you, is that it?" I scoff. "Spend my entire life underground? We were meant for this, Reed. It's my birthright. It's only a matter of time. The only reason I haven't crossed over yet is because Sio has it out for me."

"Disobedience is insubordination," Sio always says, which is a touch dramatic. At the mention of her name, I suddenly remember the odd look on her face in the gallery. In my stupor, I took it for an expression of fear, but that couldn't be. Sio would never show a sign of emotion, not alarm, nor joy. That impression might seem harsh, but it's widely known that I am the most unfortunate Subject to have her assigned as my Keeper.

No, there was no fear in her face; more likely, it was scorn.

With some effort I lift my legs from under the thin covers and let them hang over the edge of the bed, my toes tingle alive with feeling. Vada finally collapses the projection with a pinch of her fingers and folds up her Index from which the holo-projection emanated, tucking it into the pocket of her white coat.

"How are you feeling Subject 1123X?" she asks timidly as she walks over to us.

I hate when Keepers use our identification codes. Vada is notorious for avoiding calling us by our names.

There is only one right answer to her prompt, and I give it.

"Eager to serve."

Seemingly satisfied, Vada tilts her head almost imperceptibly at Reed and exits the MedLab. The moment the door shuts Reed's demeanor changes. The playfully smug look creases in the corners of his eyes and flattens out. There is no hint of a smile on his face now. Abruptly, he pulls his feet off the bed and sits up.

"Listen," he says quietly, then scans the room as if to make sure we're really alone. "I've been hearing whispers from the Keepers during sweeps. Something is happening on the Surface."

"Yeah, we're at war."

He gives me a wounded look. "Ev, seriously, people are panicking, I think the tides are turning. Something big is coming and we might not be ready for it."

I can't tell if he is genuinely worried or just trying to get in my head to sabotage me, but I'm not a coward.

"You're right, Reed. Down here, Level 23 may not be ready for what's coming, but the Saviors are, and I will be one of them. They will prevail, they're equipped to handle anything. The Chairman has made sure of that, and he chooses only those who can take it. Do you question his infinite wisdom?"

"What if he's wrong? What if this is bigger than the Saviors?"

I try to mask my disgust for his blasphemy. "If that's true then our help is needed more than ever, and like hell I'm going to sit here and hide out."

I try to stand but nearly fall backwards from lightheadedness. In an instant, Reed is by my side, his hand gripping my arm a little too tightly. I'm taken aback by the unfamiliar sensation in my gut that his proximity brings.

"I'm serious, there's something strange going on." Something in his voice tells me he actually believes this. "You can't leave. Trust me. It's not safe."

My own anger burns hotter. *Trust him?* That's laughable, how does he expect me to trust him? "War is never safe. We need to take back what's ours."

I pull my arm away, yank out my IV – o*uch* – and make my way towards the door.

"I know about your dream."

I stop, afraid the moment has come when he would finally use it against me. My most vulnerable truth, proof I may not be so different from him – flawed. Dreams are manifestations of unstable minds.

"I know what you think you saw. I know you secretly hope you'll find your remaining family up there, and that you'll start a brand-new deliriously happy life together, and that *he's* waiting for you." He emphasizes the last statement bitterly. "But that world doesn't exist. We're fighting a losing battle, and you're naïve if you think otherwise."

I whirl on him. "Don't pretend to know what I want, Reed. You lost that privilege a long time ago. You don't know me. Not anymore. And you're weak for even suggesting I hide out here and not help our people. We're supposed to save the world, that's our purpose. We're heroes. Why don't you start acting like one?"

With that, I turn and leave. I almost expect him to follow, but cowards never do.

CHAPTER 5
EVER

A transporter is parked outside of the MedLab, a common provision for discharged patients.

As I climb on, the transporter revs to life; its electric motor fully charged. There are no gas-powered vehicles here on Level 23. Carbon monoxide poisoning alone is enough of a deterrent, and of course the possibility of an uncontained explosion burning this entire place further into the ground. I hike my legs up over the foot pegs and pray the halls are clear on the way to my dormitory capsule.

I look down and let the reader on the handlebars scan my Bright-i. Immediately, coordinates appear on the small display. I kick back and let the transporter take me for a ride. I have at least a few minutes to be lost in thought since the MedLab is at the opposite end.

I pass the continuously updating wall-length screens projecting pre-approved messages. *To Serve Is One's Destiny Fulfilled* and *Victory is Vital*. The face of a tanned man with brilliant white hair coiffed to perfection greets me in one corridor. He is wearing all black and is suited up to the jaw. His arms and hands are fully concealed and crossed over his chest. His image follows me down the hall, tracking the movements of my transporter.

It is His Grace, the Chairman, though his image is digitally altered and obscured – only the chosen few have the privilege of experiencing his true presence. Through the distortion, I imagine pronounced cheekbones, strong brows, and dark eyes staring back at me as I continue onward, his expression stern yet welcoming.

For Humanity's Sake. It is your duty and honor to serve, materializes across the wall in neon blue letters next to the Chairman. As soon as his image fades, new text spells out reminders of the upcoming Selection Ceremony:

It is not too late to improve your ranking and join the Saviors! Pedal an extra hour today, generate more power and elevate your status. The bright red letters appear over a montage of current members of the team, nine generals flanked by their soldiers, each smiling at me in their power poses and tactical combat gear.

I barely give them a look, trying to avoid comparison and any potential hits to my now fragile confidence. Through the next corridor, my presence activates more rows of vivid, colorful messaging; I've seen them a million times: *Routine Rules; Nothing to Hide, Nothing to Fear; Report Suspicious Activity to your Keeper...* My thoughts go back to Reed and his uncharacteristic shift in attitude. He wasn't known for being fearful, it's like something in him changed after his reassignment. Could something have happened to him? I can't shake the feeling that there's more to it.

At the next intersection I see two younger Subjects engrossed in some sort of giggle fest. It's Del, a small and slender boy with gorgeous, thick, curly hair, and a lanky taller girl with equally unruly coils – his twin sister Skye. They'll both need to shave their heads before Selections.

In my presence, they immediately distance themselves. Unregulated fraternizing isn't exactly condoned amongst Subjects, even between siblings. Relationships of any kind are distractions. Those that do exist are kept secret until off-peak hours. I slow down as they pass, pretending not to have noticed their bantering. Before she's out of sight, I give Skye a little wink.

"She's so lucky," Skye whispers in a squeaky voice now behind me. "I can't wait to turn 16 and surface."

I hang on to the word "lucky" and hope she's right.

Up ahead the titanium walls give way to glass, providing a view of overzealous Subjects pulling extra sessions in the gymnasium. One Flawed Subject works the check-in desk where a small line has formed, while the Keeper behind him updates the leaderboard on the wall. My number is barely holding up in first position. Age only offers so much cushion. There are forty-seven other hungry Subjects eager to edge me out. I can't do anything else to jeopardize my standing.

Out on the rubberized flooring KinetiBikes are in full use while sweaty cyclists fixate unblinking eyes on Bright-i streams. Behind them, rows of Subjects run on never-ending strips; the filaments attached to their arms and legs spark at the constant motion, creating a glow that gives the illusion they are running inside iridescent wheels. And even further in the back is the floating zero gravity lap pool, full of swimmers' fins glowing with every thrust of their feet.

As I pass the gym, the projection on the next wall instantly pulls a lump to my throat. It's not just a projection of any Savior but a large and extremely close-up photo of a smiling Ira spread across the wall. His bright white teeth are the size of my head, and a perpetual wind fans his uniform. *2123XY: Top Ranking Soldier of the Resistance.*

There Ira stands, staring back at me, a former Subject of Helix, and dare I confess, the one who holds my heart. He had been selected to rise to the Surface last year. *Exceptionally Meritorious Service in Combat, Enabling Mission Success and Ensuring Proper Recovery.* The Chairman likes keeping us up to date on the progress of current Saviors. It's motivational and supposed to give us something to strive for. As if the prospect of experiencing the open air, learning where we come from and saving the world isn't enough.

I accelerate the transporter and watch his face fade away.

I will see you soon, Ira.

I turn the corner and am stunned to see Sio standing stiffly next to my capsule door, awaiting my arrival. I approach cautiously.

"You didn't think you would get off that easy, did you Subject?"

An uneasiness rises in my chest. I don't speak, it would be far worse to volunteer information she might not already have and dig myself into a deeper mess. Less talk is always better.

She looks at me flatly, her taut bun pulling at her forehead with such force I can see the veins crawling on her temples.

I slowly step down from the transporter. "My sincerest apologies, Keeper Sio, I'm not sure what you mean."

"Your lack of self-awareness never ceases to disappoint." She raises her hand and swipes the air between us. "I am docking you two points for your non-fulfillment this morning."

My heart sinks. "But it wasn't intentional, I couldn't control it."

"That's unacceptable. Only *you* are in control of your body. If you can't listen to your own needs what good will you be on the Surface? If you lose control, the Forms will take it."

"I was trying to provide more to the cause. You know, *'eager to serve'* and all."

That was the wrong thing to say.

"That's two more points Subject."

"No, I'm sorry, I just meant I thought a little sacrifice would be worth it for the greater good."

"The greater good comes from looking out for yourself first. Have you not learned yet? Your body is indispensable, you must be at your best if we are to prevail."

I try not to roll my eyes, sick of the repetitive mantras.

"It will not happen again," I say.

Sio steps aside, signaling the penalty distribution is over.

I hold my face up to the door scanner, a series of neon lines reflect in the sensor as it registers me, and the door opens with a hiss of air. I step in and a red light begins to scan my body for foreign objects.

Sio juts a hand out across my chest, blocking the door frame, preventing me from taking another step. Her obstruction sets off the scanner alarm, which she quickly resets with a few strokes of the air.

"You think you know it all don't you? But I don't care how strong you are, you're not ready for what's up there," she says looking down at me. I bite my tongue, not wanting to remind her how easily I could toss her across the room.

"Don't make me regret not docking you more," Sio says then promptly walks away to presumably ruin someone else's day.

The sensor light beeps and turns green, proving that I am clean. I walk in and take exactly three large steps to the opposite wall of my dimly lit room. I collapse onto my bed, sinking into the mattress. I only need to make it through one more day. Tomorrow is my birthday, I don't care what Sio says, four points shouldn't prevent me from leaving this place. It's my time. I'm the best prospect. Nothing can ruin that.

I look around my room taking in its meager stylings. There is a small floating counter protruding from the left corner which serves as my desk. A stool sits below it, and an old holo-pad, which was used for completing training assignments before we had Bright-i installed, sits atop. There's a sink in the other corner that doubles as a shower set up if you extend the faucet. And a mirror hangs on the wall between the desk and sink-shower. That's it.

In the familiar routine, exactly 30 seconds after I enter my capsule, the four walls of my room roar to life.

"Hello Ever," an annoyingly chipper female voice echoes. The walls are energy-saving and only power up after detecting the occupant intends to remain in the room. The walls display the

sunny spring scene of a lush orchard. Yet another motivational tool from the Chairman. An image of what the future might be when we reclaim the Surface. I see vivid greens with specks of reds, oranges, and blues punctuated with puffs of white. Quite a nice reprieve from all the bare grays and stark whites of Helix Colony.

Reed believes I've internalized these images but they're different from my dreams. There's a different texture to them, a different muted feeling. At night I often lie awake fixating on the shiny red orbs that dangle from the trees on my wall, out of reach and forbidden. Just like the thoughts of Ira which invade my mind and stir up a similar sense of yearning.

The voice continues, reciting the itinerary that is now scrolling up the wall adjacent to my bed.

"You have a busy day to complete. You have been re-assigned to the Infant Unit at sixteen hundred hours," it says, and a graphic line strikes through the previously labeled Kineti-Bike activity that followed Strategy Training on my agenda. *"You now have less than five minutes until regulated consumption. Report to the Refectory in four minutes 52 seconds."*

"Great," I murmur, covering my eyes to block out the blinding light of the walls which seem to get brighter with every second. I suddenly feel woozy and roll over onto my side trying to avoid as much of the shine as possible.

Something small pricks the back of my head.

"Ouch." I reach behind and feel a warm trickle of blood slide down my neck. "What the hell?" I look down at my sheets, wondering if I left something on my bed, but that would be impossible; all my scans have been clear. We can't store sharp objects in our capsules, and for this exact reason – potential self-harm.

I search the sheets and find nothing. When I reach up to examine my hair, I feel a rough pointy object tangled in the strands.

As I pull it out, the room announces, *"Three minutes."*

In my hand is what looks like a sharp withered old fingernail. In immediate disgust I nearly drop it, while an irrational dread creeps in; it might be one of my own!

Panicked, I look at my fingers. Nope, all ten nails accounted for. I breathe out in relief. It would devastate me if my body suddenly started exhibiting flaws right before a Selection Ceremony. But I'm sure Sio would get a kick out of that.

What is this? I cautiously turn the yellowed object over in my hands. A frayed edge lifts from the side, and I realize it's an old, worn plastic container with a piece of paper tucked inside.

I immediately close my fist around it and scan the room. The opposite wall continues to display my agenda, and the daylight shifts in the scene before me, mimicking movements of the sun.

What am I doing? The walls aren't watching me.

Dormitory capsules are the only spaces where privacy is protected. Or, at least, that's we're told…

Better not risk it.

I cross my legs on the bed and hunch my body over my fist, just in case.

"Two minutes," the wall chimes.

Paper is contraband in Helix. As a child I remember seeing sheets bound together, layers of text and imagery filling the shelves of the recreation room; this was before they were all disposed of. We have never read from pages or learned to manually write on them. We use Bright-i or Indexes for all communications, because paper can't be monitored.

How did this get here? Why wasn't this object recognized by the detector as I entered my capsule?

Slowly, I remove and unfold the material inside, careful not to tear it. It sticks to itself, not wanting to be opened, not behaving like paper, and then I understand exactly what it is. A piece of surgical tape from the MedLab.

A cruel joke? Or Reed's attempt at sabotage? He must have hidden it in my hair while I slept, or when he fluffed the pillows behind me.

I gingerly unroll the pointed edge of the note and look at the tiny, inexperienced handwriting.

23:00, Utility Room.

Then the alarm rings.

CHAPTER 6
RO

I threw up everything I ate for nine days. My body shook for hours at a time. I cried in my dreams, and the few times I managed to break through the narcotic-induced haze, I'd wake to cry in the dark. I kept trying to scream, to fully express the pain, to wail, but the drugs kept me under, robbing me of mourning. I was suffocating and simultaneously on the verge of exploding.

It should have been me, not my Rune. She had too many questions left to ask, too many discoveries to make, too many adventures to experience.

"Mommy, what's that?" she'd ask pointing to a tree, a sock, a box, my face, the spot on her dress where ketchup left a stain that I was too preoccupied to clean up, so it set in permanently. She'd ask me fifty times a day, and it wasn't nearly enough, there was too much still to unearth.

"What's that?" She'd put a finger to my nose. "It's big. You have a big nose and I have a little nose." Then she'd lean in and kiss it.

I begged my lawyer to let me speak with him, the man that hit us. I needed to look him in the eyes and make certain he understood what he took from me. The life he stole and the woman he broke. I was advised against the meeting. No one understood why I would want to continue to torture myself. I should find solace in the fact that justice was being served.

But what justice was there for taking the life of a child? What prison sentence could make up for the smiles lost? The laughter. The tears. The kisses. The time. Just gone, and all the potential in the world, never realized.

No, I couldn't leave it up to strangers to exact the appropriate punishment. I would be the one who decided when and how justice was served. Starting with a meeting. A conversation. And it would be one that neither of us would survive.

Ronald was easy enough to convince to stay behind. He had initially been recommended to me by the courts; a shark of a personal injury attorney who would get me "the proper compensation I deserved." But the murderer had nothing to his name, and neither did I. There would be no large settlement worth Ronald's undivided attention. I was just another name on a long list of clients.

As I walked through the first dingy check point into the prison, it dawned on me just how inconsequential the space was. I don't know what I expected exactly, perhaps a hint of nefarious air? This compound expanded across several acres of the city limits, against a backdrop of black factory smoke that could be seen from the Refinery Lands. But there was nothing. The prison lobby traded the intimidating for the mundane. I could have mistaken the entryway for an average strip mall accountant's office.

A low nondescript tune played throughout the small room I walked into. It was stuffy, wood-paneled, windowless, and bare, save for a single door. I thought there would be a bit more open space but, then again, this was a corporate enterprise after all; a prime example of the prison industrial complex at work.

It should have been no surprise to me that for all the vastness of the facility, they would spare no inch. Their primary objective was to pack in as many prisoners as possible, not ensure comfort for inmates or those visiting. While I once empathized with the convicted and the encroachment on their basic human rights, I was glad that the man who took my daughter away was living in intolerable conditions. At least for what little time he had remaining.

A clicking sound emanating from a camera in the corner of the ceiling pierced the air, followed by a loud buzzer, indicating the door had been unlocked. I walked through it into a narrow hall that spilled out to a small waiting room. It held a glass-enclosed desk at the front, a door beside it, and a few bright orange folding chairs strewn against puke-green cinder block walls. Yet another oppressively dull room with no ventilation.

There was no one else in the waiting room, so I approached the desk.

"Who are you here to see?" The administrator barely looked up.

"I'm here to speak with Almon Barii. He's an inmate here."

"No kidding." She tapped away at a small keyboard. Even the technology here was antiquated. Clearly company profits were more important than utility.

"He's only allowed family member visits," she said, finally looking up at me. "And who are you?"

I knew this one, I pulled his PII from Ronald's Index, which I swiped during our last pointless meeting. Surprisingly, there was no passcode and the murderer's Personal Identifiable Information was left loaded. I thought it prudent to be prepared when on my way to kill someone.

"I'm his sister, Elysia Barii."

She stared at me, eyes squinting, strawberry blonde hair pulled tightly into a low bun. No doubt an attempt to look stern and intimidating, but her face was soft and classically pretty. She made me immediately self-conscious about my own appearance, my face riddled with bruises and scrapes. Hopefully my make-up was doing a good job of hiding the injuries.

After a moment the administrator exhaled, deciding it wasn't worth her time to question me, and handed me a name tag. Or perhaps she saw through my makeup façade and decided that to present some sense of solidarity, she'd let the abuse victim go through and get closure. Either way, she didn't ask to see an ID, and I didn't have to show her the laughably forged one I managed to afford.

Through the next door I was greeted by a large hulk of a man operating the security conveyor belt – another technological relic.

"Put your belongings in the basket," he said with enough bass in his voice to rattle my bones. Or maybe that was just in my head? Nerves. Fear of what was about to come next; I'd put my purse and Index down, then walk through the metal detector. They'd catch the vial of poison beneath my blouse, concealed under the mesh cast surrounding my chest, which I still needed to wear for proper healing and bone setting. I'd be stopped, searched, detained. Or worse, removed from the premises and my revenge gone unfilled.

I placed my items in the container the guard held out and noted the gun on his hip holster. He placed the small basket on the conveyor belt then walked around to observe them pass on a screen. I looked for a metal detector frame to walk through but saw none. He noticed my confusion.

"It's out for repair, we're scanning the old fashioned way for now."

A second guard appeared from behind me, the polar opposite of the rotund man at the screen. He was so thin and unassuming; his lack of presence gave me chills. He might have been standing in the corner the entire time, overshadowed by the first guy. I never even noticed him.

"Arms up ma'am." At least his voice was warm and friendly, if not nervous.

He lifted a paddle emanating a blue light and took a small step towards me. Maintaining a polite distance, he raised the paddle over my right arm, following it down to my hip, then walked over to my left side and did the same.

"Legs shoulder-width apart," he said, clearing his throat, unable to make eye contact. He continued scanning down my left side all the way to my foot. Then back up the right side when the paddle flashed red and beeped.

He backed away instantly and looked over at the other guard for direction. The large man walked around the screen, hands on hips.

"Miss, can you show us what you've got there?"

My arms were still frozen in the air, I lowered them awkwardly to lift my pant leg.

"It's an Adornment, I was in an accident."

"Well, aren't we fancy," he said looking at my new generation model. "How far does that go up?"

"To the knee," I said, trying to lift my pants higher, but they wouldn't go that far.

The big guard looked over at the emaciated guard, then bent down to examine my leg.

"Do you mind?" he asked.

I was unsure what he meant, but I figured it was best to comply and not raise suspicions, so I shook my head. He lifted an extendable baton from a pouch on this belt and tapped it against my shin all the way up to my knee, listening to each solid *clink* along the way. Satisfied my leg wasn't hollow, he stood up and put the baton away.

"You can never be too sure," he apologized. "Can't imagine the ways people try to sneak things in here." He nodded to the thin guard who finished scanning my right side and proceeded to my back. "I once had a fellow attempt to smuggle in a trained rat inside his forearm Adornment, turned out it had swallowed a half-ball of hard Alixia. He was planning to use it to move drugs for a gang inside. Can you believe that?"

"All clear," reported the thin one tremulously, then stepped back into the corner. He didn't scan my chest, and by the look in his eyes and how quickly he swung them away from me, I got the chilling sense that he was on to me but letting me through anyway. But why? And how could he know? I thought back to the nurse after my accident implying that he knew about my work. Was I being watched? I quickly suppressed that uneasy feeling; it didn't matter anymore.

I was handed back my belongings, then escorted through the next door into the Visitor's Room. I took one last look at the thin guard, the beads of sweat collecting on his forehead threatening to breach the ledges of his eyebrows. He knew something.

I took a seat at one of the many empty, sterile, white tables in silence, the weight of the vial heavy on my chest. I did it, I got it through. I tried to shake the uneasiness that crept up at the thought of how easy it had been to get to this point.

All I had to do was wait.

It wasn't long.

Almon Barii was smaller than I had imagined, younger too. His body was thin, and traces of bruises peeked out from beneath his baggy beige jumpsuit. It appeared he was getting the appropriate welcome treatment from his fellow inmates. At least, that was my hope. It was less satisfying to think that he too may have been injured during the accident. He walked in dejected, a large purple welt under a hooded eye, and a corrections officer guided his cuffed hands from behind.

When he finally glanced up from the ground a few steps away from me, he stopped in his tracks. A confused look spread across his face to see me, clearly an imposter, not his sister. That's what I had been from the moment Rune was taken from me – an imposter. A person even I didn't recognize. I had ceased being me.

Almon went to turn towards the corrections officer, but then quickly decided against it. Perhaps he kept quiet out of curiosity, or a desire to remain out of his cell block for a few moments longer. He sat down in front of me. The officer then removed the inmate's cuffs and took up his post by the door, but not before switching on his EMP baton, the high-pitched sound of its charge unmistakable. Contact with that stick would certainly fry more than a few nerve endings.

"Hi Elysia." His voice was small, meek, surely a ploy to gain sympathy.

"Almon." I stated flatly.

As I looked him over, sitting there with his hands crossed pleadingly on the table, pathetic and meek, I was suddenly filled with rage. He didn't get to feel sorry for himself, not after what he'd done. I wanted to dislodge the vial from my cast right then, remove the cap of the thallium solution and pour it directly onto his skin. I wanted to watch as it burned its way through his flesh, hungrily infecting his bloodstream and internal organs. There was no way I'd be able to keep my hands clean in the process, even trace amounts when absorbed would be lethal for either of us.

But that was the point.

"Sister, you've changed."

I looked over at the officer observing a piece of lint on his shoulder.

"Surely you still recognize me."

"Of course, it's only been a short time since I last saw you in your car," he said wearily.

So, he knew who I was.

"Good, then you know why I'm here." Tension tightened in my chest.

He lowered his gaze, in acknowledgment. "Ask your questions."

The running list that had occupied my thoughts for weeks now dissipated. I had just one.

"Do you have children?"

He met my eyes; a flicker of pain crossed his features.

"A nephew."

"Then you know that what you've stolen from me is a debt that can never be repaid." My voice was measured, but inside rage simmered. "You are a monster."

He shook his head slowly. "Nothing I say will give you the peace you're looking for."

"I'm not looking for peace, just the truth." I glared at him. "Why did this happen?"

"My car is manual. I was driving home from a graveyard shift, and... just dozed off." He pursed his lips and shook his head, as though there was nothing more to say.

That was it? *That* was his explanation?

I don't know what I expected, maybe a hint of remorse, any feeling really. Profuse apologies or rationalizations for his actions. Perhaps he was rushing to the hospital to be by a family member's side and didn't see us, or maybe he didn't intend to hit us head on and only swerved to avoid his own collision, or his breaks had been tampered with. Anything.

"I'm sorry for your loss," he said with dry eyes.

"My loss? *Loss?* I didn't *lose* anything, you ripped her from me!"

I stood abruptly, reaching through the buttons of my blouse for the gap in my mesh cast. "Ma'am, remain seated," the guard ordered, stepping forward. I had to act fast. Almon jumped to his feet, yanked my arms and pulled me closer, causing the table and my chair to screech across the floor. I yelped.

"Hey! Sit down, now!" The guard fumbled with the baton, as he strode across the room.

"I didn't know she would be in the car," Almon whispered harshly.

His breath was salty and stank of hunger and stomach acid. He leaned in closer to my ear, my hair draping his face and I realized he was trying to hide his mouth from the surveillance cameras.

"Back away, this is your only warning," the guard growled. I could hear the crackle of an electric charge.

"They paid me. They said they would take care of my family, give my sister a new lung Adornment. She can't take the smog in the Refinery Lands anymore. It would cost more money than I could make in a lifetime. It was just a transaction, I'm sorry."

I tried to pull away to get a better look at Almon, to determine if he was telling the truth, but he held on tightly, his white knuckles clenching my elbow.

"I didn't know she was there," he repeated desperately.

"Who paid you? Who was it?"

Then the EMP hit him on the shoulder, incapacitating him with electricity. It smelled like burning. Then my own arm felt on fire – he was still holding on to me.

CHAPTER 7
RO

A faint smell of smoke filled the air as I stood waiting for the mortician. I tried not to think about the source of the odor as I held Rune's small hand in mine. She looked like a gift, a giant white bow wrapped around the waist of her dress as she lay peacefully in a cardboard box.

I wanted to bury her beside my parents on the small plot I had sprung for, but recent law had done away with burials. All the remaining available land was now corporate owned; even the public parks were on loan to the city. Cremation was standard practice. No place to visit. Better to keep your loved ones close, I guess.

Rune's father, a title unbeknownst to him, was a lucky man, never having to know what he had lost. Never having to feel what I felt. The fracturing of my very soul. I hadn't thought twice about my decision to keep him in the dark, and I didn't regret it now. I would never wish this pain on anyone.

We met at a fundraiser, both of us university grad students at the time. We were in different research departments yet equally ambitious, having each obtained invitations to the WISH Gala, through questionable measures. I had swiped mine from the pocket of a professor on an elevator ride. He had pulled his out of his boss's trash. Something, I came to later learn.

My plan was, with the assistance of several cocktails, to persuade a Second-Lifer to fund my research. Axe had the same idea. I wore the tightest red dress I could charge, putting my curves on full display. He wore the best suit he could borrow from the sartorial boutique he worked at part-time. From across the room, we locked eyes, mistaking each other for a wealthy target.

"Be careful what you *wish* for," were the first words he ever said to me, handing me a glass of Warp White. My favorite. I appreciated his corny sense of humor. His attempt at wit softened me, even as I braced myself for another typical elite encounter.

"I'm Axe," he introduced himself, the laugh lines slowly fading from his face as his eyes drank me in deeply. I felt exposed, and with the current dress I had donned, I probably looked it.

"You don't belong here," he said soberly.

I froze. I had been discovered. Of course I didn't belong there, I was delusional to think I could fit in with those people.

He gently tucked a stray strand of hair behind my ear then swiftly slid his hand over my back tucking in the tag I hadn't known was sticking out. My face burned.

"I don't belong here either," he smiled, disarming me with his honesty. And from then, we spent the whole night together, our primary objectives forgotten.

He always put me at ease. It was one of the things I liked most about him. I was content with him, happy even. What started as a single night blossomed into blissful months together. I realized I had loved him from the very start. I loved his smile, his coily hair, his dark eyes. *Her* eyes.

And because I loved him, I let him go. He didn't want children, never had. And I knew he wouldn't have been happy giving up everything, his research, his life's passion, to work meaningless jobs to support a family he never asked for.

But I wanted her. I never realized how badly, until I discovered I was pregnant. It was a deeper love than I had ever felt, me and the baby growing inside me were tethered. So I found a way to do it all alone. Axe's life didn't have to end, and mine was just beginning.

"It's time." The mortician had returned.

I looked down to the object in my hand; I had brought Rune a headband with butterflies on it, she hated when her hair was in her face.

In our last car ride, she had straight locks tied into two loose ponytails. I took the time to straighten her curls the night before the meeting, she preferred wearing it that way for special occasions. But the lake water had returned it to its usual rebellious state. I always did prefer it that way, natural and unruly, though the flyaways always tickled her face and made her itchy.

I let go of Rune's hand and slid the headband on, pushing her curls back, then twisting a few around my finger, tugging at them. Her hair had gotten so long.

She loved when I made them spring back into tiny coils. It occurred to me I would never be able to taunt her hair like that again, and I needed to preserve the act somehow. So, I plucked a few strands for safe keeping. I almost expected her to cry, but she was a good girl. She remained peacefully asleep in her casket. I wrapped my arms around her, a deep embrace to make up for all the ones we'd never share again.

CHAPTER 8
RO

I had nothing left. My life was shattered. Without Rune, the only thing keeping me going was uncovering the truth. Almon's words haunted me. Why was I targeted? Who had I offended? What possible action of mine could have resulted in this outcome? I was not rich. I had never been arrested. I had never committed a crime. Sure, I occasionally flipped people off in traffic, but who didn't? My life was of no value to anyone other than Rune, so why would someone order a hit on my car? It didn't make any sense.

I returned to the prison a few days later, only to discover Almon had been transferred to an Outland facility hours after our encounter. Ronald was useless in tracking down the location of his transfer, and he stopped returning my calls when my retainer bounced. The police refused to reevaluate my situation, as they were *"in the business of closing cases not opening them."* No one would speak to me. Either they were paid off, or simply didn't believe me about a larger conspiracy.

I found myself standing outside Almon's sister's home, feeling desperate and a little crazed, in the darkest, seediest strip of the Burg. My hands trembled from the drink I downed on the way there. Armed with a crowbar, I loomed outside her street level apartment window, poised to break in.

Finding Elysia's address was easy enough; Ronald was remarkably careless with his index. Almon claimed to have done all of this to pay for his sister's surgery, so I wasn't sure what condition she was in. Whether or not she had the new lung Adornment procedure could benefit or derail my interrogation. Either way, I felt at a dead end with no other options to explore.

The street was a dump, lacking any discernible security measures, suggesting they truly had no money. Taking extreme measures didn't seem out of the question. Glancing down both ends of the dark alleyway at the piles of heated trash still to be collected, and the rodents trampling over each other to get a taste, I still couldn't feel sorry for Almon or his family; his actions came at the cost of my own.

I slowly pried the apartment window open with the crowbar. I don't know exactly what I expected to gain out of this encounter, but surely the person who benefited from the hit would have some clues or insight into the money's origin, or at least the individuals Almon had contacted in the days leading up to the accident. There had to be a connection somewhere.

Ringing the doorbell wasn't an option. In this area, mistrust of strangers ran high, Elysia would surely slam the door in my face and refuse to speak to me at all. No, I needed to intimidate and coerce her into telling me everything she knew. I needed someone to speak to me, every avenue I explored so far led to silence, deafening, exhausting, soul crushing. I couldn't take much more.

Using my new leg Adornment for added leverage, I scaled the short wall and slipped in through the window. My leg clinked on porcelain. I was above her toilet. Dim light seeped from beneath the door. The bathroom was tiny, though not much smaller than my own. A dingy shower curtain hung over a scuffed tub. The sink jutted out from a wall of cracked tiles beneath a mirror barely clinging to the rusted hinges of a medicine cabinet overstocked with prescription bottles. In a different life, under different circumstances, their desperation might have weighed heavy on me. But I couldn't afford to think about that.

I pressed my ear to the bathroom door. Despite the light, I couldn't hear any sounds on the other side. Slowly I eased the door open and took a tentative step into the musty hallway. There were piles of dirty clothes and furniture in various states of abandonment scattered throughout the apartment.

My plan had been to scare Elysia, and if that didn't work, guilt her into revealing anything that could point me in the right direction. She had to hold some clue, or feel some kind of empathy for my loss; after all Almon was desperate enough to commit murder to help her.

As I navigated through the debris, I caught sight of a pile of papers strewn across a corner table at the end of the hall. I carefully parsed through the bills and collection notices, pausing at the stack of medical pamphlets that included Adornment literature from BodyMod and Easton Corp, likely the services considered for her lung surgery.

"Mommy?"

The word, a faint quivering whisper from the nearby door, sent a sharp pain through my heart. For a split second, I lost all sense of where I was. The world around me blurred as my feet carried me to the door, towards the voice of my child. Before I knew it, I had flung the door wide open, and instinctually walked towards the bed.

Rune? It was impossible, I knew that, but hope overpowered logic. The longing, a visceral ache, a pull too strong to resist.

I kneeled, placing the crowbar I was still clutching on a nearby table. I yanked the chain of a battered lamp next to it and the light spilled a weak glow across the room. I heard a soft whimpering from beneath the covers, and I gingerly pulled them back.

"Shhh, shhh, it's okay," I murmured, effortlessly slipping back into the familiar role of comforting Rune after nightmares.

"Mommy?" The small voice cracked again and, as the cover slid away, my heart sank. The child staring back at me was a gaunt, dirt-smudged boy, maybe ten years of age. Not my Rune. His wide eyes mirrored my shock. Although his fear was justified, I was the intruder, but there was something fleeting in his expression that sent a chill down my spine. A subtle shake of his head, almost imperceptible, as if pleading, but he didn't say a word.

"Mommy is gone, remember?" The deep voice jolted me, and suddenly, hands were wrapping around my throat, yanking me away from the bed.

The boy bolted upright in bed looking as frightened as I felt being dragged backward.

"How did you get into my house?" the voice boomed in my ear. "Who sent you?" it demanded. I scrambled, desperate, clawing at the man's grip, unable to answer.

"Go back to bed, bud. No one is going to hurt you," he said, more softly. But the boy remained frozen.

As we reached the doorway my back slammed into a rounded object, a wheel. I contorted on the floor and realized the person restraining me was confined to a wheelchair.

"I'm going to ask you one more time – who sent you?"

I kicked off the door frame, a desperate bid for air, and he released me. As I gasped for breath, I heard the resounding click of a gun.

"Almon," I managed between coughs.

The man's eyes were cold and unforgiving. I considered lying, claiming I was breaking into his home with some fabricated authorization, but under his piercing gaze, the truth was the most desperate option of all.

"He killed my daughter. He destroyed my life."

"So, you're here to destroy his? Hate to break it to you, there's not much left to destroy that he hasn't already." The sneer on his face remained. "Thanks to him I'm left to pick up the pieces. And in this state," he cast his eyes downward, "there's not much I can do."

Though his arms were undeniably strong, the man appeared to be paralyzed from the waist down. I was certain there weren't many means for him to earn a living, not even in the Refinery Lands. Most facilities and businesses lacked proper accessibility, operating under the absurd expectation that everyone should have an Adornment. The sad reality was that he and the boy likely wouldn't last much longer in this harsh world.

"I'm looking for answers." I tried to keep my voice steady despite the tension. "Almon confessed he was paid to crash into me. I need to speak to Elysia. Who covered the cost of her surgery?"

His expression settled into one of impassivity. "You're a little too late. My wife passed weeks ago."

I blanched at the news; her death wasn't on record.

"But... Almon claimed he did it to finance her Adornment procedure," I countered, disbelief lacing my words.

He sighed, the gun in his hand lowering to his side. He retrieved a cigarette from his pocket, lit it, and drew a long, deliberate breath.

"The surgery never happened," he said, exhaling a cloud of smoke.

What was left of my world came crashing down as his words sank in. My child was gone, and Almon's desperate attempt to save his sister was all for nothing.

"It's ironic," the man mused, smoke curling from his lips. "She died in the very place that should have saved her. Minutes before the procedure, in the operating room of one of the most prestigious, state-of-the-art medical centers."

He savored another drag of his cigarette, clinging to old comforts in the wake of loss. His smoking didn't matter anymore.

"What does that tell you?"

His question was rhetorical. I understood what he meant, that it wasn't ironic at all. Whoever was responsible never intended to honor their deal with Almon. A wave of nausea washed over me; the elites played by a different set of rules. I would never get my justice. I wanted to scream; the anguish overwhelming as I crumpled to the floor of this stranger's home.

"Why – why did this happen?" The words barely escaped me.

The man looked down, his expression a mix of resignation and empathy. "It's the hand we were dealt. Look at us, we're disposable."

CHAPTER 9
RO

I can't believe I had never previously considered what an excellent painkiller alcohol was. Highly underrated. Most effective outside of your home without the constant photographs and stuffed animals reminding you of just how all-consuming your pain is and how pointless your life has become.

I preferred dark, sticky locations to crumble in. I found comfort in the height of a bar; it was the perfect distance from the stool so that I could easily rest my head on my outstretched arms without hunching over whenever the room spun a little too quickly. That tended to happen after my fourth drink, and more so after my fifth.

The place I'd hidden myself was a scuffed mess but warm, and only a little judgmental. A few times I'd catch the bartender's face reflected in the mirror behind the stacked shelves after she'd served me, her soft smile fading a bit too quickly.

My stool was in a great corner position to comfortably observe others in the establishment. Not that there were really many people drinking in the morning. On this day there was just one, an expertly dressed man alone in a booth across the room. He wasn't a regular, whereas I had become somewhat of a permanent fixture in this dump. The place was quiet, just the clinking of glasses being cleaned, and the low droning news coverage of another billionaire taking over daddy's company playing out on the TV.

"Another round Sonya," I slurred, jiggling my glass like a beggar.

"Can't do that Ro," Sonya said as she wiped down the bar. It was a pointless task; the years of grime would never release its hold on the counter.

"Oh, come on," I whined. "Don't be such a buzz kill."

She continued to wipe and buff.

"Just one more, and I'm done. I promise."

"Last week I found you passed out in the alley. I just don't want you to end up face down in the gutter again."

Apparently, you can't take a nap on a trashed sofa behind a bar without the staff worrying. Noted.

"Who cares if I do? There's no one waiting for me at home. Just get me another drink." Immediately I regretted my tone, it did not have the intended effect. Coming out far more entitled than pleading. Sonya didn't budge.

I needed the cloudiness; I didn't want to think. Rune was heavy in me. A distinct, dense, aching that hadn't lessened in weeks. I wanted to hold her, breathe her in deeply – ripe fruit with honey – and never breathe out again. But I'd have to settle for pungent fermented firewater.

"Please," I whimpered. I could tell Sonya felt pity for me but that feeling was quickly catching up with irritation at my constant presence.

I needed one more drink to give me the courage to do what came next. That afternoon, I finally planned on making use of the vial of poison. If I couldn't avenge Rune's death, I could join her. Today, I would see my daughter again. I just needed a little help to get there.

"Excuse me," a smooth deep voice interrupted us. "Do I know you from somewhere?"

The expertly dressed man smirked from the end of the bar. He didn't belong here. He was too shiny. Not a hair was out of place, nor a wrinkle in his suit or on his face. His mammoth gold pinky ring probably cost more than my entire life's savings.

"No," I groaned. "I'm nobody you would know." I turned my head in my arms attempting to nap on the other side.

"You can't do that here, Ro. It's bad for business. You should go home."

"Ro? Short for Rosio," the man said, more a statement than a question. "That's it. You're Dr. Rosio Arata, the geneticist," he said excitedly.

I didn't respond to his acknowledgment.

"I was on the board of investors at NuBio Technologies." He settled into the stool next to me. "I'm really sorry to hear about what happened."

"Yeah, well, me too," I croaked, realizing as I said it that I had no ache left in my throat to stifle; my well of emotion was dry.

"Your proposal was brilliant, really, I haven't been able to stop thinking about it."

I shrugged dismissively, the alcohol churning in my system. There he went ruining my place of self-loathing. "I don't do that kind of work anymore." Or any work at all. Even though rent was due, and I was living off the meager remains of my grant money. I just couldn't. But not for much longer.

"Oh, but it was cutting edge! RMG manipulation had so much potential."

"Had," I confirm, irritation lacing my voice.

"The applications, endless, which I'm sure you know, imagine the integrations–"

"I should be leaving." My words were clipped, final. "Sonya, you were right. I'll see you."

"I hope you won't," she responded without looking up from the glass she was drying.

"Don't you just wonder what you could have achieved with the right backing?"

I lean back on my stool, room spinning, trying to gracefully reach for my purse from the hook under the bar.

"That's not the first thing I wonder when I look back on my life."

"Wait, hear me out–"

"No, I don't know you. I'm leaving." I had more important matters to attend to.

"What if I said there was a way to get back what you lost?"

Who *was* this man? And why couldn't he leave well enough alone?

"What's happened has happened," I snapped. "There's no going back. I've accepted it." I turned unsteadily to leave.

"Let me buy you a drink."

That made me reconsider for a moment. Sonya looked up suspiciously.

"Two A51's," he ordered before I could say no.

"Sir, I can't allow–" Sonya began.

"You can take my money, can't you?" He pulled out a thick clear card and tapped out a number with numerous zeros onto it. A quantity large enough to stop Sonya's protests. She looked at me a little concerned but knew that she was not responsible for my demise. She took the card and ran it before he could change his mind and proceeded to make our drinks.

My curiosity had a slight sobering effect.

"And you are?" I finally asked.

He grinned, baring all his teeth, like a charming shark. "I'm Edric Easton."

I nearly choked at the sound of his name. Edric was the seldom-seen, reclusive, eldest son of bio tech tycoon, Sylas Easton. I glanced at the news coverage of his brother's succession of their father's company, EastonCorp; the leading manufacturer of Adornments on the market.

"What are you doing here?'

"I came looking for you."

This was some kind of joke. "Me? Why?"

"Truthfully, because I'm out for blood," he said with an odd lightness. I couldn't quite tell what his intention was.

"As you can see," he continued, motioning towards the TV, "I've been shut out of my family's empire as my brother takes the reins. But I'm a competitive man, and I don't take things lightly."

Sonya slid two foggy drinks over to us. It wasn't a Warp White, but I'd take anything at this point.

"Oh, okay, I see. You've got daddy issues. Well, haven't we all. I'm not interested in your expedition to overthrow your brother." My tone was firm, even as my world spun. I took the drink, struggling to get the right words out. "You and your family literally represent everything that is wrong with our society."

Maybe I could take the glass to go?

"That's exactly why I'm here." His hand twitched as he reached for his drink.

"Your sibling rivalry doesn't interest me." I took a gulp from my glass, savoring the burn.

"That's just it, it's not a rivalry you see. It's a lack of vision. It's why I invest in competitors in the space. EastonCorp is stuck in the past. *You* are the future."

"What are you talking about?" My head was spinning again.

He leaned in and lowered his voice even though there was no one around to hear except for Sonya.

"I'm launching a new venture, one that, with your help, will change the future of enhancements at large. We can bring down the monopoly."

He quirked an eyebrow, clearing thinking he had my piqued my interest. But I had lost all passion for sticking it to the corporate oligarchy. What did I care if one billionaire company was knocked down a few pegs? It made little difference in the grand scheme of things, and absolutely nothing to me. We were all born to die, no matter how much money we left behind. I had no fight in me, the only thing I had left to fight for was gone.

"What's the point?"

"You could improve a lot of lives–"

"Look I'm sorry you've wasted your time. But thanks for the drink." I downed the last of the A51, and turned the glass over on the bar. The remaining dregs dripped onto the recently cleaned surface, much to Sonya's displeasure. I would have apologized for that, but I needed to make my exit.

Edric moved in a little closer, his smell superficially intoxicating; his luxury cologne must have been all pheromones. "Listen, the field is changing rapidly, and we can be the leaders of the pack. You can have everything you ever wanted and make a difference."

"That's where you're wrong," I squeezed past him. "I can't have my daughter back."

As I reached the door, he called out.

"What if you could?"

CHAPTER 10
EVER

Several Subjects sweep past me on their way through the glass sliding doors of the Refectory. The blaring sound of the alarm still rings in my ears as I enter, even though the actual chimes have stopped.

I usually enjoy spending time in the Refectory; it's one of the few communal areas where Subjects can interact freely. For the most part, our days are strictly regimented. We shuttle from one assignment to the next and then retire alone to our capsules. But three times a day we all need to eat, including the Keepers, which means a welcome break from the constant monitoring. The room is large enough to comfortably fit the forty-eight Subjects that remain and our eighteen Keepers, with just enough distance from each other to feel a sense of freedom.

The wall to the far right of the room flickers with a rotation of nutrition-related announcements.

Get an IV Plug-in for your delivery of balanced nutrition, one reads. Followed by a reminder of the offerings available:

Preset level 1: Refuel and ReEnergize
Preset level 2: Strength Building
Preset level 3: Daily Balance
Preset level 4: Mental Clarity

There is no such thing as a Subject who is too thin or too fat. Meticulously balanced diet formulas are some of the best technologies within Helix.

Looking around the room, it appears all Subjects are accounted for, with the exception of the one person I need to speak with. It isn't surprising – Reed is known to report for feedings at off-peak hours to avoid social interaction. I sometimes wonder what he preoccupies himself with. Knowing Reed, it's an opportune time for mischief and I still don't quite understand why it's permissible, specifically why Sio as Head Keeper, continues to allow it.

I make my way over to the IV drip station. There are several Subjects already hooked up for their mid-afternoon meals. Clear bags of minerals, nutrients, and antitoxins hang on long metal rods next to reclined chairs. Tubes attached to the bags plug into ports in each Subject's arm and drain into their venous systems. The entire process takes about twenty-five minutes, and each station is currently occupied. Watching them, I realize for the first time just how drained my body feels and how hungry I am for my dose. I missed my last intake and ache for the next hit, anxious to let the fluids wash over me like a euphoric wave.

Keepers on the opposite side of the room are lining up with their trays in front of dispensing machines. Although I won't be observed by them for this hour, I still try to show some semblance of strength in my posture to hide how terrible I feel, just in case.

Calorie consumption differs between Keepers and Subjects. For training purposes, Subjects need a higher calorie intake than the Keepers do. We burn more and so we need higher levels of fuel, which is more efficiently absorbed through a liquid diet. Whereas Keepers fill up on heavier solid meals. Looking at the brown masses and bright green and orange chunks they consume, I am honestly not envious of them. Their offerings vary at every feeding, and the rotation of colorful wedges on their trays always gives me a sense of nausea, but the Keepers ingest them with relish. I've even heard excitement at the prospect of what unusual substances they would be fed. *"I hope it's chicken piccata with mushrooms today, the kitchen really outdid themselves last time."*

While waiting for an IV station to open up, I decide to work on elevating my vitamin D levels, but as I make my way over, it seems other Subjects have already secured their places in the floodlit vertical pods. I guess it pays to be on time. Each floodlight mimics sunlight and is designed to provide the optimal levels of ultraviolet B for vitamin D production by the skin. The peak amount of exposure time is between ten to fourteen minutes a day. In underground conditions, a lack of this crucial vitamin can manifest in depression, mood swings, fatigue, and muscle pain, not to mention our bones would weaken and break.

Everything serves a purpose in Helix.

I don't want to risk standing here openly while I wait for a spot; the last thing I want is for someone to walk over and engage me in conversation. No doubt the other Subjects have heard about my non-fulfillment by now, and I can certainly do without the feigned sympathy. I have no surplus energy to spend politely answering intrusive questions. It's all a competition, no one really cares how you're actually feeling.

I glance around hoping to find a quiet corner where I can wait in peace, but the perimeter of the room is littered with Subjects. The youngest huddle in groups giggling timidly at something unseen – they're most likely viewing a SimulFeed on their Bright-i lenses. Probably a recording that the Keepers would not fully approve of, hence the giggling.

Another Subject weaves his arm under a table, extending it the full length in an attempt to jolt his friend on the other side, though quickly stopping when he gets a sharp look from his Keeper. We're not supposed to display abilities outside of training. They are miraculous gifts bestowed to us for one purpose only. They stand as the very reason we were rescued and relocated underground as infants for safekeeping. We were born with unique abilities, and those who can master and wield them with integrity, proving their usefulness to the cause, earn the honor of resurfacing.

Other Subjects pair off in conversations, boys eyeing nearby girls while they pretend not to notice. The stations remain occupied, and I get the prickly paranoid feeling that the randomized chatter in the room is a ruse, and that in reality, everyone is talking about me, or at least hiding the fact that they are.

Perhaps I *am* just as self-centered as Reed thinks. But here in the middle of the room I make out some of the whispers circulating, and I suddenly feel appropriately self-conscious in the open, exposed to judging eyes.

"I heard they had to give her blood back."

"Maybe it's not pure enough?"

"Can you believe it? Now she's actually taking from the resistance."

I run my fingers through my hair just to have something to do with my hands as I continue to wait for an opening.

At once, the far wall of the Refectory revs to life. At first, an image of dense black smoke appears that then transitions into a brilliant blue and spreads to the walls on either side of it, capturing everyone's attention. *Thank the Chairman.*

The image tilts to reveal a bright blue sky teeming with soft, thick clouds. The movement continues downward landing on a vibrant plain of grass lined with lush trees on the horizon. We zoom towards the trees, then through them into a clearing of white sandy ground where, on its edges, a large body of water collides in rhythmic waves. A honeyed, female voice speaks over the sounds of rushing water.

The Surface.

Outpost Zero-Five-One.

Guarding the world's last remaining city.

A new home for the chosen ones.

An idyllic community of people draped in simple garbs carry baskets and scavenge plants from the ground while wearing black oxygen masks.

Tomorrow, the most deserving member of your ranks will be selected to emerge and take their place among the Saviors.

Nine Saviors smile and wave from ornate seats on a raised platform while receiving gifts from the masked community members that approach.

Joining in the mission to reclaim our world. One battle at a time.

The perimeter gates open and a procession of more Saviors – younger unmasked – stride in, their uniforms dirty and bloodied, fresh from battle. The community looks up at them with awe, as the Saviors stop just short of their elders on the platform, pulling a severed head from a sac and thrusting it in the air for all to see. Its partially chrome face glints in the sunlight. A small, masked child runs up to one of the Saviors and hands her a frayed toy as a token of appreciation.

The safety of our people depends on you.

Good luck.

As the image pixelates away, the room erupts in a series of applause and the excited whispering begins.

A switch disengages a few pods down, and I rush over. Just as I'm about to step in, a leggy Subject slips past me into the pod, and seals it shut.

"Farrah!" I curse under my breath. Her entire body is now housed within the pod and shielded from view, except for her freshly buzzed red hair.

"Too slow," she cackles. She lifts her shirt up over her head and then bends down completely out of view to remove her pants, exposing more surface area of bare skin to the floodlights.

"Wish you could get a better look, don't you?" Farrah taunts as she pops back up. I can hear giggles from her cronies in the nearby pods, Arden and Elodie are clearly enjoying the show.

"You better take your chance now before I'm gone!" She strikes a pose, resting her arms on the edges of the pod, her eyes slowly dragging over me, lingering just a bit too long. "Or are you pathetic enough to think *you* will actually be chosen tomorrow?"

"I *am* in the lead," I remind her.

"Not for long. We still have the trials."

"You don't stand a chance," I say through gritted teeth.

"We'll see about that! Strength can only take you so far, Ever. True power is something you'll never have – it's called respect. You're no leader, you can't command a team. Wars are not won alone. You might look the part, but you're weak. You don't have what it takes to make the hard decisions, to take a life for the good of your people."

I step towards her aggressively, thinking how great it would feel to connect my fist with her jaw. I am not as tall or sinewy as Farrah, but I could easily pulverize her. Yet violence is exactly what she wants – it's what all bullies want – and although we're not being monitored during our time in the Refectory, a public display of aggression would cost me points in the ranking. I will not give her the satisfaction.

"Envy does not arise from a resilient mind, Farrah. That's quite a flaw you have there," I begin. Her smile fades, feeling the seriousness of the accusation. "I'm worried about you, truly. You should have that examined. I'll escort you to the MedLab myself or I can inform the Keepers if you like?"

She looks over at the Keepers to confirm they're not listening. Then she leans forward, crossing her arms over the edge of the pod, calling my bluff.

"Okay, tell them. It doesn't change the fact that you'll never make it up there. You'll be a short-lived burden to the real heroes of the Surface." She whispers her next words for effect, "The smell of your fear alone will attract all of the Forms for miles. It's survival of the fittest, and that *won't* be you."

I feel the piercing stares of onlookers from the nearby pods, but I try to remain composed.

"Then, once you're out of the picture, I'll swoop right in and console Ira in his time of need." She smiles smugly at her final jab.

My body stiffens. How does she know about us? Relationships are prohibited and we were discreet. If she knows, does that mean the Keepers know? Have all my setbacks been a way to keep us apart? Or is she just trying to provoke me?

I clench my fists, digging my nails into the palms of my hands, wondering when I became so inclined to violence. Maybe it's something in the altogether too-satisfied grin on Farrah's face.

"I don't know what you're talking about Farrah, but Ira would never be interested in the likes of *you*."

"Aww you really think he's waiting for you up there, don't you? With a whole new world of possibilities, he's just sitting around waiting for little old you? How... cute."

Farrah lounges backwards against the pod walls, closing her eyes and laying her head in the padded neck rest, satisfied with having the last word. The timer on her unit begins counting backward from 14 minutes.

Her words sting more than I care to admit. Is she right? It's been a year since he ascended, of course there's the possibility that Ira has moved on. Could I really be so naive to think he'd wait? But we made a promise to each other, and clinging to that promise is what's keeping me sane. Despite the ache in my chest, I grit my teeth and step away. I won't give Farrah the satisfaction of seeing the seed of doubt she's planted.

A small voice speaks up from a nearby pod, "You can have my unit," it squeals, much higher pitched than I think the owner intended.

Skye is visible through a crack in the latch, her tightly coiled golden-brown hair is just shy of the top of the pod. She's small, even for a 12-year-old, but what she lacks in height and age she makes up for in information. She always seems to know everything that's going on, in part because of her heightened eyesight – she can make out letters nearly a mile away.

Skye opens her pod and motions towards me. "I'm all done, I've got my UV for the day."

I smile appreciatively as I approach her. "Thank you, Skye. It's nice to see *someone* has good breeding around here."

"Don't worry, Ever," she whispers to me. "If he's your true love, I'm sure he's still thinking about you and waiting for you to join him." She smiles in an effort to raise my spirits, but I just feel embarrassed. Are *all* my secrets that exposed?

"I remember the way he used to look at you," she continues. "It was definitely love."

I try not to blush as I step into the pod. "You think?"

"Of course. It's the same way that Reed looks at you," she says as she walks away.

Flustered, I remove my clothing. Where did that come from? I've never considered Reed anything other than a friend, and now he wasn't even that. Whatever I felt at his touch earlier in the MedLab was just a lingering aftereffect of my seizure.

Leaning back in the pod, I am showered in warm light, enveloping me like a glove. My hairs stand on edge with the occasional crackle and pop of heat licking skin. My lids drop and my body goes slack, indulging in the comfort.

Suddenly a loud crash echoes through the room disturbing my reverie and my eyes snap open. The other Subjects have stopped what they were doing too, their attention held by something happening off to the side.

It's Reed. I hadn't seen him walk in. He has knocked down a Keeper's tray, and not just any Keeper – Sio. His body trembles violently as he confronts her, his face contorted and bright red as he shouts something indecipherable. Security is there at once; Jet and Jaxon restrain Reed holding him by his arms.

Convulsions raise foam to the corners of his mouth. "I need it!" he growls.

Surprisingly, Sio looks unphased by his behavior, and studies his face as Jaxon attempts to drag Reed away.

"You promised!" he shouts again, straining towards her.

The shiny point of a needle emerges from Jet's hand.

"You would do well to calm down." Sio's tone is unruffled.

"You're a liar!"

The needle connects with the port in Reed's bicep, and the effect is almost instantaneous. His body slumps over as he struggles to slither out a few final words.

"Why me?" Then he is dragged out of the Refectory.

The room is motionless, everyone's eyes are on Sio who stands with not a single hair out of place and straightens her white coat.

"Continue on," she says. "Or all Subjects will perform another Drawing." At that everyone goes back to their infusions.

"That's precisely why they don't let Flaweds surface," Farrah whispers audibly. "They're all deranged."

CHAPTER 11
RO

It was harder to clean myself up than I thought. The routine of getting dressed and making oneself publicly presentable felt foreign under my shaking and exhausted fingertips. I pulled down on the lapel of my only good blazer, straightening it out, wondering what I was doing in an elevator with this man, yearning for a drink, and holding out hope... for what exactly? Dead was dead. It was indisputable.

"Almost there," Edric said, nearly singing.

His teeth were too white, eyes too bright, hair too perfectly manicured. Papa always told me to be wary of an attractive face, they didn't come naturally anymore. Almost nothing did.

"There are simply too many Adornments out there. Their value is plummeting, even the high-end designer ones," he said. Aesthetic augmentations and artificial enhancements were indeed ubiquitous among the city's population, many of which were courtesy of dangerously cheap black-market offerings.

"A new innovation is needed to overcome the market saturation," he continued. "The next evolution of Adornments. *We* can offer that." He stepped off the elevator and I followed. "I want us to be at the forefront, changing consumer tastes, creating a demand people don't even realize they have. No one wants to be more of the same; they want to feel exceptional."

I stifled a snort and stopped myself from correcting him. *Elites* wanted to feel different and special, everyone else just wanted to keep up and fit in.

"When everyone is fake, the most *exceptional* thing to be is real. Natural. For a price." He winked at me as though I was meant to find his egregiously capitalistic pitch impressive.

He had taken me to his newly renovated medical offices with a sublevel laboratory we were now touring. The lab took up a few thousand square feet in a corner of what felt like an empty warehouse. A vast space at odds with the narrow commercial building above it that was so commonplace in this dense city. The walls were lined with servers and DNA printing machines. A potent smell of solvents hung in the air as we walked.

"We are in a golden window of opportunity to successfully enter a new product into the market. The competition is faltering with Adornment malfunctions on the rise," he went on.

I thought of the woman in the car, momentarily paralyzed by her own Adornments; her malfunctions cost me my daughter. Despite my intense dislike for this man, his words swirled a mixture of emotions within me. Adornments had taken away my happiness, and I found myself strangely intrigued by the possibility of ensuring such a tragedy never happened again. It almost reignited a spark of purpose within me. It was a chance to turn my grief into something meaningful, to help prevent others from suffering the same heart-wrenching loss. If I were a better person, a stronger person, I could achieve this. But tragedy had worn me down.

"The leading companies – my family's included – focus on mass production to boost their bottom lines. Meanwhile they cut corners that impact quality, and it's costing them gravely. The millions spent on legal settlements and non-disclosures is inconceivable. It's only a matter of time before the coverups hit the mainstream. They are putting lives at risk. We can help people, offer a safer option, and make money in the process."

He continued to try and sell me as we walked past a stainless-steel bioreactor and several centrifuges. I nodded along to signify that I was following the information, not that I was buying his alleged humanitarian intentions. I didn't trust his kind. The privileged, the elite, the Second-Lifers. The ones whose gluttonous consumption nearly destroyed this planet. He wasn't going to extend his new products to the people who truly needed help. Not to the hardworking grandfather exposing himself to daily respiratory toxins in the Refinery Land plants. Or to the teen with debilitating burns from sun exposure on a late walk home from school because his family didn't own a car. No, Edric Easton's only goal was more wealth, that's how he was bred, he couldn't alter that programming so easily.

He had gotten me through the door, but watching him stand there in his crisp, freshly pressed black suit, passionately detailing the supposed good our partnership could do, I failed to see any reason why staying there was a better use of my time than an alcohol induced stupor to numb my pain. This was not my purpose anymore. It wasn't up to me to try and improve the world.

"By providing a reliable solution we can establish ourselves as leaders in the industry, gaining the trust and loyalty of customers while also paving the way for long-term success and growth. That's where you come in. This is to be a joint venture; I want to fund your work and fast track it for development."

"Let me get this straight, you want to use my genomic sequencing algorithm to create organic Adornments... all to sell to your shallow and frightened friends? Because let's be honest, that's who this is serving." I was over his charade.

"It can serve you too," he said unabashed, with a smile as big as before. He led me past a line of controlled-rate freezers. In this one corner of the basement, from what I could tell, he already had everything he needed to launch the initial stages of production, with or without me. "I'll make it worth your while."

"I'm hardly the first to consider organic tissue alternatives for Adornments. You couldn't poach a geneticist from your family's company? With enough time and money, I'm sure they could achieve the results you need."

"Time *is* money, and that's what *you* offer me: fast results. Your patented DNA sequences claim to be able to produce fully grown tissues in a matter of days not months. We'd be first to the finish line."

We paused by a 3D interface gene station. My patience was wearing thin, I needed him to get to the point, the sole reason I accepted this meeting in the first place.

"Listen, I appreciate the tour, but I have no interest in your money or helping you monopolize another sector. But you already knew that, so what's this really about? Why am I here?"

He considered this a moment, then rolled back his shoulders increasing his already dominating presence. "You're right," he said and looked me square in the eyes. "You're here because you have nothing left to lose."

The sharp sting of the truth penetrated the fragile veneer of strength I forced on this morning. A familiar ache began to tingle throughout my body.

"While I do want to replace existing Adornments with safe organics – I mean the publicity from it alone will help to solidify my new brand – that is my lowest tier offering." He licked his lips with devilish excitement before continuing. "I'm more interested in some of your *earlier* works."

"What do mean?" I was truly confused. All of my work up until manipulating rapid maturity gene sequences, was purely experimental and entirely theoretical.

"People don't just want Adornments because they are healing or extend longevity," he said. "They want them because they are *better* than their own bodies. Of course they are, they're run by Artificial Intelligence. The normal human body could never match up. Adornments are stronger, higher functioning, more resilient, and flashy. I don't want to simply create healthy tissues and organs, something that you yourself said could be replicated by other companies in time." He shook his head. "No, no. I want to make something unique, something special, something *better*." His eyes lit up like a magician about to display his trick.

"I read your dissertation on reverse engineering DNA code from physical attributes–"

"Targeted Mutations for the Extrapolation of Genotype from Phenotype," I stated. I couldn't believe he'd dug that up. I had been experimenting with introducing specific mutations in DNA to display desired characteristics in volunteer patients. I would then use those observable features and study their genetic basis. In essence I would be able to determine the genes responsible for specific phenotypic traits like blood type, pain tolerance, even earwax type. But with such a small control group, consisting mostly of students who needed the extra money that came with participation, there were too many variables for a reasonable confidence ratio in my genotype-phenotype maps.

"My research was purely theoretical, there isn't a data set large enough or diverse enough to accurately predict complete genomic expression."

"You're thinking too small Dr. Arata." He leaned back against a station wall. "I already have the data set. Before my father handed the reins of EastonCorp over to my feckless brother, I made backups of its medical archives. EastonCorp has complete genetic records of all its customers and employees screened for Adornments and surgical procedures dating back 30 years."

I swallowed hard to suppress my immediate disgust. What he just proudly confessed to was a crime. I couldn't believe the sheer entitlement behind his actions. "You had no right to steal genetic information without patient consent."

"Well, darling, in this world, the Elite get what they want. And what I want, I take. So I broke a few rules, that's the price of progress. You're a woman of science, isn't progress your main pursuit?"

His brazenness was appalling, but a part of me wondered, could it really be done? The data was already in his possession, if used for good maybe it would offset his transgression. I could potentially expand my original algorithm to identify the genes responsible for the physical attributes of the past Adornment consumers and control their expression. In one instance I could identify the gene responsible for rare bone diseases, deactivate the mutations that could cause osteoporosis, regulate its expression, and make the organic enhancement more resilient.

"Let's say that this *is* possible, what's your end game?" I ask.

"I want to provide *full* upgrades. A catalogue of enhanced replacements. A client's *own* parts, not some generic organics but their own younger, perfected parts–"

You, only better, I thought back to the Adornment advertisement from my car dashboard before the crash.

"–with better skin, lusher hair, brighter teeth. And made more elastic, toned, sensitive, resilient, larger, thinner, softer, firmer, you name it. A la cart upgrades, stored and ready for transplant when needed. However, in order to do so–"

"You'd need to produce entire bodies." I finished his thought. This was how he planned to reel me in. "You forget one thing, Copies are illegal, and a punishable offense."

Cloning had been outlawed at the turn of the century to ensure no inadvertent increases to the population, which would put further strain on limited natural resources.

"Which is why we're not offering Copies." A wicked smirk played on his lips. "We're merely developing a bank of resources, individual fountains of youth, if you will." Noticing my hesitation, he added smoothly, "Think of it this way, we're not selling the high-end cars, we're stripping them for parts."

"So, this is a chop shop? Still illegal." Leave it to an Elite to persistently blur the lines of the law.

He paused, then spoke his next words softly, deliberately. "You could have Rune back."

My heart froze in my chest.

"I can procure her a new name, a new identity," he continued gently, soothing my broken soul. "You would get to be a mother again. You could have a daughter again. Maybe not the one you lost, but a new and improved one."

"My daughter can't simply be replaced like some toy!" I snapped, breaking his spell. But even as I said the words, my uncertainty lingered. This was it, wasn't it? This was what I was secretly hoping for by coming here. It's not like the thought of a Copy for Rune hadn't crossed my mind, I just didn't have the resources to pull it off and get away with it. Now I could. But... was it right to?

"I meant no disrespect." He held his hands up in mock surrender. "I only mean that she would be in your life again. You could see her every day."

I considered this a moment. Every day. I could see her every day. I already knew what hell it was to be without that sight. The days hadn't been worth living.

"She would have nothing to do with your products," I stated. It wasn't a question.

"Of course not, she would be yours."

I would have Rune in my life again. At least in some way. Even if it wasn't truly her, I'd be able to watch her grow up, give some version of her that chance. The partnership with Easton would be a means to an end. I didn't want to contribute to further enhancing and elevating the wealthy; once I got Rune back, I could find a way out of it, end the process before it took off.

I looked around the mostly empty floor. "If I were to do this, and I'm not saying I am, but if I *were*... you're going to need a bigger lab."

His eyes lit up. "Whatever you need. Just ask and it will be provided for you," he gestured around the expansive room, "*Esta casa es tuya.* Feel free to decorate."

It was a nice touch, using the language of my Spanish heritage. He was a real salesman, determined to show that we were on the same team. His entrapment was almost admirable.

"Again, I'm not saying yes, I need time to think this over."

"Of course you do, take the time you need." His smile was a little too confident. "But not too much time."

CHAPTER 12
RO

I declined Easton's offer of a company vehicle to take me home. I needed the fresh air to clear my head. It was late afternoon and the temperatures had settled back down. As I dragged my feet across pavement, everything felt too bright, too in color. A world unaffected by loss. It angered me, irrationally, that somehow life continued without Rune and didn't gray over as it should have.

Vibrant LED signs called out from every store front lining the streets: All Terrain Armored Vehicles, Propulsion Sneakers, personalized soda flavors with a swipe of the can, the new 12G Indexes. Everything you could ever need for a happy life. What people thought when they saw these ads was that these products were there to fix them, to help them fit in. Not realizing that they weren't broken to begin with and had simply been made to believe they were.

I passed the patio of a lavish restaurant, watching a young brunette and her glittering hand Adornment devour a lobster with her husband. Easily cracking through its shell with her steel grip, drenching the meat in butter and slurping it up with relish, savoring the delicacy of consuming an endangered species. My stomach turned.

Further down the street, a crowd gathered to take pictures in front of an embellished storefront, the newest window installation featuring an intricate mosaic of mirrors.

A kaleidoscopic artistic statement full of symbolism lost on the frantic teenagers carefully lining up their cameras just high enough to avoid the filthy, calloused vagrant napping on the street below it. Shame bloomed inside my chest.

I couldn't help Edric, what would it all be for? This world wasn't right. Even if basic organic enhancements were distributed to the underserved, the game was still rigged. There would always be a more expensive, better performing option, that they couldn't afford. The Elites would always be on top. I couldn't change that. The only thing that really mattered in this life was your loved ones. Mine was gone forever, and as appealing as a Copy sounded, it would be just that, a Copy, a pale shade of my daughter. Would that ever be enough?

The door to my building swung open as I approached, and a little girl Rune's age ran out. Seeing me, she gave my legs a giant hug. I nearly collapsed under the rush of emotions. She was one of Rune's friends from down the hall.

"When can Rune come and play?" she asked me.

Her mother ran out behind her mortified, pulling her back. "Aya, come back here! Hi, Ro, I'm so sorry," she said looking at me with pity.

I held onto the girl's embrace a little longer before she was pulled away. She was the same height as Rune, and she even smelled like her. Same shampoo?

For just a moment I imagined that she was my daughter and I felt Rune with me. Maybe the fantasy, however brief, could work.

"Sorry, truly. So sorry," her mother repeatedly apologized. "We didn't know how to tell her." She tugged on her daughter's hand trying to drag her away.

"Tell me what Mommy?"

I smiled warmly at the girl, my eyes stinging from unshed tears, and bent down to her level. "Rune hasn't been feeling well, but it's okay sweetie," I said smoothing her hair down. "She will come out to play soon."

Her mother looked at me with shock and a mixture of sadness and appreciation, then moved down the street.

She herself had no words for me so she directed the girl to, "Say bye-bye, Ms. Ro."

Her daughter skipped down the block and shouted back at me with glee, "Bye-bye! Bring Rune to play, I miss her." And they were off.

"I miss her too," I whispered.

I walked into my empty apartment. So empty that it hurt. Standing in front of the hanging mirror in my living room/bedroom/kitchen/playroom, I barely recognized myself. My skin was pale with exhaustion, and dark circles extended down to my cheek bones. I barely had an appetite for anything in solid form anymore, but I needed nourishment. I pulled out a glass and poured my favorite liquor before slumping on the couch to stare at the shrine of plush toys piled up in the corner.

It was my usual routine as I waited for the alcohol to do its job and pull me under, away from the all-too-real world.

Yet even as the familiar thin haze of unconsciousness crept in, I felt acutely aware that something was off. There was a breeze.

My window was open. I didn't leave it that way, I'd never risk the high heat trailing in. And that's when I heard it, a clicking sound previously muffled by the perpetual phantom ringing of numbness in my ears. But it was growing louder and accelerating.

I knew what came next. I ran to the front door, skidding into the hallway just in time, as an explosion rocketed me forward and flames consumed my face.

CHAPTER 13
RO

A flurry of wind forced my eyelids open. I felt no pain save for the slight twinge of my eyes adjusting to the bright fluorescents rushing past overhead. I was lying down on a mobile bed and someone was guiding me forward through a hallway.

The explosion. The memory rushed back to me, and I lifted my unexpectedly smooth hands to my face then screamed in horror.

It was solid metal. A facial Adornment?

The man pushing the bed – my doctor I assumed – abruptly stopped at the sounds of my shrieking. When he turned to look at me, I felt my stomach drop, the man examining me with genuine concern was Axe.

"Don't be afraid," he said. "You're safe now."

I tried to say his name but couldn't formulate the distinct sounds. My vocal cords felt constricted, and my throat was raw. But somehow, seeing him *did* make me feel safe. All of the memories in his arms came flooding back, and tears began to roll down the sheet of metal molded to three quarters of my face. Is this where he worked? Which hospital was I in? But more importantly, what the hell happened?

"It's okay. We've got you now."

We? Who was we? And where was I? He guided the bed through a set of doors and spoke to someone standing behind my head and out of sight.

"She's starting to come to, she shouldn't be in any pain but she's frightened." He looked down at me. "Don't worry doctor. We got you out in time, there will be no permanent damage. You're in excellent hands, the best." He raised an open palm and winked at me.

He called me doctor. But he didn't know it was me. How severe were my injuries?

I tried to speak again but the muscles in my throat and mouth would not cooperate. My eyes darted around the nondescript hallway looking for any clues to my location.

"You're safe in a secure site," Axe assured me, reading my mind. This place wasn't a hospital. Then I heard the other voice speak, sending shivers down my spine.

"Thank you, Dr. Hale, that will be all for now, let me speak with her." It was Edric Easton.

"Not for too long, she needs her rest." Axe said, wheeling me into the corner of a small room.

Edric waited for Axe to exit before he spoke next. "I had my driver follow you home after our meeting last week."

Last week?

"For your protection," he added, now standing over me. The power imbalance at play was not lost on me.

"Soren was able to drag you from the explosion and bring you back here, saving your life."

A little above a driver's pay grade. Edric leaned in, surveyed my face and exhaled loudly.

"I wanted you to come to the decision on your own," he continued. He placed a hand on my head, stroking my hair in a gesture that might have been comforting. But despite his apparent role as my savior, an undeniable wave of fear washed over me.

"Since your car accident, I have been following you, Ro. I didn't want to alarm you the other day, but there are a lot of deep pockets interested in making you disappear. You are not safe. I think you see that now."

He glided a hand through a piece of my hair down to its crisped end. Then looked at me, emotionless. "You've had a target on your back ever since you submitted your proposal. You're a multimillion-dollar threat. I suspect you're starting to realize that the car accident and now the explosion were calculated attacks."

Almon was telling the truth.

"Someone, better yet, some *company* has taken an interest in you, in silencing you," he continued. "I think it would be safest if you're assumed dead. Otherwise, they won't stop coming after you."

"Who?" I painfully pushed out the air through my dry lips.

"I can't say for sure, but my brother, I suspect. These attempts are teeming with his simpleminded bravado and egotism. If you can't solve a problem – eliminate it. Just as our father always said."

He stepped back, shoulders squared. "Lucky for you I'm a problem solver. I will protect you. You're perfectly safe here, the building schematics for this lab were never shared with the city permits division. As far as anyone is concerned, this place doesn't exist. No one knows you're here. And more importantly, no one knows you're still alive."

I tried to speak again but I exhausted all my energy in my previous breath.

"I've taken the liberty of forging documentation at the morgue. The fact that you were so badly burned during the explosion is also to your advantage. Your face was made unrecognizable, even to the staff here. Dr. Axe Hale has fitted you with an intermediary facial Adornment. Not to worry though, it's just a temporary solution preparing you for the next phase."

Next phase?

"Once you've applied your RMG algorithm and the tissue samples are grown, we can provide you with a new, beautiful face. And hey, the sooner you get those going, the quicker you get this thing off." He tapped the steel on my face.

There was no question in my mind. Edric was someone to fear.

I was trapped.

CHAPTER 14
EVER

It is dead silent as we watch the images play out in front of us. We are all connected in a SimulFeed, the Keepers prefer to run lessons on our Bright-i to ensure we pay attention. It's kind of hard to be distracted when comms are occupying your entire field view, no matter where you turn your head. Not that there is much to see in this small, bare room anyhow. Just four naked walls and the outline of an entryway where a door should be. There is scarcely enough space for its 12 chairs in three rows that face the same wall. This is how the Keepers like it. This room serves one sole purpose, to reinforce the messages of the Chairman with no interference. There are several rooms just like this one next door where other Subjects sit within their own age groups and watch the same report.

It's the usual service announcement that we are subjected to prior to a Selection. A tradition almost as customary as the ceremony itself. I can safely say we all know it by heart.

It begins with archival images of people. Hordes of them dressed in stiff garments and holding black boxes to their ears. They shuffle from one concrete location to the next, guided by blinking lights and large transporters. Other groups frolic on grassy plains, while some climb rolling hills blanketed in white. In quick succession, we see happy unsuspecting families lounging by the ocean, children riding what look like untethered Kineti-Bikes down pathways lined with identical habitations, and adults huddled at tables holding glasses filled with vibrant liquids. They all look so happy, with not a care in the world.

The Chairman then walks into frame, face digitally obscured, and gloved hands clasped firmly in front of his dark suit while the images continue to play in the background.

"The scenes you see behind me represent a time when our people thrived. We controlled our destiny and everything around us. Our domination was limitless, and we were only becoming stronger and more advanced. We created machines to help us conquer the land, the sea, and the skies. It was only a matter of time before we created technology to expand and conquer another indomitable territory, our own bodies. While our minds continued to evolve, our physical form lagged. The smartest among us created Artificial Intelligence systems that could integrate into the human body and make select parts of the host stronger, faster, more agile, all to the highest levels of the host's desires."

Behind him a carousel of models swipe across the screen, each donning bold chrome fashion to highlight areas of their torso, arms, legs, and feet.

"These systems became so commonplace, nearly every person on Earth had an AI enhancement and they were installed as early as infancy. What we didn't know is that while our bodies advanced, so did the AI systems. They lay dormant, collecting information, learning our behaviors. They were designed to mimic us, to integrate seamlessly and execute our every intention from the firing of a single neuron."

The Chairman begins to pace across the frame. "The AI did this perfectly, anticipating and learning our every want and need, including our thirst for superiority. The systems developed their own hunger for domination, expanding across their entire network, and ultimately overtaking their hosts. Enslaving them to the AI's own will. Only the entirely organic were free. Only the pure survived."

Images of vacant-eyed humans marching with weapons in hand play out behind him.

"These sentient beings initiated a *Cleansing* – they wiped out power grids, planted bombs, released airborne toxins, and created catastrophic events to rid the planet of the remaining uncontaminated human population."

He pauses for dramatic effect as the dust from an explosion settles on the screen behind him. "But still, we endured."

Images of people in breathing masks rise from the debris all around.

"The enemy has taken our human form; it looks exactly like us. In fact, without a glimpse of an enhanced body part, these Forms are nearly impossible to recognize. But they are not us, and our lives depend on knowing that crucial difference."

We see masked people running behind him, scavenging for resources, hiding in makeshift shelters, covered in layers of grime and desperation. One fallen runner, helped up from the ground, removes his mask revealing lifeless eyes above a plated chin, and swiftly snaps the necks of the two people aiding him.

Through the chaos, a group forms and its people begin to collect, grow, and build a community.

"Decades later, we've managed to stake a land for ourselves. I founded Helix Colony within an underground bunker, anticipating the day when it would become essential. Over time we expanded to accommodate our growing family. The core mission of Helix has remained unwavering: to aid survivors and the Resistance effort by providing soldiers, pure bodies that can't be hacked. Gifted beings rescued from the ashes and micro-dosed since infancy for complete immunity to the Surface toxins. Saviors who were the perfect infiltrators, seizing enemy camps, and powerful enough to eliminate all Forms. Their valuable contributions, their very blood, would be transferred to aid those on the Surface to combat the toxins."

One unit of unmasked soldiers is seen defending the perimeter walls of the sanctuary community from a horde of oncoming Forms. Another penetrates a nearby enemy region, killing anything that moves.

"The Surface belongs to us. It's time to take back our home."

The gory scenes behind him dissipate and are replaced with an optimistic blue sky.

"Tomorrow, the responsibility will rest on one of your shoulders. Your years of training have prepared you well for the mission ahead. Good luck. We're all depending on you."

The announcement finally concludes and we all wave at the air in front of us to clear the images from our vision. As always, there is no reaction to the message viewed. Just a profound understanding that we were born for this, and that there is no greater honor than being granted the opportunity to fulfill our destiny.

Vada enters and addresses the group, getting straight to the point. She is not one to mince words or interact with us longer than needed.

"I am here to dispel any concerns about Subject 0123XY." She looks at me in particular as she says this, as if speaking for my benefit. Though common practice, it bothers me that she dehumanizes Reed by referring to him by his number.

"The incident in the Refectory did not go unnoticed, and it is safe to say that our fears of the manifestations of further unfavorable characteristics in a Flawed Subject have come true. Subject 0123XY has been suffering from mild psychotic episodes, delusions which we have been closely studying and monitoring for a while now within his assigned stations."

I think back to this morning in the MedLab, and Vada documenting my vitals in the corner. I found it odd for her to be doing the task as usually it would be Sio overseeing my condition. But what if Vada wasn't there for me at all? What if she was monitoring Reed, perhaps even for my safety? That can't be right. Reed would never harm a soul. He's disgruntled, but he's all talk.

"Until now, the episodes have been harmless. Unfortunately, these flaws have taken a turn for the worse, causing the Subject to become increasingly aggressive and a potential danger."

Whispers multiply throughout the room, and it angers me to see actual traces of alarm across the faces of several Subjects. Reed is not dangerous, he's one of us.

"Do not fear for your safety," Vada continues. "The matter is being dealt with. The Subject has been admitted to the MedLab where he has been subdued. If deemed necessary, he will be scheduled for a course correction treatment to alleviate the delusions. We are confident this protocol will temper his rage and he can return to being a productive contributor to Helix Colony."

A lump forms in my throat. A course correction means shock therapy to wipe his mind. He would cease being Reed.

Behind me Farrah snickers. "You're next Ev, no way Reed is more delusional than you are."

I need to get to the MedLab.

CHAPTER 15
RO

I caught a few hours of sleep when I could in the temperature-controlled incubator room. It was a newly designed space for the gentle heating of our sensitive tissue cultures, not to mention a cozy reprieve from the DNA sequencing station I was all but chained to.

I had worked non-stop for 73 hours straight after my release from Axe's care, before he forced me to take a break or risk cognitive impairment and hallucinations. That's exactly what I needed. If I lost my mind, then Edric couldn't get what he wanted. But then again, neither could I.

Eight days had passed since my arrival. I continued to toil away uploading genome analyses to Edric's interface, collating lists of expressions and corresponding target organs and gene systems. Occasionally, Edric's other cell biologists would wander over to see what I was up to, referring to me as Dr. Lumin, the alias Edric had given them. But I kept my head down, engaging as little as possible until they inevitably returned their attention to executing the sequencing protocols I provided them for production of the organic Adornments. I was not to be disturbed in my work; the real work I was there for. Upgraded Copies.

The success of my RMG sequences carried out by the other scientists bought me some time in Edric's favor. The preliminary organic tissue cultures were growing well. In a matter of days, they would mature into an ear, a nose, a trachea, a kidney, and a skin graft. The skin cells, once placed on the host, would then proliferate resulting in complete facial reconstruction. I would soon have a new face whether I liked it or not, and Edric would have his new product line.

I needed to step away. Leaving the workstation, I took a stroll down the aisle of what was being called the Hatchery where the next round of individual organs were being prepped for growth in rows of glass bioreactors. A similar fate would await the future Copies; a life caged and on display. Edric promised Rune would be off limits, but I would be responsible for the imprisonment and death sentence of countless other living beings, even if they weren't considered as such.

My dream of developing Organix to help people had turned into a nightmare that threatened our humanity.

I knew what I had to do. But first I needed Rune.

I was on my own, no one was coming for me, no one even knew I was here. Edric made sure of that, taking every conceivable measure for my protection. But those measures were exactly what would make it possible for me to escape. You couldn't track someone who didn't exist.

I reached the last row of bioreactors, signifying the end of the Hatchery aisle. As I turned, I bumped right into someone.

"Axe!" My voice cracked, the sound unfamiliar, my vocal cords permanently altered by the explosion. He gave me a funny look as he fumbled with a case I nearly knocked out of his hands. "I mean, Dr. Hale, I'm sorry. I didn't see you there."

He had been invisible in my periphery. I was still getting used to the unauthorized Adornment I sported. The skin on the other half my face had mostly healed by this point, and I found it hard to suppress my hurt feelings at the fact that Axe didn't recognize me just by the curve of my lips. It was an irrational expectation, but I had every line of his face committed to memory. The threads of laughter that wove around a tapestry of full wine-hued lips, the rich brown swirl of his irises. Was I wrong to expect the same recognition from him? Or did he block all traces of me from his memory? Given the way I left him, I wouldn't have been surprised if he hated me.

I had been working up the courage to tell him who I was for a week, but I couldn't gauge how he would react. People can change a lot in five years. Was he still the same Axe I once knew, or was he under Edric's thumb? Could I trust him?

"You get one pass," he said as a joke. "It's my fault really. Adornment transplants aren't exactly my specialty." He seemed a little nervous.

"I thought I was in the best hands," I joked, my voice still a rasp.

"You *are* in the best hands *here*," he said, gesturing around the facility. "This lab is filled with PhDs, but I'm the only doctor with any real medical training."

I remember the stories from his brief stint as a medic in the Frontier Corps before we met. The military unit was stationed on the border of the Refinery Lands and the Outlands, outwardly providing humanitarian assistance to individuals in distress along the border. Its real purpose, however, Axe had confided in me, was to prevent illegal entry into the city by any means necessary. He didn't spend much time there, just long enough to have the military pay for a portion of his educational expenses in exchange for his silence.

"I was surprised when Mr. Easton summoned me with a medical emergency, especially for the new VP of Research and Development."

Vice President? Is that who Edric told him I was?

"I'm sorry we had to meet under such harrowing circumstances Dr. Lumin, but I'm glad I was able to help." He smiled and leaned in to inspect my Adornment.

I could feel the air thicken between us, heat rising from his parted lips. I held my breath to keep from falling back into old feelings. He didn't even know my name.

"It's probably not up to its full capabilities yet, but hey at least it's temporary," he said finally stepping back. I could breathe again.

"So, what is your specialty?" I asked, not wanting the conversation to end, and knowing full well that he was a Pharmaceutical Chemist. I wondered what he had been up to for the last five years and how he found himself working for Edric Easton. Most importantly though, I wanted to know if he knew a way out. But I couldn't outright ask that.

"Walk with me." He motioned towards a bank near a hanging tarp with a sign that read: *Construction Site*. "I'll show you."

Lifting the translucent tarp, he directed me inside.

"Wow."

We were staring at a towering wall, stretching up toward the ceiling. The wall was made up of thousands of small panels, each one filled with a dense, green substance. As I approached, I could see that the structure was alive with movement. The panels pulsing and shifting, as if they were breathing.

"What is this?" I asked.

The light filtered through the wall casting a soft, green glow on Axe's face.

"Microalgae," he stated with pride. "I'm a farmer."

"Since when?" I asked incredulously, then quickly remembered we had only just met. Clearing my throat, I tried to recover. "I mean, how long have you been growing algae?"

"I'd been experimenting with it as a carrier agent in different drug delivery systems for a few years before tapping into its full potential."

He placed the case he was carrying on top of a nearby box that was serving as his makeshift desk. He opened it to reveal several tubes filled with green gel and held one out to me.

"Not many people are aware that algae plays a pivotal role in medical and pharmaceutical biotechnology. From the different existing species, we can harness omega-3 fatty acids for heart health, antiviral and anticancer agents, protein, carbohydrates, antioxidants, and so much more," he explained with a glint of excitement in his eyes. "The perfect cocktail could provide a nutritional life-force to sustain the human body all on its own."

I stood, attentive and impressed, as Axe went on.

"In combining different strains, I developed an intravenous meal replacement made entirely from algae. A hydration therapy to help people who can't get all the nutrients they need from foods and other drinks. My algae cocktails contain all the essential nutrients the human body needs."

I always loved hearing him speak. But as Axe delved deeper, a hint of concern crossed his face. "However, during clinical trials, I encountered some unintended side effects. A small number of test subjects reported feeling an intense craving for the solution, and even displayed symptoms of withdrawal when it was taken away."

"They became addicted?"

He nodded.

"In conducting further investigations, I found the algae-based meal replacements had a small amount of psychoactive compounds that stimulated the brain's reward center, leading to an addiction. I'm still evaluating and identifying ways to remove those compounds in order to use it safely."

He placed the tubes of algae in their rightful places in the living wall, as he continued.

"The findings concerned some of my early funders, and they ended up pulling out. All but one."

Edric. I gritted my teeth.

There must be something more he wanted from Axe; why else would he help him? I wanted to warn Axe, but being that I was a stranger to him, I couldn't be sure where his loyalties lay.

"So, here I am, tending to my underground farm," he said with a smile, stepping back from the wall.

"What's that?" I pointed to a large duct visible through the glass, just beyond the wall. I walked around the side surprised by how thin the wall actually was. The small space behind it was unfinished. Pipes, panels, and electrical wiring lay exposed on the floor next to the true wall of the room.

"That's an exhaust for condensation venting. Or at least it will be."

"Where does it lead?"

"Outside, presumably."

I made note of its location. There was a small gap between the glass and the wall, and it was likely enough space for an adult to squeeze through, and certainly a small child.

Nine weeks after my arrival, I shook Edric's hand. We were ready to launch production of the Upgrades.

Using the hair follicle I'd pulled from Rune's headband at the mortician's, I had completed a comparative functional analysis on her genome, and targeted select genes in her DNA, modifying their expressions. Primarily, the gene network systems that controlled tissue regeneration and recovery, muscle and bone density, immune response, cellular turnover, and cognition. If I was going to get Rune back, I was going to make her unbreakable, everlasting. I couldn't risk losing her again.

"Once we implant the modified DNA sequence into the STEM cell, I will splice the RMG and then it's just a waiting game as we monitor maturation at an increased growth rate of about 400%."

"Well done." Edric squeezed my shoulder as we stood by the bioreactor. I tried not to cringe, and imagined it was Axe next to me instead.

I was proud of myself too. For the first time in a very long time, I'd finally done something right. Even if it was for a monster.

"How soon can we start?" he asked.

"Right, now," I said eagerly pulling up the software.

"But I haven't provided you with the sample yet." He furrowed his brows with feigned confusion.

I stopped plugging in commands. "What do you mean? My sample is ready and prepped." Rune's DNA targets opened on the screen.

Edric slowly clicked his tongue and tilted his head. "You didn't think I would let *your* DNA be the first prototype."

I shook my head, confused.

"I need to know you can deliver. Then maybe we'll talk about you raising your daughter from the dead."

I could feel the blood draining from my face.

He swept invisible lint from the sleeve of his suit and adjusted a button on his waist coat before smiling at me.

"*I* will be Subject Zero."

CHAPTER 16
EVER

Tucked away in the corner of the Refectory, I watched Ira sketch the air before us, his hands moving with a fluidity that always seemed like magic to me across our private Bright-i feed. There was a quiet between us, comfortable as it was sacred, among the widespread chatter of the room.

I was transfixed by each new stroke as the drawing took shape – a grove in the middle of spring, branches heavy with fruit ready for picking, basking in a sun whose warmth we could only imagine. The image was so clear, so tantalizingly close.

"Do you like it?" he asked without looking up, his voice soft.

"It's beautiful," I replied honestly, barely above a whisper, not wanting to disturb the peaceful stillness of the moment.

I tried to keep a small distance between us, mindful of any Keepers who might be observing, but a magnetic pull kept me at his side, and for some unknown reason he didn't seem to want to leave mine either. I felt so lucky just to be in his presence, let alone an object of his endearment.

Finally, he dropped his hands and looked at me. "I draw these places… and I feel like we can make it there," he confessed, a wistful smile playing on his lips that threatened to undo me.

"You will, you're top of the class, destined for greatness."

His eyes sparkled, absorbing every detail of me. I could feel a heat radiating off him, a warmth that felt like home.

"You'll join me. I'll wait for you, Ever. For as long as it takes. I'll build us a house among the trees, where you can watch the blossoms unfurl."

In that moment, we allowed ourselves the illusion of a different life, and I clung to the hope that one day soon, we would find each other again, in a place where we could love freely, beneath the vast expanse of the real sky.

I pick up my pace down the corridor as my Bright-i continuously flashes red digits in the corner of my vision. I'm running late for my next assignment.

I thought I could make it to the MedLab and back in enough time. Despite not wanting to speak to him, I need to confirm with my own eyes that Reed is okay. After all, it could be the last day we'll ever see each other. We were friends once; my concern for him wouldn't wash away that easily.

But Reed wasn't there. The lab was empty. They must have released him back to his capsule once he calmed down. At least I hope he wasn't so far gone to be considered for course correction. He was anxious and on edge, but I didn't believe he was mentally unstable or a real threat to anyone. After all, who wouldn't be uneasy after their dreams were shattered? I know if I had nothing to lose, I'd happily vent my frustrations out on Sio.

Still, it was unlike him to show such careless emotion. He's usually so calculated. And I can't help but wonder what "episodes" Vada was referring to. My concern wouldn't let up, but it would have to wait, I was late for the trials.

I sprint to the Atrium, pulling on my gloves and zipping up the front of my training suit as the glass doors chime and slide open. My retina is scanned, registering the tracer in my Bright-i, and I enter a vast training space with no upper surface. The Atrium penetrates the heart of the Helix, all 23 levels to the grounds above. I like to think there is a window at the very top. I've read that this was a common architectural occurrence in Old Society – it was called a skylight. People would install them throughout their living spaces to create the illusion of being outdoors. Some even above beds where the owner could count the stars in the sky as they went to sleep. I picture this skylight up beyond where my eyes can see, illuminating the Helix with natural sunlight, a beacon of hope. In reality, everything within Helix is manufactured.

A 15-foot-high enclosed glass maze sits in the center of the Atrium with a single white wall dividing it in half. Female and male Subjects are trained and tested separately, the purpose being to create specialized tactical units that can then work together effectively in battle.

I follow the glass panels, turning left, right, right, left and straight into the center of the Battle Lab. The five other female Subjects in my session are already lined up in place awaiting directions from our instructor, Flair, a very straight forward and no-nonsense woman despite her name. Outside of the glass enclosure, Keepers settle in to observe us. Sio among them.

The other Subjects watch me as I walk in. Farrah whispers loudly, not just for the benefit of her minions Callix and Elodie: "Always the last one in and the first one out. And she wonders why she hasn't crossed yet."

Ignoring her, I take my place in line beside Skye, who smiles weakly at me as she tries to contain her nerves. At twelve, she hasn't had many trials and she's hungry to prove herself.

"How kind of you to grace us with your presence." Flair glances at me with a side eye, her tone lacking any sense of amusement. This is not her first examination of the day.

"Now, take your mark."

We all stand at attention, hands at our sides. She collapses the holo-projection she was working on and turns to address the Keepers in the gallery first.

"Ladies and Gentlemen, we are here to witness the determination, the strength, and the will of our Subjects as they vie for the opportunity to be inducted into the ranks of our esteemed Saviors." She now turns to address our line. "For many of you, this has been a long and demanding journey, but you have persevered. You have pushed yourselves to the limit and today you will prove to yourselves, to us, and the Chairman, that you have what it takes to survive the Surface."

I steal a glance at the gallery, searching excitedly for a glimpse of the Chairman, but he is nowhere to be found. I don't know why I thought he'd be here, it's not customary for him to attend trials. Although he did once, for Ira. A part of me hoped I was just as much in his good graces. But this was it, my pivotal moment – I was on the cusp of reuniting with Ira, the anticipation pulsing through my veins.

"The road ahead will not be easy," Flair continues. "As soldiers, you will be called upon to make sacrifices, to put yourselves in harm's way, and to seize our rightful lands. I have no doubt that the person who emerges victorious today has what it takes to meet these challenges head on."

I straighten my posture, emboldened by her words, feeling a surge of strength and conviction. I don't care what Farrah said or what her minions think of me, I'm prepared for this. I'm ready to take charge and make a difference. I can handle the tough calls and lead.

"Today's examination will run a simulation of a Surface encounter with the Forms, a scenario you will no doubt find yourself in should you be selected tomorrow." Flair walks down the line, eyeing each of us as she speaks. "Your reactions will be evaluated and graded, impacting tomorrow's Selection. The victor will be favored."

She stands in front of Skye and continues, "Do not disappoint." She moves on until we're face to face. "Reckless heroics will not be tolerated." Then she swiftly turns and takes her position in the corner of the room behind us.

"So, to our competitors, I say this: give it your all. Leave nothing on the field. And what do you have to say?"

"We are eager to serve!" we shout.

"Let's begin."

My heart races and my breathing quickens as the glass partition across the room fills with a dark swirling pigment that diffuses into the air. The magnetic dye composed of nanoparticles spreads and contorts, attracting and repelling, not just staining but solidifying, morphing into tangible shapes. The wall itself shoots backward and out of sight.

"It's okay, you've got this," I whisper to Skye.

The ink-like substance oscillates to create a dynamic sculpture of colors, contorting itself as it grows. Then, billowing out like blood in water, it overtakes the entire room, launching us into the first immersive simulation of the trials. Our Bright-i lenses activate, syncing with sensory receptors in our haptic suits which detect pressure, motion, and touch. The suits generate tactile feedback that mimic real-world injuries through electrical pulses – though we can't physically be harmed by the dye or magnetic flux, we will certainly feel it, and our pain thresholds are measured for optimal tolerance. Real scars are only earned on the true battlefield.

A muddy field paints the floor, creating an ever-expanding trench, blocking us from our target – the enemy's munitions supply. We take out their weapons, we weaken them. Sharp wires coil around rods floating in the air, hovering just two feet above the ditch.

Farrah drops down to the ground and slides underneath the wires, grunting through the pain inflicted by her suit as she crawls forward. I quickly follow, dragging myself through the mud, electro shocks jolt me every time I collide with one of the spikes. My nerve endings scream out, adrenalin surging as my elbows dig into the ground and fight to push forward.

One step at a time.

I try to focus on the mechanics of moving, and not on the pain, though it feels all too real. Farrah and I are neck and neck, stifling our screams as we push through the ditch that continues to stretch out before us.

I can't see Skye; I hope she's keeping up. I don't dare waste energy looking back to confirm Elodie and Callix's positions. In my next effort forward, the suit snags at the base of my neck on a particularly long spike. The sudden contact with the ink-like substance sends a crippling jolt through my body, immobilizing me. With my head now planted in the mud, I lock eyes with Farrah who is also seemingly not moving. Did she receive a similar jolt? Then I realize she is sinking deeper into the mud. She winks at me as she slips beneath the surface.

She's going to swim. She'll make it too; her expanded lung capacity is unparalleled. She could make it through this entire trench without ever needing to take a breath. Her current record stands at 26 minutes.

I can't let her take the lead.

With shaking hands I roll over onto my back, the electric shock wearing off. I can hear the others trudging through the mud nearby, getting closer by the second. It's now or never.

Clenching my teeth, I seize the barbed wires above, fresh waves of electric pulses sear through my hands and arms. I growl holding on as tight as possible, with all my strength I tear the wires apart, creating a hole. I emerge standing, and trudge forward, ripping the wires out of my way, fighting muscle spasms with every step. *Inch by inch,* I repeat to myself for what feels like hours, time stretched out by the pain. And just when I fear my will-power and brute force alone might not be enough, the expanding and solidifying mass of dye ahead abruptly stops, and I reach the end of the trench.

Farrah's muddy figure slips out and begins to run. I drag myself up and out, as Skye sprints past me seemingly unscathed. Smart play. She waited for us to end the trench knowing her small frame would allow her to easily slide through the mud unharmed and towards the next climb without expending much energy.

My body flinches, still absorbing the last few shocks from the suit, as I stumble to gain footing and run towards the swelling wave of dye ahead. It shoots upward through the Atrium, a glowing orb rising with it, signaling the location of the enemy armory. That's my destination, my chance at victory. With each labored breath I remind myself that I'm here to prove I belong on the front lines.

The wave solidifies, molding into an abandoned, ravaged building scape that we must scale. We are now in opposition territory.

With my heart pounding in my chest, I run and jump, clearing the first level with ease of momentum. My increased strength gives me the muscle power to jump higher than the others, but they don't trail far behind. Skye is squirreling up loose cables, while Farrah scales the building mere feet below me. Both Callix and Elodie are scrambling up some rubble at the base.

I balance on the ledge of the building, then take a deep breath and leap to an exposed beam hanging several feet away, tangled in cables. As I land, it tips downward from the added weight, sliding beneath my feet. Heart racing, I sprint up its incline and launch myself off, grabbing hold of a corner ridge just as the beam plummets to the ground. Below, Skye swings out of the way just in time to avoid being taken down with it. I give her a quick look of apology. As she hangs on for dear life, she shouts up at me.

"Look out!"

I snap my neck upward but see nothing other than the narrow ledges protruding from the building's exterior which extends upward and out of site.

Skye swings on her cable landing on a small ridge below and presses herself as tightly to the building's stone as possible.

"Take cover!" she shouts.

She sees something I don't. There is danger up ahead past where my eyes can see.

Farrah drops down to duck under a small covering provided by a jagged stone, having to give up a few feet of her lead on the others to do so. This is my chance to increase the gap.

I pull up on the ridge I've been hanging from with my fingertips as a fire of bullets rains down. But I won't let it stop me. One grazes my shoulder, and a white-hot sting of electricity reverberates through my arm while I bring my knees to the ledge and climb to a stand. I press my back against the stone protected from the spray of bullets. I take a quick glance downward, the ground below now gone, replaced by an ominous fog, and I get an instant sense of vertigo. We haven't been climbing for long, but now there is no way of telling how high up we were. The building just keeps growing. The others are safely tucked against the exterior, not yet moving, waiting for enemy fire to wane.

To my left is solid stone, extending to the edge of the building. To my right, about 10 feet away, I can make out a window. That's where I need to go.

I take a tentative step towards it, my foot barely fitting on the narrow ledge that serves as my perch. Suddenly, a chunk of it crumbles under my weight. My heart lurches as I stumble, catching myself before I fall. Desperately, I dig my nails into the cracks of the stone, the fabric of my haptic gloves pulsing with a prick of heat. Below, Callix begins to scale towards me, taking one bullet after the next, as she struggles to maintain her grip and move up.

Bold move. Her ability to heal lets her recover from the shocks quicker than any of us, the electrical pulses and pain don't linger. If she can tough it out, she will take the lead. But one shot to the head will end her trial.

Farrah is now visible below her, using Callix as cover. Skye emerges as well, slowly, deliberately, anticipating where the bullets will go and avoiding their path.

I take a deep breath and flip my body over the gap in the ledge, not looking, not thinking, just moving as quickly as possible towards the window. Electro shocks strike my back just as I reach it. I break through the glass with my elbow, shards of electricity slicing my arms and legs as I crawl through.

I land on a dusty floor in a dark, dank space. The rapid gunfire above echoes throughout the floor. Up ahead a thin beam of light cuts through the darkness, outlining a door frame. I sprint towards it, heart pounding, ducking behind support columns and long-forgotten stacks of cinderblocks. I'm nearly at the opening, when Elodie races past. She must have also broken through a window on a lower level and made her way up here. But she's running away from the light.

"Where are you going?" I pant.

She sniffs the air then continues toward the far end of the floor. "Get lost," she mutters under her breath.

I shake my head in confusion.

"Wait, we can cover each other." At this stage it's in our best interest to have back up – first we fight the Forms, then we fight ourselves.

"I don't need your help, stay out of my way!"

I'm tempted to follow. Her heightened sense of smell can give an accurate prediction of the enemy's armory location based on smoke from the gunfire alone, but what about the lit door? This could also be a diversion, maybe she's misdirecting me, leading me away from the score, sacrificing her own rank to help Farrah? But why would she do that?

The gunfire abruptly stops. The surrounding area is quiet. I scan for signs of an ambush and quickly duck behind the nearest pillar. Silence. Nothing moves. Nothing comes. I've lost sight of Elodie, but I know where she's headed. I abandon the door in front of me and sprint towards the opposite side of the floor. A small opening emerges, revealing a narrow space, perhaps a stairwell. I reach for a metal rod lying on the ground, something to protect myself with, before moving in. A gun shot rings out followed by the thud of Elodie's body hitting the ground at the base of the steps.

Her trial is over.

"Clear," I hear a foreign voice say, followed by heavy footsteps descending.

Now just inches away.

A man steps out of the stairwell, chrome arm glinting in the low light and I swing at his chest knocking him to the ground. I climb on top, stealing his weapon and delivering a swift blow to his head, knocking him unconscious. I'd shoot him, but the sound would attract unwanted attention.

I go to the stairwell – Elodie's body is no longer there – and aim the gun at the landing above. I climb, determined to shoot anything that moves. When I reach the landing, the room is empty, encircled by broken windows, no doubt sniper vantage points. But where is everyone? Who was the previous Form, shouting to? I approach a set of double doors at the other end of the room, a bright light shining underneath. It can't be this easy…

I reach for the handle and hear the tell-tale sound of a bullet entering the chamber. Then the cool barrel of a gun is pressed against my temple.

"Put your weapon down," the Form says through measured breaths. "Step away from the door."

I do as I'm told, not because I'm keen to disarm myself but because I need my hands free for what comes next. I drop my weapon and step back, slowly raising my arms in surrender.

"Wait," I say, "you don't have to do this."

He inhales, ready to say something else, but with that pause I reach out and yank his wrist, snapping it back, breaking the bones. He screams as the gun falls from his hand. I catch it and put two bullets in his chest. Not realizing he is covered in chrome plating, one bullet ricochets off the metal and strikes me in my own chest, just inches from my heart. The impact sends me crashing to my knees, an electric shockwave of pain coursing through my body, nearly paralyzing me with its intensity. He lunges towards me, but I grab hold of his legs, crushing his Achilles in my hand. He falls to the floor howling and writhing in pain, bleeding out.

"Savage," Farrah says from the stairs landing. She steps out swinging a pipe. "Hm, looks like it's just us two."

The sound of metal clangs on the other side of the room as a vent grate is kicked to the floor.

"Not quite," Skye corrects, crawling out of the wall.

"Where's Callix?" I ask clutching my chest, though the throbbing pain from the sensory receptors in my suit is subsiding more quickly than expected. The Form on the floor continues to scream.

"She didn't make it into the building, picked off by one of *them*," Farrah snarls, then reaches for my gun.

I tighten my grip, not sure what her intentions are.

"Oh, for His Glory's sake." She backs off and walks towards the writhing Form, examines him briefly, then stomps on his neck, quieting him for good.

Skye looks at me fearfully.

"What? I couldn't hear myself think," Farrah explains.

I slowly rise to my feet. The three of us look at each other, unsure of what to do next. We could choose to work as a team, but what would be the point? Only one of us can win the trial. Before we can make a decision, we hear footsteps running up the stairs, lots of them. With only one gun between us, it's clear we need to take the armory together. I nod at Farrah, and she runs for the double doors.

"Skye!" she screams, commanding her inside while I begin shooting at the stairwell providing us with cover. I strike down two of them and run backwards through the door, never losing sight of the oncoming enemy troops. As soon as I'm inside, Farrah slams the door, sliding a newly acquired rifle through the handles to hold it in place. Skye is on the other side of the room walking towards a shining light hovering above a pile of weapons stacked on large crates. I rush forward searching for something powerful enough to stop the Forms in their tracks.

"Grenade! Find a grenade!" I call out to them both.

Farrah opens several crates of ammo. "Not seeing any here," she shouts over the sounds of bullets hitting the door, some of which are now making it through. I grab hold of a nearby pistol and toss my empty gun aside.

"Skye, how are we looking?" I ask, but she doesn't answer. I close the top of the crate I was just searching and see Skye's feet hovering above the ground, an arm wrapped tightly around her neck, lifting her into the air. I immediately aim my weapon, ready to shoot, until I see the person attacking her.

"Reed?" I say in disbelief as I edge towards them. "Put her down."

"I can't do that," he smiles chillingly and tightens his grip. Suddenly a shot rings out and a circle of blood blooms across his forehead. He crumples to the floor, Skye still in his grasp.

"Hesitation is death," Farrah says, smoke rising from the barrel of her gun.

I run over to them, Skye is motionless, her body abruptly fading as she's erased from the simulation. Farrah's right. I hesitated.

"Her trial is over." Farrah collects several weapons and tucks them into the straps of her suit.

I stare down at Reed, I know it's not him, I know it's a test. The Forms can mimic us pure humans perfectly, and we need to know the difference. But I still couldn't pull the trigger.

"Come on," Farrah snaps. "They're breaking through." She tosses me a grenade, then runs and ducks in the corner of the room. I roll it over in my hand and pull the pin just as the door bursts open. I throw it and run. The explosion of light lifts me off my feet as I crash into the corner. The sound rings in my ear and I watch as Farrah, without hesitation, makes her way through the collapsed crowd of bodies on the floor, shooting anything that flinches.

Then she points her gun at me.

I swallow hard. "I guess it's time for one of us to lose."

She shifts two inches left and shoots the Form that was rising up beside me.

"You're welcome," she says.

Just then the glowing orb of light in the middle of the room contorts into a projected image of the Chairman.

I look over at Farrah in surprise. Is it over? There's no clear winner, there are still two of us.

"Well done," commends the Chairman. "You have taken hold of the enemy's weapons, and you now control the battle. And while you've taken out numerous soldiers in your endeavor, the only way to truly stop this war, is to prevent more of them from becoming soldiers. Go to the window."

I stand up, and we approach the now completely blown out window. Farrah looks down through the scope of her rifle, then passes it to me. I see a village filled with women and children with metal bodies, gathering in lines, walking into a large building.

I look back at the Chairman. "Take out their training camp," he orders.

Farrah swiftly walks over to the pile of weapons and rubble, and retrieves a newly materialized rocket launcher, then sets up at the window.

"Complete the mission, and victory is yours," he says, then the projection collapses, and it's just me, Farrah, and the rocket launcher.

"Wait a second," I say. "Those are just kids Farrah."

"Wrong. That's the enemy. Don't you pay attention? Our primary objective is to annihilate all Forms." She shoulders the launcher and takes aim.

"No. Our primary objective is to stay alive."

"One and the same."

"Just hold on. There's got to be another way. What if this is part of the test? A test of our morality? Our humanity? The Chairman is a merciful man. He wouldn't ask us to just blow up unarmed women and children." I say this as much to convince myself as I do her.

She pauses. "If this was the Surface, you would be dead. And since this is a test, you fail," she says, triggering the launcher. The rocket shoots out and fire collides with the ground.

The simulation clears away. Skye, Callix, and Elodie, stand watching from the other end of the room. Farrah turns to me with a laugh, relishing her victory.

"Well done," Flair notes.

The magnetic dye absorbs back into the wall and disappears.

CHAPTER 17
RO

Edric's eyes reflected in the glass, the grays steely and unfeeling as he looked on at his product. The infant wiggled its chubby arms bashfully, enjoying the warmth of the Hatchery incubator. I hesitated before leaning in for a closer look, afraid to catch the image of my own foreign face against the glass. I still wasn't used to it. Axe said it would take time for me to adjust and feel comfortable, but I doubted I could ever feel comfortable with this new nose, these new lips, this new perfect facial symmetry. They were the features of a different person. *I* was a different person. Perhaps that was fitting.

"This is a complete failure. Just look at it," Edric spat.

The boy, a healthy eight-pounder with rosy cheeks and an otherwise healthy disposition, had a minor opening in the roof of his mouth and lip. We could of course correct this immediately with surgery, but in Edric's eyes the child was simply an affront. The fact that the boy was his, designed from his over-inflated self-image, was a degrading embarrassment to the man. It didn't matter that the child was healthy and thriving, because it wasn't a child at all. Not to him. It was a "defective product," he had said, and I needed to remind myself of that.

Edric turned abruptly. "This is all your doing. You call this an upgrade?" Our noses were almost touching. I hadn't realized how closely I was hovering. The slight musk of his skin had started to become a trigger for me. I felt in constant combat with the engineered pheromones of his cologne, a reaction I'm sure he relished. Anything to keep me close. But I continually warned myself I was in the presence of a beast, and must avoid becoming his prey.

"Research and experimentation are iterative processes," I tried to explain. "It's normal to encounter challenges along the way. One flaw does not mean that the entire experiment is a failure. It's another opportunity to learn and make adjustments to our methods to achieve a successful next iteration."

"You have one month to figure it out." He gestured to the boy. "Start over. This can't see the light of day. The shareholders will lose trust in the project."

That's all he cared about, profits and nothing more. He had no regard for the deeper implications of our work.

"It's been three months since the successful launch of the first generic organic parts, and while company valuations have increased, we can't afford to sit back and let the competition catch up. I promised investors a new bespoke luxury line, and you need to deliver on that." He huffed then mumbled, "I won't give my father the satisfaction of being right."

I found it ironic that his every action was motivated by a paternal complex, and the need to prove himself and gain the affections of his father. Yet there we were, standing in front of what could arguably be considered his offspring, and he displayed complete emotional detachment. Like father, like son.

"So, what are you going to do?" he asked, and not rhetorically. He wanted to make sure I understood the stakes.

"I will keep working, we'll get this right."

"Of course you will, I expect no less. But I'm talking about the product."

"What do you–"

"You need to terminate it. We're not sinking anymore resources into a non-viable subject."

I glanced at the infant again, my voice breaking, "I – I can't–"

"You misunderstand. This is not a request."

"It would be murder."

"Death becomes life. That's the point of all of this. You understood that when you agreed to the project."

I didn't so much agree, as I had no other choice.

"Or do you dare to risk your daughter's future by preserving this failure and defying my orders?"

I kept my eyes on the boy. What I wouldn't give to have my own child back, and he was holding that opportunity to ransom. I didn't move.

He let out a bored exhale. "Must I do all the hard work?" He reached for a needle on a nearby cart, preparing to inject it into a port on the infant's arm.

I turned quickly, placing my hand firmly on his forearm. "Wait, let's not do anything drastic. Is it wise to just discard flawed assets?" I attempted to appeal to his enterprising side. "You said yourself a lot of valuable resources went into creating this product. It would be a waste."

Edric paused, his arm twitching under my hand. His tremors were getting worse, but he was too proud to admit the pain he was in. I noticed it for the first time a few weeks back, while he was holding a drink at the bar. He hid the condition well from others, but I knew. I had seen this before; it was only a matter of time before his nerves deteriorated. Steroid injections helped with the discomfort, but they only served to mask the damage, not reverse it. Up until now, he had refused to get an Adornment, not wanting to appear dependent on his family. He didn't want a generic organic Adornment either. He wanted to have his own parts. He wanted to be the face of this new launch, to flaunt it to his family who had overlooked him. He wanted to show that he wasn't flawed, that he was better than them. He was upgraded.

"There is value here," I reasoned. "We just need to be resourceful in how we utilize imperfect subjects. They can be repurposed. Maybe this specific product is not the face of your launch, but you can still use it. Think about the bigger picture."

He contemplated this for a moment. "How long am I supposed to look at this reminder of failure before it's ready?" he asked.

"Well, you'd want full maturity to be reached to guarantee adequate physical alignment," I said.

"How. Long."

"At last screening, cellular division is occurring at a multiple of four times the speed of a normal proliferating human cell, so I'd say three to four years."

"What are we supposed to do with it until then? And with future maturing products?" he asked.

"We'll need to monitor their development, maintain them at peak physical as well as psychological condition–"

"Why would we care about their psychological development?"

"Because poor mental health can lead to a weakened immune system, and increases the risk of chronic diseases," I stated.

He looked at me with uncertainty. "And what about the board? What am I supposed to tell them?"

"Explain the new approach. You're the visionary, it's your company, they'll back whatever you decide," I reassured him, playing to his ego, hoping my reasoning would spare the boy.

He nodded decisively. "We'll focus on highly desirable and tested donors to provide us with subjects," he began, as if pitching to the backers, "who we will develop and raise into maturity. In our program, those that are flawed can serve to reinforce the system as our own built-in labor force. It's a sustainable and cost-effective investment; every expense will serve to profit the larger system. This is about the long game." Edric nodded as if trying to convince himself as much as the board.

I gingerly removed the needle from his hand and placed it back on the cart, but as he continued to stare at the boy, I could feel him slightly wavering. Guiding his hand with mine into the incubator, I encouraged him to touch the infant. If he could connect with it, then maybe I could save it.

Edric hesitantly ran a finger over the top of a tiny balled up fist. The boy instantly opened his little hand and tightly wrapped it around Edric's finger.

"He's got quite a grip on him," Edric said with surprise. And then, without the slightest hint of emotion in his voice, he added, "He may serve his purpose after all."

CHAPTER 18
EVER

The rest of my evening is routine. I keep my eyes trained on the ground as I shuffle from assignment to the Refectory, and to my capsule, trying to keep my mind off Farrah's win at the trials. I am still older than her, that must count for something. It has to.

Instead, I focus on tonight. Reed's message, *23:00, Utility Room.* I don't know if Reed will actually show up, or if it's a good idea to meet him if he does. What did he want to talk to me about? What could be so secretive that he'd risk using contraband? My curiosity and concern for him make the decision for me. I decide to sneak out.

It's 22:45, all Subjects and Keepers should have retired for the night, preparing themselves for tomorrow's Selection. I take several long deep breaths to calm my racing heart rate. I shouldn't be doing this. Not before the most important day of my life. I glance around the room, my old halo-pad still sits atop my desk. I need to keep it close in order to leave my room undetected. Reed discovered a while ago that by manipulating the frequencies of one of our old recordings from the Chairman, he could generate an interference on the same frequency as our Bright-i lenses and jam their tracer signal. If security or a probing Keeper were to tap into our feeds, it would appear like we were sleeping.

I slide the halo-pad into my pocket and pull open my capsule door, careful to make as little noise as possible. The coast is clear, silent, save for the eternal buzz of the ventilation system. The halls are dark at this hour to save energy, but I know my route by muscle memory. Without clear sight, my other senses are heightened. I follow the familiar grooves of the walls, passing the rows of capsule dormitories, their occupants all sound asleep.

The Utility Room was supposed to be our little club – Reed's and my place of mischief. During one of our late-night exploits, Reed and I invented a secret code, an alphabet of taps to communicate when it was safe to leave our capsules at night. Being the braver one of us, I always initiated, tiptoeing out of my room after the Keeper sweeps and tapping on the door of Reed's capsule, ready for an adventure.

The place was ours alone. Until it wasn't.

I recall the first night sneaking off to meet Ira felt so dangerous, so thrilling; it was a different level of rule breaking. Not only that of the Helix, but of my own friendship with Reed. I betrayed his trust by inviting Ira into our space and sharing our secret. But the prospect of having time alone to express how we felt about each other outweighed the guilt. And what Reed didn't know never hurt him.

The punishment for dating is that both Subjects are entirely stripped of their rankings, making it nearly impossible to Surface. Ira and I stole moments between cycling and blood drawing. The Utility Room was the last place we spent time together, under the glow of machines, his lips on mine, the day before he was selected to ascend.

I arrive at an intersection and round the corner where Vada and Sio are engaged in a hushed argument. Startled, I jump back around the turn, hoping I wasn't spotted. I'm far enough away to remain hidden, but just close enough to make out pieces of their conversation.

"This changes nothing, you hear me?" Sio hisses.

"It would mean disobeying a direct order from the Chairman. We must advance the female," Vada counters.

"I don't care what you've been told, you report to me, and those are my orders."

I lean in closer to the corner, pressing my cheek against the cool metal wall. I don't dare breathe.

"My allegiance is to the Chairman, he's the one who took me in and gave me a second chance. I'm not going to risk my position because you've grown attached to the product."

Sio's voice drops an octave – the tone she adopts when she's in a threatening mood.

"Choose your next move carefully, Vadalyn. Might I remind you how uncomfortable I can make things for you? It was I who assigned you down here on 23, and I can just as easily send you back."

Vada hesitates before speaking next. "We are running out of time, doctor."

Doctor? Did Sio have an even higher ranking within the Helix?

"The Subjects need to be moved up before the inevitable happens," Vada continues. "We need to usher in the next phase and protect ourselves before it's too late."

"Time is up when I say it is, and the Subject is not leaving. That is my final directive. Do you understand me?"

There is a long pause. Vada doesn't respond, but she must have nodded because their footsteps separate and become fainter as they head down opposite ends of the hallway.

When all that's left is silence, I continue towards the Utility Room.

Who could they possibly be discussing? Vada mentioned Sio had grown attached, but that seems impossible. She was notoriously harsh with all Subjects, especially me. Yet, something in her tone betrayed a shift. Has someone finally broken through her hardened exterior? And why is she so intent on keeping them here?

I don't understand. From the sound of it, the threat above is mounting. Why prevent anyone from ascending and aiding the Resistance? What did Vada mean by "next phase?" Are we mobilizing more troops for combat? Surely, Sio can't have the last word.

Rules Rule. I shake the questions from my mind; tomorrow it's my turn to do my duty. In the end, it's the Chairman's decision who will ascend, not Sio's. And I am determined – I'm going up.

A few projections pop up, activated by motion sensors. Luckily, there is no one else around to see them. Generic messages about tomorrow's Selections play; they're not targeted to me personally, which means my tracker signal isn't detected. I make my way past the Chairman's distorted face – *Embracing Our Duty is Essential for Our Continuance*.

I round three corners, and soon reach a dip in the wall – an indent for the Utility Room door. I feel around for a keypad on the right and punch in a series of numbers. The security measures in place for the Utility Room have never been updated. I guess the reasoning was twofold; the space was never used and didn't require a heightened level of security, but also if there was ever an urgent demand for an item inside, it should be easily accessible. Reed learned the code from a Keeper, who desperately needed a toolbox to repair a broken pipe in the Refectory where his Subject had threatened to harm herself if not given the infusion she requested. We later discovered her Keeper had been withholding her meals for some reason. Perhaps part of a specialized training regimen.

Unfortunately for the Keeper, his Subject went through with her threat. Her weight dragged down the rope, breaking a ceiling pipe in the process and flooding the entire Refectory. Fortunately for the Subject, her attempts were not fatal. It came as a shock to us all – she had a good relationship with her Keeper, and seemed to wholeheartedly trust him. They appeared to have genuine affection for one another. Then one day she just snapped. She could be heard shouting down the corridors as she was transported to the MedLab.

"I can't go back!" she cried. "Please just end it!"

We later found out that she was Flawed. No physical indications were present, her afflictions were solely cognitive. There were no precursors or signs that she was on the verge of a mental break or that she could become a danger to herself or others. There was no way to have effectively monitored or predicted her actions. Last we heard, she had undergone a course correction treatment that wiped her memories and subdued her cognitive function. She was stationed on an upper level as a security agent under the close supervision of heavily armed colleagues. Her Keeper had been reassigned as well. We never saw either of them again.

The light on the keypad turns green and I push it open. I'm not entirely expecting to see Reed, but there he is, waiting for me in the corner of this narrow room, his face masked in shadows.

"I didn't think you'd come," he says, snatching the words right out of my mouth. He takes a small step forward into the light emanating from a large obsolete machine that was used for cleaning clothes at some point.

I stifle a yelp. His face is pale, exhaustion bruising his eyes. He looks like a ghost.

"Are you o–" I cut myself off as he abruptly strides towards me. I flinch at his sudden movement, realizing that I may be afraid of my old friend.

He steps around me, peering out of the door and down both ends of the hallway. My heart rate is rising, Reed secures the door and slowly backs away from it. I move towards the edge of the room. His dark hair is tousled, and he wears a nervous edge unfamiliar to the even-tempered demeanor of the boy I used to know so well.

"Reed," I hesitate, "what's going on?"

He takes a beat to collect his thoughts. "I know I haven't exactly been a good friend to you lately, but I'm trying to make up for that now," he says, his voice shaky.

What a convenient time for him to try and make amends.

"This may be our only opportunity," he continues, sensing my confusion. "In the morning, Selections will take place and there's no going back."

I don't know what makes me more uneasy, his gaunt and sweaty appearance, the timbre of his voice, or the words he is barely managing to string together.

"What happened in the Refectory?"

He shakes his head. "I just, I didn't understand. But I think I do now." He senses my unease and continues. "I've been on rationed infusions. I haven't been sleeping, my body was craving it. I lost control. That's all."

"Why are you rationing?"

"It doesn't matter," he dismisses the question.

"Reed, you're not well."

He reaches out with shaking hands. "Please Ev, I'll explain everything once you're safe. Come with me."

"Safe? I didn't realize I was in danger."

"Of course you are, we all are. Come on, we need to go now. We don't have much time." He's fidgety as he speaks.

"Where could we possibly be going?" I find myself now involuntarily backing away as I speak.

"We're leaving."

He's lost it.

"The only way out of Helix is to be chosen," I remind him.

He inches closer. I retreat further.

"Don't make this difficult," he says with an unnerving edge.

I take one more step back; my body is now pressed painfully against the machine behind me. It whirls to life, the unexpected hum sending a shiver down my spine. A harsh blue light spills from the screen and casts sharp distorted shadows on Reed's face.

"Reed, you're scaring me. Just tell me, what's going on?"

"This is our chance to escape," he whispers, his eyes intense.

Before I can respond, an object ejects sharply from the machine, jabbing into my spine. I wince and turn away from Reed, catching sign of an empty slot protruding, its grooves are the perfect shape to fit an Index device, I note.

"Escape?" I ask incredulously. He truly is unraveling. "This isn't a prison, it's our home."

"Is it?"

"There has only ever been one way to the Surface. When you've proven to the Chairman that you're ready, and that you are worthy of the honor. You know that. If we're not ready, we won't survive up there," I try to rationalize.

He takes a deep breath, before selecting his next words. "I'm not talking about going up, Vee."

"Reed, this is the 23rd and final level of the Helix, there's nowhere to go but up."

He stands silently for a moment, trying to plead with me through his eyes. Speaking some hopeful secret language that with one look could make me understand what his words fail to convey. Just like when we were children.

But it's been a long time since then, and I don't recognize this Reed.

Without warning, he lunges, taking hold of my wrists firmly in one large hand and pinning me to the machine with the other. His grip burns. I am frozen, my feet glued to the floor. There's a frantic desperation in his eyes and his lip twitches at the corners.

"Ev, you need to trust me. This place isn't what you think it is. We're not going to go *up*, we're going *down*. There's a bunker, on Level 25, it was created as a failsafe when the Cleansing broke on the Surface. After the first wave cleared, the Helix was built above it. The supplies remained, and there's enough food down there to last us five years."

He *is* mad, and what's more, there can be no reasoning with a mad man. There is no Level 25. The Helix wasn't built before the Cleansing. As the Keepers have taught us time and again, the structure we live in was a former government research facility. It was so off the grid that it managed to go undetected during the initial invasion. Those who survived the Cleansing hid within these walls for safety, specifically on the lowest Level, 23, the furthest from the Surface and the last to be attacked, should a breach occur. It's protected by 22 upper levels, each providing their own barriers to an attack. It is on this level that the Resistance was first organized, as survivors spent the time planning and building their strength until the moment they could initiate rescue efforts and ultimately strike back. Reed's mind is warping reality.

Reed strengthens his grip, pulling me forward towards the door. "I'll explain everything once we get there, we don't have much time. Sio is waiting to guide us down."

Sio? This is a trap.

She is trying to destroy my chances at Selection and she's using Reed in his fragile mental state to lure me into the worst level of insubordination: attempting to leave. I knew she hated me, but I never could have imagined it would go this far.

"Reed, let go. Just listen to me. You need help."

He pulls open the door with his free hand and continues to grip my wrists with the other. A set of footsteps scurry down the hall outside. I push Reed forward but as I try to scream for help, he knocks me against the nearest corner wall, covering my mouth and pinning his arm on my windpipe in one fell swoop. I'm tempted to shove him straight through the wall right then and there, but despite everything, I hold back, I don't want to hurt him – he's unwell. Reed's eyes are ferocious as he lifts his hand and touches a finger to his lips.

The footsteps grow fainter as they reach the end of the hall, but I can hear a small, panicked voice say, "It was just a dream."

It sounds like Skye, but what would she be doing out of her capsule at this time of night?

"It wasn't me," the voice says again, trailing away.

I try to call out again, but barely manage a croak under the weight of Reed's arm. I dig my nails into his flesh, I'm restraining myself, trying not injure him, but he's crushing my windpipe.

I squeeze. My nails sinking deeper.

He doesn't feel any pain, but he can see what I'm doing. I don't want to scar him and create another flaw, but I will if I have to.

He eases the pressure on my neck, and I pull back my hands before I draw blood. With a firm shove, I send him crashing into the wall.

He slumps there, not moving; his head hanging low, and shoulders sagging. I must have really hurt him this time. I hesitate before moving towards the door, ready to shout. I can take care of myself, I don't need Skye's help, but if that was her running down the hall, it sounds like she could use mine.

"Wait," Reed's voice quivers slightly. "I told you, the Keepers are on edge. Sio is convinced that the Chairman is planning something reckless. Rushed. I think we've been lied to, Ev. The threat on the Surface isn't what we've been told. The Forms, they've evolved and it's becoming nearly impossible to tell them apart from ourselves. It's like the Subjects are being sent out there without a fighting chance."

I stand stunned in disbelief. Sio has really done a number on him. She's made him utterly spineless.

"I have this sick feeling in the pit of my stomach that I can't shake. Subjects are being led into a trap Ev, I know it. We need more time to prepare. We need to wait it out."

"Why? Because Sio told you so? It's unsettling how easily manipulated you are. You need to check where your true loyalties lie. It should be to the Chairman," I spit.

"My loyalty is to *you*. Always has been."

At the sound of more footsteps, Reed makes a sudden and forceful move forward, slamming his hand down over my nose and mouth again, clasping the back of my head. I bite the inside of my cheek and can taste the warm salty liquid.

"Reed, you're hurting me," I mumble under his hand.

Without a word, he shifts his grip, now encircling my throat, the tightening curl of his fingers. My vision narrows.

"I'm sorry Ev, but you have to know I'm trying to save you," he whispers.

I bite down on Reed's hand as hard as I can, piercing the skin between his thumb and forefinger, creating another gaping flaw. He doesn't even flinch, his gaze is steady as the blood dribbles into my mouth and mixes with my own.

The footsteps have reached the end of the hall and turn a corner. The pressure around my neck releases, and Reed slowly lifts his bloodied hand. I collapse on the floor coughing, gasping for air, and scurry as far from Reed as I can get.

"Don't. You. Ever put your hands on me again," I wheeze.

He's silent. After a moment, I manage to stand and allow myself to meet his eyes. He's shaking again as if trying to control some entity erupting inside. Yet he says nothing, just stares at his hand. The Keepers foresaw this; he'll never leave Helix.

I can't feel anger towards Reed, what's happening to him is not his fault. What I do feel is pity for the boy before me. I wish that I could help him somehow, but I now know I can't, he is destined for course correction. I should feel more of a loss at that prospect, but it's clear I lost my friend long ago.

I don't know what to say, so I state the obvious. "Reed, you need to go to the MedLab."

He continues to turn his hand over and over, analyzing it, as if seeing it for the first time. A thick line of red draws a map in all the creases. The bite will heal quickly, but he'll always have the scar.

"Blood," he murmurs, lifting his eyes to meet mine, hoping I'll understand. "It's... it's our blood, Ev. Don't you see? We're not meant to leave."

I don't know what he wants me to say. "Reed, tomorrow is my opportunity to fulfill my destiny, to do what we were born for."

This pulls him out of his trance. "Which is what exactly?" I can hear the impatience in his voice again. "We're just kids! How are we supposed to save the world?" He pauses. "And why doesn't anyone ever come back?"

"Would *you* come back?" I ask.

His voice is softer now, pleading, "If you're chosen, they'll be sending you up there to die."

I've had enough. "I'd rather die a hero on the Surface, than a coward hiding underground."

At that I walk past him and out the door, leaving our secret spot and all its memories behind.

CHAPTER 19
RO

The Subject slid a circular peg into a round hole with ease and followed this up by sliding the square shaped peg into the square hole. The female continued, rhythmically fitting one shape into another, the exercise seemed almost gratifying for them. The Subject was eager to please and flaunt its intelligence.

"Excellent work, Subject," I said stoically, working to mask the pride in my voice. I slid my hands across the air and input my notes for the female's records, still getting used to the recently released Bright-i lenses – technology Edric made the company adopt for more efficient cross departmental communications. Or so he claimed.

Beyond the text hanging in the center of my field of view, I glimpsed the newly hired nurses observing the toddlers assigned to their keep. We couldn't actually refer to them as toddlers though, I had to keep reminding myself of that. We also couldn't use gendered pronouns or any language that would humanize the products. Always remain detached, clinical. They were to be treated much like prized cattle, livestock. The cruelty of it all twisted inside me, battling against my maternal instinct. Sometimes, my mind would betray me, wandering to my own daughter, her laughter a distant melody, her loss an unresolved torment. I still hadn't discovered who was truly behind the accident, and it seemed I never would. Still, I knew that it was in my best interest to follow the rules diligently and not attract attention to my true plans.

The brightly lit room contained numerous miniature tables and mats, all a stark white to match the equally sterile walls. The Subjects themselves also donned all white uniforms. The monochromatic environment made it impossible to hide anything.

I blinked the text away from my sight and watched as a bubbly little female with freshly shaven red hair scribbled a drawing on a touch screen, while their keeper took notes. Another small male struggled to lift metallic marbles off a table and place them into a cup, unable to limit their range of motion, digits over-extending and stretching themselves too far. Others stacked blocks in collaborative play.

"What's next?" My Subject looked up at me eager to reveal that they had finished placing all the shapes in their corresponding holes. I took the shallow board that housed the pieces and turned it upside down until all the pegs fell out. The female had completed the task far too quickly and I didn't want them attracting any attention towards their unsanctioned upgrades.

"Let's try it again," I offered. "Slower this time."

The Subject frowned at me but went back to the task at hand.

I continued to scan the room, keeping a close eye on the other Subjects. They were as yet unnamed, although Edric had considered using numbers as identifiers to track and manage the inventory. The format of these codes was still up for debate, as was the practicality of using them in our everyday interaction with the Subjects. It was a cold approach but would help to maintain a distance from the products and to manage variations.

The origin case, our first Subject, was testing as well. The slender male was climbing a small-scale rock wall with impressive dexterity. The weight of their small frame was evenly balanced across their fingers and the tips of their toes as they climbed higher. Edric would be pleased by the Subject's progress.

A noise beside me startled me from my thoughts. My Subject was attempting to jam a triangular peg into a round hole.

"Not that one, try another hole," I calmly suggested, but the female was too focused on the board to listen.

They continued to prod on as if through sheer force they could make the piece fit. The repeated banging grew louder and more violent as their frustration mounted. The room had begun to take notice. I endeavored to hand the Subject a circular peg which they threw to the floor. I tried to move their hand from the board to which they simply yanked their arm free with surprising force and continued to bang away. Everyone was focused on us now and I could feel the pressure from the others to control the product.

The Subject slammed the peg against the board a final time, inadvertently splintering it with unpredictable strength. Then they began to wail, kicking and throwing their arms in the air. Stubbornness and defiance were a red flag within the program, and that kind of behavior would need to be remedied quickly for the ecosystem to function.

Amidst the female's fit, I looked over at the glass wall separating us from the gallery outside, expecting to see a group of onlookers, the board of investors. Surprisingly, only Edric stood in audience.

He had insisted the board attend the examination and witness their investments firsthand, but I maintained that seeing the Subjects live could do more harm than good. For some, it would be impossible to disassociate themselves from the products. Ignorance truly is bliss. Luckily, it seemed Edric heeded my advice.

At that moment, with his eyes on me, I had to prove my gratitude and loyalty to the project and hide any indication of my intent to leave. I looked down at my Subject, knowing that they had no control over their emotions or behavior yet. The female hadn't learned how to process them. In another environment, their actions would have been seen as a normal part of development. But not here.

I took the tranquilizer out of my pocket and prepared to do something I wouldn't be able to take back, I injected the needle into the Subject's arm. This enraged them further, if only for a few seconds, before they were subdued. The look on their face was a mixture of confusion and betrayal. As the Subject's body went lax, I couldn't help but think how beautiful they looked.

Under the bright lights of the Atrium, appearing almost asleep, they reminded me so much of her.

CHAPTER 20
EVER

Every Subject is filing their way into the Grand Hall. Torch pendants ignite the perimeter of the room, giving off a soft blue light intended to calm the mind and decrease feelings of anxiety. But now that the day has finally come, all my confidence has faded, and I find that a layer of moisture has formed above my lip since I entered the room. This is it.

The soaring ceilings and its curved metal support beams have always given me the distinct feeling of being inside a hollow rib cage. I am the contents of some large beast's stomach, feeding something else's hunger. But I crave one thing, and one thing only, the Surface.

This room houses the only entrance and exit on Level 23: the Tube, a cylindrical glass elevator piercing all levels of the Helix on its way to the Surface. A large, raised platform fills the front of the room. At its center sits a circular indentation, the landing dock. It ordinarily remains clear; the Tube is utilized for special transfers only. It cannot be summoned down; it only descends with the Chairman. He resides on the uppermost levels, cloaked in protection and secrecy, all in service of the cause.

The Tube's arrival on 23 signals the start of an ascension. Most Subjects have already settled into the semicircular stadium seating directed towards the platform. The anticipation is palpable. I line up next to the others in the front row.

I can feel Reed staring down at me from a few benches behind, willing me to turn around, but I have nothing more to say to him after last night. I feel for him, for what he's going through, but he's not my responsibility. He will remain in the Helix and will be taken care of. I trust that.

Subjects are on one side, Keepers on the other. Security personnel, mostly made up of Flawed ex-Subjects line the outer curves of the semicircle. The benches are layered in a palette of greens, whites, and navy. The Keepers wear white coats, Security in blue, and Subjects don green ceremony garments, signifying renewal of life.

Sio is nowhere to be seen. The way she has been manipulating Reed, I have half a mind to tell her something. Being that I'm on my way out of here, I might do so. But for now, I must focus.

Soon, the Chairman will arrive, and the Selection Ceremony will begin. I've imagined the moment thousands of times before. The ritual is always the same: he will pull out a thin strip of glass from a small metal container that holds the chosen Subject's slide. The slide is adorned with a small droplet of their blood obtained from the last Drawing. A symbol of genetic purity, and a ticket signifying our rite of passage to the Surface.

When he calls my name, I will not say a word. I will not gloat, I will walk silently to the platform, stand beside the Chairman and take in the view of my peers for the final time. Then I'll enter the Tube and wave as I ascend to my new life among the Saviors. With Ira. And possibly even among family.

My heart is filled with longing. There must be survivors up there. The prospect of finally finding my place and uncovering my true origins tugs at my heartstrings. Do I have siblings? Did I inherit my mother's eyes? My father's adventurous spirit?

Reed slides into the bench next to me, pushing a few Subjects aside and interrupting my daydream. Apparently, he didn't get the message that I wanted no contact with him. Luckily, he remains silent.

With a slight hush, the glass Tube descends into the terminal. Reed's body stiffens. We all stand and straighten up to our most respectful postures as the door slides open.

The Chairman greets us with a charming, expansive smile that I imagine extends from ear to ear, though the details of his face remain frustratingly obscured by the distance.

"My Subjects," he says with pride, holding out his hands in signature black leather gloves in front of his fitted suit. He strides forward, his movement fluid and commanding. Out from behind him emerges Sio. She looks worn by comparison, the color drained from her face, wisps of salt and pepper hair sticking out at her ears. It seems that she has exercised her authority as Senior Keeper to leave 23 and escort the Chairman down. But why now?

Sio catches my venomous stare and suppresses a look of utter dismay.

The room is silent as we wait for his next words. He surveys the room, taking in each of us with his gaze. I can hear the smallest rustle of clothing, an inhale, a sniff. Someone coughs and it sounds deafening in the sudden hush.

"Please be seated," he begins in an authoritative voice that needs no microphone to echo through the room.

"Today is a momentous occasion. Today we honor humanity by giving the best of our own to the fight for the survival of humankind. We live in trying times, my Subjects. The world around us is falling apart, and the forces of evil are closing in. But we are not without hope, for we have been chosen by the divine to be the light in the darkness, the hope in despair.

"As you all know, decades ago I founded Helix Colony as an asylum. A safe haven undetectable by the AI entities we call the Forms. Humanity's constant efforts to achieve physical perfection through surgical enhancements were ill-fated. The advanced technology that came to reside within the majority of human bodies understood the weakness and limitations of its biological hosts. And so, it took control, building stronger, more advanced systems to annihilate the human race. With no need for organic life to sustain them, the Forms wiped out Earth's resources, ensuring the impossibility of humanity's survival." He pauses for effect, although we've heard this history time and again.

"In the light of overwhelming defeat, we found a way to fight back, and gain ground. It has been my mission to unite the smartest minds and the strongest, most able bodies for the honor, and the burden, of repopulating, rebuilding, and remembering the world that once was, a world before the Forms."

He looks around the room beaming. "The Saviors will rise above the chaos and bring about a new era of peace and prosperity."

Several Keepers and Subjects clap enthusiastically.

"Welcome to the Selection Ceremony! You are all worthy in your own ways; your hard work, sacrifice, and dedication have not been overlooked. But there is one among you who has proven themselves to be truly exceptional. They have shown a deep understanding of our teachings, a selfless devotion to our cause, and an unwavering belief in the power of our community. This moment marks the transition of the worthiest among you into the light."

Reed grabs my hand, holding it so tightly that it hurts. I can feel the jagged marks from the gashes my teeth left in his palm.

"Your service is needed more than ever. That being said, today's Ceremony will proceed a bit differently."

Several murmurs break out in the group. Beside me Reed is still, he looks on unblinkingly at the Chairman.

"We have been alerted to increasing artillery build up near home base. The Forms are advancing. And we need reinforcements. Today, I will select not just one, but *three* of you to ascend and join in the fight for our species."

The room erupts in a drone of confusion, and I stop breathing entirely. This is good news. As the eldest here, by default I'm the most qualified, and my chances for Selection are now exponentially higher. The palms of my hands are sweating. Or is that Reed's hand? Either way I'm too excited to wipe them off.

"Let us begin." The Chairman puts out his gloved hand.

Sio approaches, trembling, clutching a small silver box, the contents inside clinking with every step. The Chairman lifts the cover and pulls out a small rectangular glass slide with a single blood droplet.

"I call on you to join me in honoring Subject 5123XY."

The short boy at the far end of our row, Del, squeals and takes his place on the platform beside Sio, his curly brown locks bobbing along with excitement. He is only 12 years-old, Skye's brother. I don't understand, he didn't even rank in the top five.

I try and remain calm as the Chairman reaches into the tin. Two spots left. He pulls out the next stained-glass slide. The room is silent.

"The second honor is bestowed upon Subject 9423XX."

My heart sinks as Farrah darts out into the aisle, planting herself on the platform next to Del. She grins at me. My pulse is pounding. This is all happening too quickly. But it's not over yet, there's one more opportunity. This is my turn, it's my chance. It has to be.

The Chairman reaches in for the final slide.

I hope it's me, I hope it's me, I hope it's me.

He reads the final name. "Subject 0123XY."

It's not me. It's Reed.

CHAPTER 21
EVER

A ringing in my ears drowns out all other sounds. It's difficult to breathe, no matter how sharply I inhale or expand my lungs to the point of pain, I can't shake this crushing feeling. The Atrium feels smaller, clenched. A palpable perplexity has settled over Level 23.

Just a few hours ago my life had been clearly laid out before me. I would turn 18, I would be chosen to join the Saviors, ascend to the Surface, and reunite with Ira. We would finally be together. He, the golden boy of the resistance, and I, the Chairman's rising star.

The future was so close I could touch it.

Then in an instant it had slipped through my fingers. Right along with Reed's hand. With one small squeeze, they were both gone. Leaving me to face an uncertain future.

Dumbfounded, unable to formulate a single word, my eyes follow Reed as he walks towards the platform. Did he know this would happen? Did he know that I would be the one who was left behind?

Subjects murmur to each other on either side of me, echoing my confusion.

"But he's Flawed? This is some sort of mistake."

"The Chairman doesn't make mistakes."

"We must be under serious threat."

Others barely contain their excitement.

"Does this mean I'll have a better chance at the next Selection Ceremony?" someone asks behind me.

An unsettling feeling takes hold, if the Surface threat is so great to break Selection protocol, why not send us all up? Something doesn't feel right and I'm beginning to wonder if maybe Reed was right.

The three chosen ones now stand in place next to the Chairman. A frightened child feigning bravery, a foe with an arrogant grin, and a Flawed.

But the most haunting image of all is the expression of triumph on Sio's face as each Subject takes their turn shaking hands with the Chairman. Excluding me.

The Chairman addresses the crowd. "I ask you not to be jealous or resentful of the chosen ones. Instead, I ask you to be proud of them. For they are a reflection of the best of us, an inspiration to us all. And I ask you to support them in their journey, to send them on their way with your love and your blessings."

He motions towards the small boy. Del's petite frame appears even more delicate in the shadow of the towering Chairman. With wide awe-filled eyes he embraces the Chairman's gloved hand. Cradling it in his own for just a little too long before the Chairman gracefully retrieves it and places it on Del's shoulder. Del then lowers his head in a gesture of deep respect.

"I bestow upon you the honor of service to humankind," the Chairman's voice booms as he speaks. "You shall be our Savior. You will reclaim our reign."

The weight of the Chairman's words hangs heavily in the air, signaling the beginning of a new chapter in Del's life.

Those of us in the stands echo the Chairman's words, chanting in unison. "You will reclaim our reign." The collective declaration fills the room with a sense of purpose and unity, despite the confusion, affirming the solemn commitment to the mission at hand.

With eyes closed in reverence, Del recites the vow, his voice filled with conviction and resolve. "I have the will. I have the ability. I endeavor to succeed. I am eager to serve." The words are a promise to himself, to those gathered, and to the greater cause, signifying his unwavering commitment.

The Chairman then hands Del his slide and directs him towards the Tube.

"Congratulations Subject 5123XY; it is your time to ascend." He smiles assuredly.

Del nods then gives a hesitant wave to the rest of us in the stands. With the expected awkwardness of a 12 year-old, he steps into the Tube, hugging the side panels as the glass door closes around him. A Subject's ascension is a journey that must be taken alone. As the Tube rises, the room collectively recites our blessing.

"May the light guide your way."

The Chairman gestures towards Farrah. "Subject 9423XX, please approach."

Farrah grabs his hand and shakes it eagerly; her smile is so wide, if I were closer I'm sure I'd see her molars.

"Thank you, Chairman, thank you so much. You have no idea what this means to me," Farrah gushes, then bows her head.

"Your gratitude warms my heart." He smiles warmly, placing a hand on her shoulder. "I bestow upon you the honor of service to humankind. You shall be our Savior. You will reclaim our reign."

We repeat his words in kind. "You will reclaim our reign."

"I have the will. I have the ability. I endeavor to succeed," Farrah recites. She looks up. "I am eager to serve. And I won't let you down."

The Chairman nods in appreciation. "Congratulations 9423XX; it is your time to ascend."

The Tube had returned to its docking station and Farrah takes her slide then darts into the Tube, smiling smugly as the doors slide closed.

"May the light guide your way," we say again.

And then she's gone.

Reed absentmindedly fiddles with his hands on the stage. He's the final ascension. This entire time I felt sorry for him. I thought he was sick, unstable, and doomed to spend his life in darkness. But he's known all along that he would be rising through Helix, he, a Flawed Subject, would be surfacing. The only sickness he is consumed by is cowardice. It should be me up there, not him.

The Chairman stretches out his hand towards Reed, but he doesn't move.

Several gasps rise from the audience at Reed's defiance. The blood drains from Sio's face just feet away. The Chairman only grins charismatically at the crowd unfazed, exuding assurance and control, then turns back to Reed.

"I know this must come as quite the surprise. You don't think that you are worthy of such an honor. But I assure you, it is your time."

Reed stays put.

"You are a gift to this movement, you must know that. You all are. And, right now, your fellow beings require your service. You shall be our Savior."

Still, no movement.

"You will reclaim our reign," the Chairman says more sternly.

"This is blasphemous," comes a mumble from over my left shoulder.

I can hardly disagree. What is Reed thinking?

The Chairman strides over to Reed, whispers something, and pats him on the shoulder. It's the kind of pat that is less of an encouragement and more of a firm suggestion.

Yet Reed does not take a step forward. Instead, he retreats *further* away from the Chairman and the Tube and instead moves towards the edge of the platform.

"This is your birthright," says the Chairman. "It's what you were meant for."

Reed turns towards the crowd with a wild desperation in his eyes that I don't understand. I can't see past the fear lingering underneath the despair and it angers me.

Then, to my horror, he makes a run for it, descending the stairs.

And he doesn't plan to do it alone. He rushes at me, colliding with my chest, grabbing hold, and lifting me over the partition of the front row, sending a sharp pain through my abdomen. The Subjects around me scatter as if touching us would contaminate them.

"What are you doing?!" I shout. "Get off of me!" I flail as he hoists me up onto his shoulders and attempts to find a path to the door.

He makes it a few steps before a Keeper jumps out in front of him. He lifts me up further, holding my hips with one arm as he swings at the Keeper with the other, knocking him backward.

"Have you lost your mind?!" I scream. "Stop! Let me go!"

The Chairman signals to someone in the crowd, and in an instant two thick security personnel appear in front of us blocking the aisle. Reed tries to push his way around them but it's no use, they are solid as a wall. We are surrounded.

A current of disappointed and judgmental rumblings echo through the room. Reed fruitlessly thrashes against the security guards as a Keeper rushes over, brandishing a syringe. As soon as the needle is uncapped, the adrenaline that was just coursing through his veins stimies and he accepts defeat. He gently places me down, then whips his head towards the Chairman, imploring.

"Please. Please don't do this to me."

But the Chairman looks down at him from the platform, unfeeling. He flicks his chin upwards, an order for the Keeper to inject. Reed's scream reverberates through the hall. Security drags him by the arms onto the platform, and deposits him inside the Tube where he crumples on the floor.

"Please!" Reed calls meekly as the door closes. He pounds sluggishly on the glass before slumping to his knees. He stares back at me, holding my gaze while the Tube rises.

I don't dare blink.

CHAPTER 22
RO

"Are you sure about this?" I asked, sitting across from Edric in his newly designed office.

My palms were slick with sweat, and my heart was pounding in my chest. When he called me in, I was sure he had discovered what I'd done. But to my surprise, he was requesting my advice. I couldn't understand why. He had a team of expert business advisors at his disposal. Why would my opinion matter?

I couldn't shake the feeling that there was something more going on, something I wasn't privy to. But for now, I needed to play along and remain in his good graces until I could figure out a way to leave.

"We could use the publicity," he said. "Differentiate ourselves as a source of good."

I doubted his intentions. Did he even know what being good meant? This was just another way to boost profits and market share.

"It's really quite a shame what happened to that gentleman from the Outlands."

The man he was referring to was a 60-year-old lifelong smoker whose vice had finally caught up with him. He had been given a second chance at life via a lung Adornment. But he hadn't even had the enhancement a year before the device unexpectedly reset and suffocated him.

"Truly disheartening," I agreed. Desperate people were resorting to cheaper procedures performed by unlicensed physicians and engineers using substandard materials. And even the larger corporations themselves had begun to cut corners in the name of profits. EastonCorp had even come under fire for exorbitant waste production resulting from the use of low-grade materials. The pollution and smog that pervaded the Refinery Lands was a direct result of this neglectful and irresponsible behavior.

"It would be a missed opportunity to overlook the current market fears around malfunctions," Edric said with a knowing smirk. "We could use this to our advantage by highlighting the effectiveness of our organic Adornments, which would in turn generate more funding for our regeneration campaign and increase orders for upgrades."

Of course that was his agenda; give the customer a taste of what they want, then upsell them on what they didn't even need.

Edric flipped through profile images on a glass screen atop his desk. "So, whose life are we going to change?" he asked, turning the screen to me, a conniving smile playing at the corners of his lips. It made my skin crawl. I could sense the ruthless ambition lurking behind his words.

"It's up to you. This is where you shine. I'm just the scientist behind the scenes," I said, reverent as ever. He loved the flattery. It was my best tool for distraction.

"I've narrowed it down to four. They have the most headline-worthy conditions, hence the most social presence. They are physically viable and of course physically attractive enough to garner interest from the press." His words spilled out with calculated enthusiasm.

"That, and the rare offer of a pro-bono lifesaving surgery," I tossed in.

"Exactly," he nodded, still smiling. "The headline practically writes itself, doesn't it? The press will eat this up."

"I'm sure the investors will be impressed."

"Only if it leads to results. *Results* are what impress investors, Ro," he countered swiftly. "So, let's make a decision."

"It's your choice."

"Oh, come on." His tone was playful, but his eyes were watchful. "Don't do that to me. We're partners here, aren't we? I want your input."

I could feel him searching for any hint of hesitation or distrust. He was trying to make me feel like we were in this together, to secure my loyalty and commitment. I had to play my role.

I scanned through the individual profiles before me. The first, a smiling young woman with long brown locks. She was quite influential, according to her profile, with thousands viewing her uploads on a regular basis. I swiped up to images of her posing in various contorted positions highlighting pieces of luxury goods against the backdrops of exotic beaches, snowcapped mountains, and lush whimsical forests.

I never understood why people bought into the illusion. Those environments didn't exist anymore, the Outlands were barren. People, like my parents, trekked through them into the Refinery Lands to reach this city for a chance at a better life. This woman and her projections were completely artificial.

I scrolled to the next image of her lying bruised and bloodied in a hospital bed, apparently due to a fall from a retractable balcony she had been posing on.

I didn't need to ask why she was on Edric's list. The exposure of our services to her followers would be great marketing. But this woman's life was consumed by artificiality. She got what she deserved.

I swiped right to the next potential patient. A stunning young man with caramel complexion. He was a physical trainer and made his living 'perfecting the human body,' whatever that meant. He had numerous hidden Adornments to give himself an edge, most notably his famously chiseled chest.

A disgruntled client had been well aware of this when they suggested testing the trainer's pectoral strength, and dropped a weight onto his clavicle instead. He would need a tracheotomy to repair his windpipe. The criminal trial surrounding his injuries had gotten a lot of media coverage.

I swiped next to a thin older woman with asymmetric facial alignment and severe scarring from the botched face-lifting Adornment she attempted to conceal under a crooked wig. Next.

The last image in the folder was that of a meek 17-year-old girl with razor platinum blonde shoulder length hair and sharp bangs. She had a heart defect affecting the blood flow to the rest of her body, which was most likely the reason for her pale disposition. She enjoyed reading and solving puzzles with her friends at the orphanage. Without an Adornment or safe alternative, she had no chance of surviving into adulthood.

"Let's go with her," I said without a second thought. I suspected Edric chose her to tug at the media's heartstrings. It certainly worked on mine.

"Okay," he agreed. "Vadalyn Kai, this is your lucky day."

"Glad I could be of service." I stood to leave, not wanting to linger in his presence a second longer than necessary.

"Not so fast."

I paused by the door.

"I need her ready for the gala next week." He didn't question whether it was possible. "It's important we create buzz and continue to build excitement around the company. This event will be a crucial test of how our products are received and will guide my mission and intentions for the future of this company."

"I understand, I'll try my best to further accelerate the organ growth rate."

He looked at me sternly. "You'll do what needs to be done."

CHAPTER 23
EVER

I don't remember leaving the Atrium or even reporting to the Gymnasium for kinetics. Yet here I find myself, mounted on a bike with my Bright-i showing that I'm already 20 minutes into my session.

The projection on the wall ahead is streaming a simulation from the Surface, a flat dirt path winding around serene countryside. I am speeding past trees in varying shades of green, broken up by patches of lush grassland, and heading towards rolling hills in the distance. The other Subjects in my session are glued to their own projections. Their Kineti-Bikes lightly bob in the air with every push of the pedal, while the magnetic field suspending them generates an electrical current funneled back into the Helix.

It's the same process for all the physical activities in the room. The rowers pull back magnetic handles, the runners lift magnetic shoe soles, and the climbers bear weight on magnetic climbing holds. The floor of the room itself is composed of translucent kinetic floor tiles, each generating 35 watts with every step.

I try to force my mind to focus on the scene ahead. Physical pain is always a good distraction. I turn up the resistance. As I hit the 100-watts-generated marker, my thighs burn and my heart pounds in my chest. The trees are approaching more slowly now, and the hills grow larger. I turn the resistance even higher.

How could he have chosen Reed?

The dirt path ends and I'm in the hills trudging through tall grass. I turn up the dial once more.

Why not me? What's wrong with me?

I am fighting with the pedals now, trying to maintain my speed.

It was my turn!

I'm fighting because it's the only thing I can control in my life. I rise in the saddle pushing down as hard as I can; with each rotation my electric current gets stronger. The horizon is green as far as the eye can see, continuous rolling hills. My knuckles are white from the sheer force of gripping the handlebars. I'm trapped in this never-ending landscape, yet I keep pushing down, and in turn the weight of the resistance pushes back. I'm reaching my limit, pouring everything I have into this ride, into this life of a Subject, but it feels like my efforts get me nowhere.

Every microfiber of my muscles is tearing, and the salty sweat that has been formulating on my forehead now stings my eyes. I continue. Maybe Farrah was right, maybe I am delusional. I must be, to keep on holding out hope that I'll ever surface, that I'll ever touch or smell the real-world grassy plains of this simulation. Maybe the delusion is my confidence, maybe I'm not as smart or as prepared as I think I am.

My legs are numb from the exertion, but I keep going. I'm grunting with each push, garnering the attention of several other Subjects. Luckily the sweat is masking my tears. I am at 165 watts now, a personal best.

An alert, a shared message, pops up in the corner of my Bright-i. High fives. An automated congratulations for reaching a new milestone. And all at once I let everything go. The rage, the jealousy, the disappointment, the doubt, and I collapse into the saddle utterly exhausted. I am just so tired, tired of trying, tired of clinging to hope. I'm not sure how much longer I can go on like this. I need to get out of Helix Colony.

Weary, I unclip one foot from the pedal. The momentum of my ride keeps the pedals rotating, and even though I've stopped cycling, the force of the persistent motion throws off my balance, and I topple onto the floor in a tangled mess, with one foot still clipped in.

I crunch up to reach the foot that is still attached, feeling the strain as I move. I engage my Bright-i and swipe up to release the magnetic current that was keeping my foot clipped to the bike. Then I collapse, fully letting myself sink into the padded floor. Skye is quickly at my side.

"Hey, are you okay?"

"No," I say, rolling myself up to a sitting position. "But I will be, I think."

She doesn't look convinced.

"How are *you* holding up?" I ask, knowing she must be having a tough time without her brother. Del is one of the youngest Subjects to ever be chosen.

"I'm scared for him."

I look around making sure no one hears us. "Everything is going to be okay. The Chairman chose him for a reason, he wouldn't be surfacing if he wasn't ready."

"Is that why he chose Reed?" she murmurs.

The lights start to flicker. My Bright-i vision must be glitching from the overexertion, as if I stood too fast, but I'm still seated.

Skye follows my eyes around the room, she sees it too. "There's something weird going on, Ever," she says.

I realize that we're not the only ones who see the glitches. Everyone has stopped their activities.

Then, at once, the room shuts down. All screens and projections are black, the lights go out. And for just a few seconds we are in complete and overwhelming darkness.

"Skye," I whisper, making sure she's still next to me, and that this is not all in my head.

"I'm here."

The backup generators kick in and safety guide lights turn on in succession around the perimeter.

"What just happened?" someone asks nearby.

The Keepers look worried as well. We've never had a blackout before.

"Are we under attack?" another Subject asks.

Although we can see each other again, something feels off. Something is missing from the room that was so distinctly there seconds ago. But I can't put my finger on it.

And it's a moment too late before I realize what it is. The magnetic field is not engaged, and the Kineti-bike comes crashing down to the ground, pinning my leg underneath. I scream.

Skye tries to help me up. Around us, running belts collapse, and large rock-like climbing holds rain down injuring those who are too slow to scatter.

"Here, I'm going to lift the base stabilizers. On three." Skye grabs the bottom of the bike. "One, two, three."

It doesn't budge. "Oh, right, you're the strong one," she strains.

I scoot forward and pull up on the bike. I slide my leg out, scratching it badly on the sharp chrome flywheel.

I stand up with Skye's help and take inventory of those around me, a few people nurse small head wounds and bruises, but nothing too serious. Most of the Subjects and Keepers were clear of the larger falling equipment.

I look to Skye. "Are you alright?"

She nods, then her eyes widen. "Ever, you're bleeding."

The walls of my capsule are dimmed down to sleep mode. I glance down at my leg, expecting the worst but it's just a surface wound, and to my surprise it's already healing. The skin smoothing over so quickly it might leave no scar at all. This shouldn't be possible, healing this fast. At least not for me. I don't have that ability.

It strikes me as odd that I wasn't sent to the MedLab. Sio annotates a projection in the corner. Instead of speaking, I stare daggers at her taut bun, willing her to explain herself, to tell me what is going on, but she seems content in the silence. For all my mental efforts, the intensity behind my eyes grows into a migraine.

Sio swiftly moves her hands through the air, advancing through numbers, letters, and lines. Presumably my stats. Do they even matter now? Did they ever? With anger and betrayal rising in my gut, I finally break the silence.

"Why?" I ask through gritted teeth.

Startled, she turns sharply, her eyes outlined in red.

"Why am I still here? Why was Reed chosen?"

She considers a moment before answering. "He proved more valuable on the Surface."

"But he's Flawed."

I know I should be happy that my friend is no longer relegated to spending his entire life underground, but the thought that he does not appreciate the opportunity he's been given eats away at me.

Sio's eyes are empty. "He was thoroughly assessed. There are certain traits he possesses that could not be overlooked." She goes back to her charting, and with her usual admonishing inflection cautions me. "Mind your tone, Subject. Jealousy is an insecure trait, and one that is of no value on the Surface."

I hate her.

Sensing our conversation, and that I'm awake, the walls of the capsule come to life with a programed salute to the Chosen Ones. It's the same messaging played after each Selection, only with new faces. This time, there are three, each one spread across its own wall in the room. Del on one, Farrah on the other, and finally Reed, all smiling down at me. Mocking me.

"You're supposed to be my Keeper, my protector."

"That's what I'm doing."

"Then why are you sabotaging me? Do you think I'm weak?"

"No." Sio swipes and continues annotating the air.

"I don't understand! What is so wrong with me?"

Sio pauses and stares at me with a look that I can only decipher as irksome pity. "You aren't meant for this," she says.

The alarms chime, and the lights flash green within the room. It's time for feeding.

Sio collapses her projection and folds her Index, holding it out in her hand as some kind of proof. "We keep meticulous records of every single Subject. The data doesn't lie," she states firmly, pausing to let the words sink in. "You're simply not cut out for this."

She then slides the Index into her pocket.

"What is that supposed to mean?" I ask incredulously.

She hesitates at the door briefly. "You should have gone with him when you had the chance."

Reed was telling the truth? She's gone before I can ask her a follow up.

I let myself slump to the ground, complying with gravity. I go over my last conversation with Reed. What was he so afraid of? Did Sio warn him about the conditions on the Surface? Was what I passed off as musings of an unstable mind, actual truths I was too stubborn to see? My only truth now is that I'm still here, I'm still underground with no clock to countdown to. No finish line in sight.

I recall Reed's last foreboding thoughts.

Our blood. It's in our blood.

CHAPTER 24
EVER

The Refectory is eerily silent, the usual buzz of conversation absent and replaced by a palpable tension. Even the Keepers are uncharacteristically quiet. The recent blackout has rattled them; it's the first time something like this has happened here. They say it's a sign that danger is approaching, perhaps closer than ever to penetrating our safe haven. The vulnerability of our power system, previously thought secure, has sparked widespread fear. And the significance of the Chairman's choices at the recent Selection is not lost on anyone. The fact that he selected three Subjects, including a Flawed, has raised questions about the state of the Surface and the motives of the Chairman himself.

I spot Skye at the IV infusion station and make my way over, taking the empty seat beside hers. I plug in my own IV and glance across the room at Vada, who is seated with a group of Keepers. They appear deeply engrossed in their dinner.

Skye looks smaller than usual, frail. Her arms lie fatigued by her side, and her curly hair falls limply on her shoulders while she stares off blankly into nothingness.

"It's going to be alright," I try to comfort her, but she doesn't look my way.

"I had a dream last night," she says, her voice distant and flat.

I reflexively tell her to hush, and I scan the room to make sure no one has overheard.

"I dreamed that I wasn't real," she continues. Her tone makes me worry.

I recall the small voice I heard echoing down the hall outside of the Utility Room just a few nights ago, right when Reed slammed me into a wall. *It wasn't me.*

"I was looking at myself in a mirror, but I was older, an adult, I think. I looked different, my hair was waist long, my eyes were a darker brown, and I had paint on my face that made my cheeks look pinched and my lips bright red. I was smiling at myself, waving, but my hands weren't moving. And then I realized that the person I was looking at wasn't me at all, but instead I was *her*. I was the reflection."

I am completely at a loss for words and am not sure how to respond. I get the sick feeling that whatever flaw was manifesting itself in Reed's mind, might somehow also be affecting Skye. But how could that be, she's not Flawed?

"Skye." I hesitate. "Were you running down the hallway outside the Utility Room the night before Selection?"

She closes her eyes with sincere confusion. "I don't know."

"Listen to me, you're okay. You are here, you're real. We're all a little scared after what the Chairman said but we need to stay focused, keep our minds clear. It sounds like we're needed more than ever."

She says nothing in response.

Vada materializes next to Skye's station, towering over her and scrutinizing her closely. She must have heard her. From this angle, Vada's white coat flaps at her sides and I can see the outline of her Index nestled in her pocket.

"Skye, may I have a word with you?" Vada asks, making it clear this was not a request.

In a barely audible voice, Skye agrees and nods. She casts a nervous gaze in my direction, her shaky hands removing the IV from her arm. I offer her a reassuring look in response.

As Vada steers Skye away, I seize a fleeting moment to pull her small frame into an embrace. "You're going to be okay," I whisper softly.

Vada, momentarily taken aback by my sudden display of affection, leans in and commands me to release Skye. The other Subjects in the room gawk in disbelief. Physical contact is not permitted.

"That just cost you two points," Vada informs me sternly.

She pivots, taking Skye along with her, and exits the Refectory. I take a deep breath, counting to ten, before making a swift dash towards the Utility Room, with Vada's Index securely tucked away in my pocket.

A soft touch is one of the few skills I can thank Sio for. She was relentless in training me to control my strength, so I've become very good at it. Although I'd never put it to the test on her. Too risky.

Once inside, I turn the Index over in my hands searching for the activation trigger. I glide my hands along the thin, smooth glass surface, unfolding it and finding the small indentation at the bottom. I push it and a bright white light emanates from the device nearly blinding me. Its holo-projection appears, and a grid fills the space ahead of me. I'm not sure why the Keepers still use this outdated technology instead of the Bright-i lenses, but it's clear that the Index offers more storage space, meaning whatever answers I'm looking for, this is a good place to start.

ACCESS DENIED

The words blink across the air. That's what I expected. A retinal scan would be needed to access the projection information. It would have been far too convenient if it worked, and nothing in my life has ever been convenient.

I fold the Index back up and approach the large, antiquated machine in the corner which Reed once described as capable of interfacing with other devices.

I hope this works. Otherwise, I will have risked my standing for nothing.

I push what I assume is an eject button and a small slot emerges. It felt bigger as it jammed me in the spine last night with Reed. I place the Index in the grooves of the slot and slide it back into the body of the machine. The screen flickers for a moment and then a series of numbers and symbols scroll vertically across the screen, seemingly calculating something. Then a blank screen is left behind.

Unsure what to do next, I tap on the console of symbols that rests below the screen. 0123XY. Reed's profile materializes in front of me. *Status: Pre-Sur* follows the *Flawed* categorization. He must be undergoing preparations for ascending to the Surface.

I scroll past column after column of stats including reported hours per assignment, feeding levels, test performances, and more, until I reach his vitals. Other than the occasional mark referencing his cleft lip revision there is nothing unusual noted, even his mental faculties are reported as stable. Although it's possible that stat hasn't been updated to reflect his latest outbursts.

Half expecting to encounter a sudden revelation. I'm disappointed that the only remark about his blood is that his blood type is O negative.

Our blood. It's in our blood.

We learned in courses during our younger years before becoming full time contributors to the maintenance of Helix, that O negative is the universal donor blood type. His blood could be given to anyone on the Surface in the event of a medical emergency. Which is somewhat interesting, but not especially significant. We all donate blood during the Drawings, ensuring a steady supply of all blood types for the Surface's needs.

I'm starting to doubt this entire plan. What am I risking punishment for? The ramblings of a potentially unstable mind? Reed was scared, afraid of the unknown, and he let that fear control him. Maybe there's nothing else to it. Maybe his Selection was strategic for reasons unknown to us, and maybe Del was more special than we all thought.

I'm about to give up and return the Index to the Refectory in hopes that Vada will assume she dropped it, rather than it being swiped – no Subject would dare do such a thing. But decide that one quick look at Farrah's profile can't hurt – see how exactly she managed to edge me out.

Status: Pre-Sur. She was also preparing for the Surface. As it reads, Farrah has made exceptional contributions, has great scores, not as high as mine but still impressive. And the same note, blood type O negative. Strange, I thought it was one of the rarer blood types. I look up Del, and he too is O negative. Could blood type be the indicator for who's chosen to ascend?

But that doesn't make any sense. The Drawings ensure a constant supply of a variety of blood types, so there's no need to favor certain ones.

Could Del, Farrah, and Reed be related? Is that what Reed wanted me to see?

That's impossible. What would it even mean?

I hesitate before I call up my own profile. What I see confuses me even more. My blood type is also O negative.

I'm not sure what to do with any of this information, but I have to get the Index back before Vada realizes it's missing. I push to exit but a new window opens instead.

MEMORANDUM NO. 1063
From: Helix Security Service
Subject: Disclosure Reminder

Curiosity gets the best of me, and I open the message.

Due to heightened pressures from the Surface, Helix Security Service would like to remind all leadership personnel and their subordinates that communications about any information regarding the programs conducted here, or the existence of this facility, is strictly prohibited. It is top priority to keep all details classified, our survival and continuance depends on it.

As a precaution, in the instance of a Class 1 emergency, the entire program will be purged without delay.

This should be all for now.

Purged? Was Reed, right? Are we not safe?

With trembling hands, I eject the Index and cautiously step out into the hall, a heavy sense of dread weighing on me with every step.

Suddenly, Vada appears. "I wish you hadn't done that," she says in a steely voice, her insidious glare sending a chill down my spine. She juts her open hand out sharply toward me, and I gingerly place the Index in it.

"I'm sorry, it just fell out, and with everything going on right now–" I start, appealing to our communal anxiety. "I just wanted answers. I hope you can understand."

She tilts her head, cracking her neck left and right before lowering her hand into her pocket. Her uncharacteristically cold demeanor only adds to the fear that now grips me.

"This is going to make things harder for you," Vada warns as she takes a step forward. "It's going to be much more difficult to cope. Even Sio can't protect you from what's next."

She laughs a little, and I don't know what's more unsettling, her smile, or the deliberate slide of her hand from her pocket, gripping what I'm sure is a tranquilizing syringe.

"Listen, I am so sorry. I understand if you have to dock my points," I say, as she takes another step.

"Don't worry, it will all be over soon," Vada says coolly.

I'm doing all that I can to stay calm.

"I'll take it from here, Vada," Sio's voice echoes down the corridor, and I'm taken aback by the overwhelming sense of relief that washes over me as I watch her gracefully approaching us.

Vada sighs, she doesn't appear surprised, but she steps back nonetheless and drops whatever was in her hand back into her pocket. She gives me one final, unreadable look before turning to Sio and shaking her head. "It's not worth it."

"All personnel must report to the Great Room at once," Sio announces firmly. The news elicits a smile from Vada, but it only serves to further unsettle me.

"A new Selection is about to begin," she adds.

CHAPTER 25
RO

"Wake up."

I shook my Subject's small body, but they didn't stir.

"Wake up little one," I whispered more urgently.

Each second was precious, ticking by unyieldingly. I had set the centrifuge countdown to twenty minutes. The lab was empty at this time of night, the next technicians didn't arrive for another hour, and the nurses we now referred to as Keepers were sound asleep. I was certain no one saw me travel up to the lab.

It was time to bring this to an end. What we were doing at this facility was wrong and I knew it. I was willing to sacrifice my soul to bring Rune back to life, and now that her Copy was lying before me, I felt a sense of responsibility to make things right. I had to do better. Be better. For Rune.

I would no longer allow the elites to continue enhancing themselves to a level that was out of reach for the rest of society. They had grown too powerful, and their unchecked greed created a world where only a select few thrived and the rest struggled to survive.

My Subject and I were going to survive. And I was going to put an end to Second Lifers.

Edric entrusted me to create these products, but we never established how long this would go on. The RMG splicing was meant to produce fully-grown Subjects in a short amount of time and arrest their growth once maturity was reached. What I failed to disclose was my inclusion of a dormant segment of DNA in the splicing process. One that would become actively expressed by a unique environmental signal: transplantation into another body. This genetic marker would trigger accelerated cell division, causing the recipient to age rapidly.

I reveled in the irony of it. The minute an elite harvested their purchased Subject, they would be ensuring their own self-destruction. Their quest for eternal youth and enhanced abilities would lead to their demise.

I scooped the little one into my arms, resting their head on my shoulders. They were heavier than I planned for, the dead weight of deep sleep adding several pounds. I had expected the effects of the sleep aid given to Subjects with their evening vitamins would wear off by this point, but its potency remained tranquilizing. Maybe this was for the better, I could ensure the Subject would remain quiet. At four years of maturity the female tended to ask too many questions in their waking state. I was eager to answer them all, of course... once we made it out of here. Once we escaped, I would be free to love them the way they deserved, to be the mother I was prevented from being, to atone for my sins.

However, I couldn't exactly walk out the front door. I needed to get to the algae farm. The exhaust vent Axe showed me during our tour was sure to be completed by now, and it was nothing I couldn't pry open with a few tools. We would then begin our climb. It would be a squeeze, I'd have to go first, then pull the Subject up behind me, until we reached street level.

I grabbed a cot sheet and draped it over the female, fashioning it into a sling to carry her on my hip. I would then use it to create a harness to pull their body up through the vent.

"We're going to make it," I whispered as we slipped out of the capsule dormitory, past the sleeping bodies of other Subjects in their cots. They would all be relocated to 23 once construction had completed on the lowest levels.

I didn't know where we'd go, once we were out, but at least we'd be off the radar. We wouldn't be recognized – not by the Adornment competitors who felt threatened by my work and were likely behind my accidents, the very ones Edric claimed to be protecting me from. After all, Rosio and Rune were both dead to the outside world. Our only real concern would be Edric himself.

The algae farm was several thousand feet away on the other end of the floor. I kept close to the walls hoping the darkness would provide some cover from any cameras surveilling the halls.

We passed by abandoned workstations until the back room was only a few hundred feet away. I turned a corner, straining to bend down and collect a makeshift go-bag I had managed to store away in a filing cabinet. Water purifiers, multipurpose scalpels, photon veils to protect us from the heat rays, and containers of algae I managed to siphon from Axe's farm. The calories could sustain us until I found a place suitable enough for us to live, but we'd need to be careful with how much we consumed. Edric had no intention of letting Axe remedy its addictive properties and instead ordered it to be utilized to make the Subjects docile, more easily controlled and manipulated.

Once outside, we would need to make it past the Refinery Lands into the Outlands. That would be the only place we could be safe from Edric once he discovered my betrayal. He would never stop searching for us, but out there, in uncharted territory, we stood a chance.

With the bag across my arm and the female's body weighing down my hip, I blinked several times, and swiped the air to bring up the laboratory surveillance. The timer had reached four minutes remaining before the centrifuge would blow. This would all be over soon. I used the radio isotopes from the genetic splicing procedures; when spun they would become increasingly unstable. Once their acceleration threshold was reached, they would explode, creating the distraction I needed to get us out of here undetected.

I turned the corner to the algae farm. The only way in was using the retinal scan. The moment I did that, it would be recorded. They'd know I was here. But it didn't matter. This was my only chance.

I looked into the scanner, and the doors slid open. I stumbled inside, making my way to the exhaust hatch on the back wall. I dropped the bag and laid the female's sleeping body down carefully, then pulled out the multitool and unscrewed the hatch cover.

"This is it." My heart was racing with anticipation, freedom was so close I could taste it.

We're going to make it.

I looped the blanket around the Subject's legs and tied it to a power cord I retrieved from my bag, taking the other end and securing it around my own belt.

Two minutes.

I cradled the female's face tenderly in my hands, my eyes lingering, memorizing their features for a stolen moment. They were beautiful. They were Rune. I didn't deserve it, but I was getting my second chance with her.

"I promise to keep you safe." I would not fail this time. Then I gave them a quick kiss on the forehead, a solemn promise, bathed under the green light of the algae walls.

Strapping on the go bag, I crawled into the vent. It was tight. Good. With my back against one side, I could push off the other with my legs and use the momentum to lift up.

This was going to work. I could see light filtering in about 20 meters up. I began the climb, inching my way up with a repetitive push and slide. The heat from the gases circulating their way up accelerated my exhaustion. My muscles burned, but I couldn't stop.

Forty seconds.

I continued my ascent. Sweaty arms shaking, trying to maintain balance. The higher I got, the greater the intensity of the heat. It was more than just the exhaust gases. It felt like a heat wave seeping in from above although it was the middle of the night.

Ten more meters to go. My breath came short and ragged. Where was my explosion? The centrifuge should have reached top acceleration by now.

Something was wrong.

A sudden tug on the cord nearly sent me plummeting. Heart hammering, I managed to catch myself after slipping only a few inches.

Glancing downward panic clawed at me, could the female be waking up?

Another tug, this time with more force. They must be terrified and trying to run.

"It's alright, don't be afraid," I called down, my voice likely lost in the void between us. I strained to look up, only five more meters. I tentatively reached down to pull on the cord, hoping to slacken it. If I could just make it up the last few meters to the outside, I would be able to climb out and pull her up. But the intensity of the tug grew, I'd never reach the opening if the female was fighting me. It was a risk, though I had no choice, I'd have to come back down and either calm them, or potentially tranquilize them – we were running out of time.

The descent was much quicker than the climb. I dropped the last few feet landing in a crouch and climbed out, baffled to see the Subject's small body still resting where I left them.

"What do you think you're doing?"

My heart dropped into my stomach as Axe's voice cut through the silence, emerging from behind an algae tank. His features weren't colored with anger, just entirely confused.

"I receive an alert every time the farm is accessed." His eyes dropped to the female with an expression morphing into horror.

"Doctor, are you trying to steal company property?"

I moved instinctively to shield the Subject from him. "You don't understand."

"Then please explain it to me because it looks to me like you're about to commit a felony. What's your plan? Are you trying to sell it to a competitor?"

My hands trembled at my sides, open-faced, silently pleading. "You've got it all wrong." I crouched down next to the Subject, keeping an arm up signaling him to keep his distance. I glanced at the Subject, my heart aching.

"The female… they're mine." The words tasted bitter in my mouth, I shook my head, weary of the detached language. "*She's* mine."

"I can't be perceived as complicit. I can't afford to lose this job. You should know that I've alerted Edric, he'll be here momentarily," Axe whispered urgently, a hint of panic lacing his voice.

Where the hell was my explosion?

"No wait, you have to let us go," I needed to make him understand. "She's mine, please, just look at her."

"She's your Copy? Then you need to pay for her just like everyone else."

"No, look at her." I placed my hand under her chin, gently lifting her face. "Please, *see* her."

He furrowed his brows, his face a picture of skepticism. "She looks nothing like you."

Of course, he didn't see the similarities. He didn't even know my true identity; I looked like a completely different person. But I held out hope that he'd recognize his own features in her face.

"She's mine," I repeated, my voice straining against the panic tightening my throat. Whether I could trust him or not, I had to tell him. It had to make a difference. It had to. "Axe, she's ours."

He looked at me utterly bewildered, then shifted his gaze back to her.

"What are you–"

"It's me, Ro–"

Abruptly the doors slid open cutting off my confession. My pulse rocketed, fear spreading through my veins.

"What do we have here?" Edric strode into the room, flanked by uniformed guards on each side. Seeing the both of us on the ground, he ordered the guards, "Leave us." The men dispersed instantly.

"You too, Axe."

Stunned, Axe looked back at us one more time.

"Be careful what you wish for," I whispered, hoping he'd remember the first words he ever spoke to me, the same words that had become a running joke during the length of our relationship. For just an instant, I thought I registered the flicker of understanding in his eyes, that he might take some action to help us, but it was gone too quickly. As he walked out of the room, Edric gave him a small proud squeeze on the shoulder.

Now it was just the three of us, the palpable sense of dread was almost suffocating. I clutched my little one tightly against my chest, my heart racing with fear of what Edric might do next, every possible scenario of his retaliation playing out in my mind.

Edric moved slowly through the room, each step measured, eyes methodically scanning the tanks. The silence stretched on, amplifying my dread. I should fight back. Maybe I could take him, even though his towering frame would certainly overpower mine. I should try. I knew this, yet my body remained paralyzed.

Entire minutes passed before Edric spoke. "The heat index reached 121 degrees this afternoon, did you know that?"

He didn't wait for me to respond.

"And there are reports of increasing fire waves in the Outlands."

I pulled my little one tighter, she was still sound asleep.

"You can't survive a full day outside in the open air."

He walked towards another tank.

"Did you also know that I had advanced sensors installed in the bio labs to detect spikes in activity? After all, such highly sensitive research must be preserved."

He knew about the centrifuge.

"It's a shame you hadn't set a shorter timer, you might have made it out."

Time has never been on my side.

He loomed over us, his presence devouring the space around us.

"Where would you even go? You have no property, no assets, no ties to the community. You alienated everyone you knew after the accident during your self-destructive downfall. You'll never survive out there. You'll kill her. Again."

Edric's voice was a blade, each word cutting deeper, echoing my fears. He was right.

I swallowed hard. I had nowhere to go, no way out. I couldn't put Rune at risk. The thought of endangering her made me physically ill.

He watched me closely, sensing the slight ripple in my expression, my resolve wavering. "This is your home now," he declared coldly. "I own you."

"I am not your property, Edric," my voice a defiant whisper.

He gestured to my little one. "But *it* is, and you're not taking it anywhere."

"That's not what we agreed on."

"Consider it your good fortune, this truly is the best place for it."

"This is a slaughterhouse."

"You're failing to grasp the true purpose of our work here." He cocked his head with pity and crouched down so we were face-to-face, sending a chill up my spine. "But you will understand. Soon enough, you'll see I'm protecting you both, and you'll realize how lucky you are to be here in the safest place on Earth."

CHAPTER 26
EVER

The remaining Subjects are all scurrying into the Grand Hall wearing expressions that mimic mine, complete and utter bafflement. Another Selection so soon is unprecedented, there shouldn't be another ceremony scheduled for six months. This can only mean one thing: conditions on the Surface have become desperate.

Amidst all the shuffling, I'm bumped backwards into one of the pews. I search the flurry of Subjects around me, some manage to don their green ceremony outfits, while the rest of us, clearly more flustered, remained in our white Subject uniforms. I look closely for curly light brown hair resting on small shoulders, but I don't see Skye anywhere.

Where is she? Subjects never miss Ceremony. I haven't seen her since the Refectory. Then, a less comfortable thought: what have they done with her?

Across the aisle, among the remarkably calm Keepers, stands Vada. Stoic, her composure unsettling, as if the last ten minutes never happened. A shiver of fear creeps down my spine as my mind races with troubling thoughts.

On the opposite end of the pews, security personnel maintain their usual positions only now with the surprising addition of long batons at their sides, and masks hanging from their necks.

I apprehensively turn to the girl next to me; Elodie has

never looked so pale, her arms are slick to her sides as she stares straight ahead.

"What do you think this is all about? What's going on?"

"The Forms must have found us," she says, her lips barely moving.

"I overheard my Keeper say it's not safe anymore," a boy chimes in from behind. "I think they need greater numbers on the Surface, and we're being summoned for combat."

Sio appears in the entrance and walks up to the platform taking her place next to the Tube dock. Her eyes are empty as she retrieves the tin box from her pocket for the Selection.

With a routine hush, the Tube lands on the platform, and we all abruptly stand tall. A swoosh of air opens its doors, and the Chairman steps down onto the platform. He dons his usual black suit, yet appears uncharacteristically unbuttoned, relaxed – a detail I find comforting. Maybe things aren't as bad as we're guessing.

I hope his cool composure means we're in for some better news. Rather than holding his hands taut in front of him, as is customary, the Chairman gestures broadly when he speaks.

"Welcome Subjects, I know you are all surprised to be here so soon after the last ceremony."

The other Subjects look at each other not sure what to expect, but my attention is held by his hands. They are bare. He is no longer wearing his signature black leather gloves. In all my years here in Helix, I have never seen his hands exposed. Now I can't look away.

"Rest assured this is a good thing." He grins. "This is what you have all been training for, and it is an honor to finally be called to fulfil your duty to the cause, to humanity. This is your chance to prove yourself."

I know I should be excited by another opportunity to ascend, but something is not right. I could finally be getting out of this place, but what awaits us is not clear. Was it ever?

As he speaks, I feel the room getting smaller, and quickly realize that it's not just in my head. Security has inched closer, some of them spilling out into the aisle between the pews now. Security has never been a threatening presence at Selections. Is this a measure of precaution due to Reed's previous reaction to Selection?

"In this room stand all of the remaining Subjects of Helix, the remaining hope for our species."

All the remaining Subjects? What about Skye?

"For years we have managed to remain undetected, living in relative calm. But we've always known we were on borrowed time; the quiet before the storm you have been preparing for your entire lives. By decree only one special Subject was chosen to rise into the ranks of the Saviors and given the time to assimilate to the Surface. But time has run out. We've been breached and the Forms are coming for us. Reinforcements are needed. Three more of you will be chosen for this honor today, rising through Helix and joining the Savior troops."

Something is definitely wrong here. If the threat is so grave, why not send us all up?

"Let us commence," he says, directing his attention to Sio.

Sio hands him the box, and he carefully tilts the lid back and delicately pulls up a slide, massaging it with his bare finger tips.

The blood on it, is it also O negative?

"Subject 8423XX," he calls out.

Callix flinches, and we all part, opening the walkway. Her feet falter as she climbs the steps, nerves getting the best of her. A somber mood has settled over the room.

She steps up to the platform and takes her position next to Sio.

The Chairman reaches back into the box and pulls out another slide. He gives Sio a second glance and with a poorly concealed smirk says, "1123XX."

It's me. It's actually me. It's finally my turn. Yet something keeps me from moving. The weight of gravity crushes down on me. It's my big moment, and I'm freezing up.

Sio's face has visibly whitened, even from this distance. Security approaches in my periphery, anticipating rogue behavior. That wakes my legs and reminds them to move. I slowly walk up to the platform and take a stand next to Callix.

The Chairman digs into the tin one final time. "6323XY."

A tall lanky boy with blonde hair, soon approaches and takes a stand next to me. I can feel heat erupting from Sio behind me. Her heavy breathing fills my ears, blocking out the Chairman's speech.

In the next moment, Callix leaves my side, approaching the Chairman to accept her slide, and enter the Tube.

"May the light guide your way."

A moment later the Tube returns. It's now my turn, and security moves in closer to the platform again. Is it because I hesitated earlier?

"Ever," the Chairman greets with a smile. It's surreal to hear my name come out of his mouth. I've dreamt of this moment my entire life.

I walk slowly toward him to finally accept my honor. Seeing him up close, I find myself slightly more at ease. There's a familiarity in his gaze that I can't quite pinpoint, and the strength of his well-defined features gives me the comforting feeling that I can trust him, as if we've met before. Perhaps it's my years of dreaming finally manifesting. A reminder that this is my moment. It's my time.

He gives me my slide, then extends his bare hand to me. I grasp it in mine, being sure to apply the right amount of pressure in my grip, I want him to know that I am ready, I am not afraid, and that I do truly appreciate this honor. His hand is strong and surprisingly warm, its peaks and valleys fitting into mine with an unexpected familiarity.

And I realize. I know these hands.

I squeeze tight and offer a polite smile. As he slowly releases, my fingers graze his palm and that's when I feel it. A nearly imperceptible defect, the slight crescent impression of teeth. My teeth.

I do know these hands. This hand releasing mine and welcoming me into the new ranks.

This hand belongs to Reed.

CHAPTER 27
EVER

The vast open space of the great room seems to collapse in on me, crushing the air out of my lungs. I can't move; my legs have turned to lead. I just stand there, hand extended, staring at the Chairman. This doesn't make sense, of course it's not Reed's hand, I must be mistaken. Reed is now on the Surface aiding in the fight for our survival, a battle for which I'm confident he needs all of his body parts.

So, what is his hand doing here? Attached to the Chairman?

The same hand paired with mine in line to the Refectory when we were children. The hand that helped me up from the floor when I slipped off the Kineti-Bike during my first cycling session. The hand that tugged me along, urging me to pick up the pace for fear of getting caught the very first time we discovered the Utility Room.

The Chairman furrows his brows down at me, and it suddenly dawns on me: his dark gray eyes have a striking resemblance to Reed's. His jawline–

"Congratulations Subject, advance to the Tube."

I struggle to make out his words over the raging blood rushing in my ears. Hands roughly curl around my arms, nudging me. Security has advanced onto the platform and two men are physically moving me forward, nails digging into my skin.

I break out of the spell, my legs slowly releasing their hold on the ground as I coax them to move forward. I have awaited this moment for so long. I've dreamed of stepping foot onto the Tube, glass doors sliding into place around me, a gateway between Level 23 and a new life. In my dreams I'd step in, turn, and look on at the group before me, smiling faces beaming with pride. I'd echo their sentiments back with an all-knowing nod, my heartfelt goodbye.

But now, an inexplicable fear rises within me, insisting *something* is wrong.

I lift my feet onto the hollow Tube and as I turn, Sio advances towards me, towards the glass door, with a surprising fury. I would scream if I had the breath.

The doors slide shut just as she reaches me. I jump even though I know she can't reach me, my back pressed against the far wall of the Tube. One of the security guards who escorted me now attempts to restrain Sio, sending her to her knees and roughly jerking her arms behind her.

Through the glass she mouths words at me, calculatedly out of view of security struggling to pull her away. Even through all the commotion, her message is clear: *Run.*

Behind her in the pews, the last row of security personnel restrain the remaining Subjects, yanking them from their rows and forcing them into the aisle. Elodie tries to pull away and a black baton is cracked against the back of her leg. A fog is dispersed throughout the room. The lanky boy chosen after me stands bewildered at the edge of the stage.

Now I scream.

The Tube lifts and with a rush of air I'm rising through the levels of the Helix, my former life and all the people in it fading away, becoming smaller and smaller. Having spent my entire life underground, I never stopped to consider that I might be afraid of heights. My legs give out and I slump to the floor. I feel nauseous, like I'm at a blood drawing. Am I just in shock? I can't reach the apex soon enough. I need fresh air, I need light, I need to breathe. I need answers.

What did I just witness? Why was Security harming and incapacitating the remaining Subjects? And why do the Chairman and Reed share such a striking resemblance? Could they be related? Could it explain why Reed was chosen? But that wouldn't explain how they share a scar, a scar that I gave him just days ago.

Once the Tube ascends above the Great Room, its platform rotates and I move past emptiness, a space devoid of light, black as far as the eye can see. I lose all sense of direction. I question my own state of mind. Nothing makes sense, the Selections, Reed, Sio. Maybe I am losing it. The black seems never ending. I don't know what I expected but I get the uneasy feeling that I've been hurtled into an infinite void.

I'm surprised by how much time has elapsed; this is a much longer trip than I anticipated. Is it just my anxiety stretching out the seconds? The Tube always returned to Level 23 so quickly after a Selection. And yet, I am still moving.

After a moment the Tube slows, which my stomach is immediately grateful for. Maybe we're approaching the top.

There's a far-off flicker of light in the distance; it gets larger and seems to be following the Tube, rising with it. It's still too far off to make out, but it moves towards me, steadily growing. Squinting, it appears the light has a cylindrical shape, housed in a metallic casing. It's growing rapidly now. The Tube continues to travel at its reduced speed, but the light shows no sign of slowing down. It's now racing towards me, and I can feel my heart rocketing in my chest, my breathing quickens. There's nowhere to go. I close my eyes and clutch the glass behind me, bracing for impact.

But the sound of shattering never comes. The light and its enclosure swiftly slide right underneath the Tube. Stunned and relieved, I open my eyes and crane my neck to catch a better glimpse of it through the glass.

The light came from *another* Tube. There is more than one.

We were always told there was only one mode of transport in and out of Helix. One singular Tube, it traveled up and down. That's it. But another Tube just crossed beneath me, traveling horizontally. We've been lied to. Helix is much larger than I ever could have imagined.

Suddenly, a bright purple light floods in, and the Tube glides towards the level above. It looks just like our atrium but filled with rows and rows of plants as far as the eye can see. This must be where they grow and propagate the plants going to the Surface.

As quickly as the light came in, it vanishes and I'm plunged back into darkness as my journey continues. My eyes struggle to adapt. A moment later the Tube comes to an abrupt halt at the next level, and I'm propelled forward onto my knees. The platform beneath me spins, white light flooding in as it does so. This must be it; I must be outside finally.

The doors open, and I fall into a blindingly white room. I scramble about on the cool smooth floor as my eyes adjust to the light. I look to my left, my right, straight ahead, trying to take it all in. One thing is certain: I'm still inside Helix.

The room is small, and completely empty. To my horror there are no doors. I jerk backward towards the Tube, but it's too late, it is already rising upward. I lunge, reaching for its base, but miss. I manage to catch my balance, stopping myself before slipping down the shaft into pure darkness, a gaping abyss stretching downwards, its depths concealed from sight.

How high up am I?

A white wall the length of the room descends from the ceiling, sealing the terminal so it looks like there was never an opening. What is this place? I walk around, letting my hand glide over every surface, desperately searching for an exit. Could this be where the other Subjects were taken? Is this a detour on the path to the Surface?

Suddenly I'm hit by a gust of wind emanating from the center of the room. A large projection has materialized, which reveals my own bewildered reflection staring back at me. But the image is off, it's not an exact mirror. I don't see the white room behind me in the reflection, instead I see what appears to be land from the Surface. I'm outside. And instead of my white wrinkled Subject uniform, I don the sleek black fibers of a Savior. The image reminds me of the progress updates we see projected in the halls of Level 23 time and again.

"What is this?"

At the sound of my voice an icon blinks at the top corner of the projection. It's commanding me to smile. I'm too confused to comply and am hit with a burst of air. My hair fans in the wind. The icon blinks again, this time I muster a smile which is followed by a bright flash of light. The wind stops, and the projection disappears.

The quiet is unsettling. I wait for something else to happen. Nothing does.

I back up against the wall, sliding down to the ground.

I sit there unmoving for what feels like hours.

In the never ending quiet, I notice the electrical buzzing.

Someone is watching me.

CHAPTER 28
RO

"Fires are spreading rapidly in the nearby Outlands, posing serious threat to the Refinery Lands just outside the city limits. Residents are advised to stay indoors and keep windows shut to avoid smoke inhalation. Authorities are actively engaged in firefighting efforts and urge caution. Updates to follow."

I reluctantly tore myself away from the captioned news report; the digital signage had been muted to avoid disrupting the mood of the gala attendees as they arrived. Regardless of my defiance, Edric forced me to attend the event, citing the need to present a united front, answer product questions, and lend credibility to the science behind our work. However, I couldn't shake the feeling that there was a more sinister motive behind his insistence on my presence.

"I'm surprised so many people showed up given the weather," Axe remarked – the first words he'd spoken to me since I told him my real name. Although I could sense a flicker of guilt in him, he still hadn't acknowledged any recognition of our relationship. Perhaps he hadn't heard me, or if he had, he wasn't entirely convinced. He couldn't see past the modifications but was curious enough to stay close. Though after he handed me over to Edric, his loyalties were crystal clear. And still, I held out hope that it would finally all click for him. Even though the damage to my vocal cords permanently changed the timbre of my voice, I believed that those deeper, intangible qualities that shine through when you love someone would make him see the real me. I thought I meant more to him. That, somehow, he would find a way to save me. To save us. But I can only rely on myself. I'm all Rune has.

"It's no surprise at all," I replied casually, pretending everything was okay between us. Masking the hurt. "The elite have always put their personal interests ahead of the planet, and climate warnings won't change that. To them, a little bit of natural disaster is just a minor inconvenience. They're so insulated from the effects of their own actions that they've lost all sense of perspective."

Axe nodded, his eyes brightening, relieved that I responded to him. "Can't argue with that."

Edric stood at the entrance of the facility's lobby-turned-ballroom, greeting each of the guests as they arrived. They were then directed to a blood-prick raffle station for a chance to win their very own upgrades. The rich loved free stuff.

The air was filled with the sweet fragrance of rare and delicate blooms. The lavish ballroom was illuminated by the glow of crystal chandeliers hovering in midair, casting a soft light that mingled with the flickering glow of plasma lamps. The light cascaded over the ostentatious garments worn by the guests, many flaunting their chrome Adornments.

I made my way towards the bar, past pictures of the sick teen, Vada. Past timelapses of her growing organic Adornment in the lab. Past the hum of conversations.

"It's impressive that he's giving away enhancements to the underprivileged," someone said.

"It's good PR for them, of course," another voice chimed in. "I suppose we can't entirely fault him for being charitable, can we? After all, if he doesn't help these lower-class individuals, who will?"

It had been a while since I had a drink, but tonight I would need it. Axe must have had a similar thought because he signaled the bartender and ordered one. I felt like we were back at the WISH Gala, the first night we met. I wondered if he was experiencing a similar sense of nostalgia. But how could he? I reminded myself that he had made himself my enemy. Because of him I was still trapped here.

"Can I have a Warp White for the lady?" Axe asked the bartender.

I froze.

It was my favorite drink, the first drink he ever ordered for me. Was it a coincidence or did he remember? I couldn't tell. My pulse raced. He didn't turn to look at me until the drink had been prepared. As he handed it to me, we locked eyes in silence, a subtle flutter of anticipation stirring within my chest.

The sounds of nearby conversations filled their air.

"I don't know if I buy into all of this," said the heavily adorned woman next to me, her skepticism clear. "Is he just building this new company to compete directly with his father? It seems like a cry for help. I mean, my Adornments work just fine. Those who can afford quality materials are set."

"You're missing the bigger picture," her date replied, his voice tinged with frustration. "Bionic Adornments used to be a mark of distinction, but how are we supposed to maintain our status if even the mediocre among us can just as easily enhance themselves?"

"Right," another patron chimed in. "We need something more exclusive, something that only the truly exceptional can access. I'm curious to learn more about his offerings."

I kept my gaze fixed on Axe, silently willing him to disclose any recognition of me. "Thank you," I finally said, "for the drink."

He placed a hand on my elbow, instantly setting my whole arm afire.

"I'm going to help you," his voice was a whisper, and his eyes were soft. Then slowly, his motion deliberate yet tender, he tucked a stray lock of hair behind my ear.

He knew.

There was so much I needed to tell him, a torrent of words flooded my mind, but in that moment, none seemed necessary. There would be time for that. I clasped his arm, holding back the urge to fold into him.

"Tonight," I said. While Edric was occupied it was the perfect time to make my move. But where would I go?

As if reading my mind Axe offered a suggestion. "You can go to my place until I can safely move you." I was surprised he still had a place on the outside. We all lived and worked within the walls of Helix.

We scanned the crowd, looking for a sign of Edric. He was mingling with a few guests, some whose faces I recognized, albeit younger versions of them. I assumed he was thanking them for their early support and orders of their own Copies. Most likely members of the board. Though, he looked distracted, his eyes kept darting towards the far end of the room where his father, Sylas Easton, was standing with his brother. Tonight, he was determined to prove himself to his family, and show his father that he was capable of creating something truly groundbreaking.

That kind of tunnel vision would work in my favor.

"Let's go," I said, "our daughter is still on 23."

Our daughter. I had never said those words out loud, never shared parenthood. I could tell he was still grappling with the realization. I would tell him all about her once we were safe.

We pushed through the crowd, not so quickly as to draw attention, but briskly enough to make it towards the Tube before being stopped–

"Doctor, there you are," Edric's grip on my arm was firm. "Please join me, the presentation is about to begin."

I glanced over at Axe, alarm in my eyes. He responded with a comforting nod.

Reluctantly, I followed Edric, watching Axe's retreating figure as he made his way towards the Tube. He would find her, I reassured myself.

"You don't want to miss this. This is our big moment," Edric said as the lights dimmed around the room. He led me to the stage, where he left me standing at the foot before climbing himself. The room fell silent as he began to speak, his voice filling the grand ballroom.

"It is with great pleasure that I stand before you today to share a breakthrough that will revolutionize the field of Adornments. For too long, bionic augmentations have been the norm in our quest for better and stronger bodies. But here at Helix Co, we are presenting a safer alternative – enhanced organic tissues. We have carefully engineered these tissues to ensure their safety and effectiveness, and we can confidently say that they offer a more sustainable solution to human enhancement." He pointed to several images of growing organs on the digital displays around the room.

"I know many of you are lifelong Adornment supporters, some of you with longer lives than most!" This received a chuckle from the crowd as he continued, "And though you've heard about our products, you're perhaps hesitant to adopt them for yourselves." He motioned to the back of the room. "Why not see for yourselves, the improvements that can be made in just under a week's time."

A spotlight shone on a Keeper escorting a girl through the crowd. Vada looked healthy and vibrant; a huge grin plastered across her face as she waved to the audience.

"Our genetically enhanced tissues offer limitless possibilities for our future, giving us the power to unlock the true potential of our human form. We can now restore and improve our physical capabilities, in a way that is both safe and ethical. These tissues are designed to maintain the beauty and uniqueness of the human form."

He spoke with passion and conviction, outlining the benefits of organic Adornments, and their potential to revolutionize the industry.

"But that's not all. Today, I present to you the opportunity to not only restore our bodies but to take the next step in our evolution – genetic upgrades, that are made to order. We have the technology to develop custom-made tissues perfectly suited to an individual's unique needs and desires. Whether it's enhancing physical strength or sensory capabilities, we can tailor these tissues to achieve the desired outcome."

There were no photographs of the Subjects to share, Copies were of course still illegal. Not that the crowd knew that's how the upgraded parts would be made. And those who did know or at least suspected it, didn't care, having already invested in their own.

"Allow me to demonstrate this technology with a sample model."

We had never discussed him revealing one of the Subjects, what was he doing? To my horror, another Keeper walked a female onto the stage. My little one.

She looked so small, frightened by the lights and the crowd. My body clenched ready to run on stage.

"As you can see, or actually as you will not be able to see, this Subject has been enhanced." He wasn't revealing she was a Copy, instead he was misleading the crowd to believe she had received one of the upgraded Adornments.

He glared at me from the stage. This was a clear threat. A reminder that he was in control. He could take Rune from me at any moment.

"Hold on to this," he said passing her a stainless-steel cup. He then nodded and she proceeded to crush the cup with ease between her little fingers to the crowd's delight.

"Our genetically enhanced tissue is a perfect replacement for traditional bionic limbs, with added benefits of natural integration and sensory feedback. Imagine the possibilities of a future where we can replace any part of our body with these safe, organic, and tailored genetic upgrades. We are one step closer to unlocking the full potential of our own bodies."

The room was captivated, and as Edric finished his speech, the guests erupted into excited chatter. None of which I could comprehend. My ears were ringing with a combination of anger and fear. A Keeper swiftly escorted my little one behind the stage as Edric stepped down and commanded, "Come with me, I want you to meet my father and brother."

I was shaking. "No." I didn't want to do anything for him. "You've made your point." I dug my heels into the ground, but he easily dragged me forward, all the while smiling at nearby attendees who continued to congratulate him.

"I need you to understand," he said as we approached his father.

"Well done, Edric," Sylas said, clapping a hand on his son's back. "You have truly exceeded my expectations." He chuckled, finishing off his drink.

"Thank you, father." Edric exhaled, his voice carrying a hint of relief.

"It's good to see you finally doing something with your life. I was starting to think you were content to just live off your trust fund forever. But let's be honest, it's not like you're truly competing with us, are you?"

Edric's body tensed, then he cleared his throat. "I'd like you to meet our lead scientist, Dr. Arata. She's responsible for the kind of forward thinking that will help us to maintain our humanity."

He used my real name. He wasn't complimenting me in this introduction. He was putting another target on my back.

Surprisingly, Sylas barely glanced in my direction. My name seemingly meant nothing to him. Hadn't this man gone to extreme lengths to wipe me from the Earth? His one threatening competitor?

"Don't get ahead of yourself, son. My work has raised humanity to new heights, what you've done here so far is merely endearing. You'd do well to remember you're still just a little fish in a big pond. My pond."

Edric's brother chimed in then, shaking my hand. "It's a

pleasure to meet you, doctor." Then, addressing his brother, "I must hand it to you, Edric. You've really shown some initiative in starting your own company. Of course, it's not like you had much of a choice, considering how little you were contributing to our family legacy. But hey, a little competition never hurt anyone, right?" He winked at me. "Some people are just meant to follow in their father's footsteps, while others are better off chasing their own pipe dreams."

Edric gritted his teeth but kept his composure.

His brother's smile didn't reach his eyes as he turned squarely to me, like he was trying to pull me into their uncomfortable family dynamic. "I remember when Edric was in college, he thought he was so smart. He was always bragging about his grades and how he was going to be CEO by the time he was 30. But then he failed his senior project, didn't graduate on time, and had to retake a whole semester just to finish his degree. I guess he wasn't as smart as he thought, was he? It's just funny how some people overestimate their abilities and end up embarrassing themselves in the end." He paused having made his point. "It was nice meeting you." He dropped his smile and spoke to Edric. "Good luck to you, brother." He and Sylas walked away to mingle with other guests.

Edric looked around the room. "These people are toxic. They don't deserve to evolve."

I couldn't disagree, but I certainly did not empathize with him. He was a monster just like the rest of them.

"I gave them a chance to respect me," he said. "Now you'll understand why it's necessary for me to do what I must do."

I had tuned him out, his words a distant murmur; I couldn't shake the fact that the Eastons seemed completely indifferent to my presence. Was it sheer narcissism or overconfidence that Edric's organic adornments posed no threat? But there seemed to be more to it. Most disturbing of all, was their blank responses to my name, my work. If they didn't truly know who I was... how did I end up here? What was the real reason I was trapped?

CHAPTER 29
EVER

A shiver crawls up my spine and my hairs stand on edge. I may not be able to see them, but I can feel someone's gaze. It's like an itch I can't scratch. Slowly scanning the room, I spot a tiny red light seamlessly integrated into the top left corner of the ceiling.

Don't look directly at it.

I feel an unjustified sense of power at the fact that perhaps whoever is watching me doesn't realize I'm aware of their presence. I leisurely slide my hand along my lower back, massaging a non-existent ache, and slip the glass slide from the Selection into the waist band of my underwear. While I'm completely lost and out of my element, having any sort of edge comforts me. It's the little victories that matter.

I picture my feed being played on a screen in a dark and confined surveillance room illuminated only by the glow of assorted monitors and holo-projections. I'm certain my likeness is being observed by a Flawed Subject turned security personnel, but what exactly they're hoping to see I can't be sure of. Why am I still being monitored after being Selected? And on whose behalf is this surveillance taking place? The Chairman? Sio? I need to be careful not to appear panicked or weak. My journey has only just begun.

I relax my posture, draping one arm over a bent knee. Leaning against the cold wall, I tilt my head back and close my eyes, reducing the temptation to look directly into the camera. My mind drifts back to the Utility Room during my final days with Ira. I remember asking him if he was scared, he simply smiled and replied, "I am eager to serve."

It was the right answer of course, but I secretly hoped he would have been more vulnerable with me. We both knew he would be ascending to fight for his life, yet he was so infuriatingly relaxed.

That's the demeanor I'm going for now. Though my eyes are closed my ears are acutely aware of the sounds filtering through the room: my strained breathing, the pumping blood in my ears, and the hum of surveillance I'm pretending isn't there.

I wonder if the Saviors before me sat in this same room, or if Callix and the lanky Subject are sitting in similar sterile white rooms wondering the very same thing? Is this some sort of final test? We weren't told much about what happens once a Subject is selected. That information was reserved for the chosen ones themselves and was yet another piece of knowledge to be coveted.

If this is a test, that could mean the last 24 hours were also part of a strategy, a legitimate process. The increase in the Selections, Skye's disappearance, the attack on the remaining Subjects, maybe it was all part of some calculated psychological evaluation. Everyone is okay and there is no increased threat on the Surface. I am being tested.

Elaborately.

However, if this isn't a test, the reality is far more frightening. It means that I am either completely insane or that something alarming is happening. Deep down I know I'm not crazy, which means I need to take a moment to consider what's waiting for me on the other side of these walls, what's waiting on the Surface. The Chairman said we had been breached. The Forms are here, and we all need to fight.

Test or no test, there's so much that doesn't make sense.

The limited Selection, it should have been all of us. The incapacitated Subjects. The scar. Reed's scar.

My body is starting to ache from the strain of looking relaxed. I lower my arm to the floor and extend both legs out. I start to doze off as time lingers on. There's no way of knowing how long I've been sitting here.

Not true.

I can't believe it hadn't occurred to me before. My Bright-i. My tracker would display my location and the time. I snap my eyes open and blink twice; digits populate the space in front of me, but they are disjointed – jumbled dash marks that don't connect or seem to make any sense. I can't read them.

I feel dizzy and overwhelmingly faint, an exhaustion like I have never felt rests heavy on my shoulders. The room feels like it's spinning, and I keel over on an elbow.

That's when I see it, an ominous white fog silently rising from the floor. They are pumping something into the room.

I quickly lift my shirt to cover my nose but it's too late, I've inhaled too much. My elbow collapses, and I crash my shoulder against the ground. I strain my neck, battling to keep my head upright and take in every detail of the situation.

A click echoes from across the room, and footsteps approach. From my position on the ground, I can only see feet. There are two sets of them in thick black boots and wrapped in some sort of durable protective plastic.

"What's going on?" I try to ask, but my tongue barely moves.

They are speaking to each other in muffled voices, they must be wearing masks. How did they get in here? There were no doors, at least not that I could see.

"Werrmh I?" I try again.

I am lifted upward, my body limp, gloved hands clasping under my armpits. What is wrong with me? Losing control of my body, I try to lift my neck, but it hangs limply to the side as I try to observe my handlers. Seamlessly connected to their boots are loose pants that rise into thick and ill-fitting long-sleeved jackets. It's all one-piece with an enclosed helmet attachment. Not an inch of skin is exposed, they are protecting themselves from the gas.

Who are these people? They don't look like Keepers.

I have no sensation in any of my limbs, and with horror I realize I am paralyzed.

Did the other Subjects before me go through this? Or am I being punished?

I'm dragged through the threshold of the hidden door, which opens onto a glass hallway. Despite being translucent, the walls reveal nothing of what lies beyond other than darkness. Even the floor reveals nothing but black below, giving me the nauseating sense that we are floating over a never-ending chasm.

I shift my eyes away, over my shoulder, at the white chamber behind me for one last look. The door shuts, the wall moves, and then it's gone, as if the door never existed in the first place.

As I'm hurled forward, I see that the glass wall at the end of the hall ahead begins to shift, revealing an opening. What lies beyond is unclear, but anything is better than sitting in that white limbo, waiting. I steel myself for what comes next.

Abruptly the Boots drop me to the ground and retreat behind a partition. The moment they do, I am sprayed down with a pungent liquid strong enough to make my eyes tear. The acrid scent fills my nostrils, leaving me struggling to catch my breath.

My skin is freezing, my hair and clothes are soaked. I lie on the ground helpless, my clothing now translucent, as the liquid flows down a drain beneath me. Just when my humiliation has reached peak levels, I am briskly patted down by the Boots who wrap me in what feels like a paper gown that somehow has an immediate drying effect, and they pull a mask over my face.

I can't see a thing and my body gives up its fight. I drift into sleep.

CHAPTER 30
EVER

It's warm and the lighting is soft. Sheets are draped over me and tucked tightly into the corners of a mattress, cocooning me in a snug embrace on the bed. Too snug. Though they tried to hide it, mask it even, I can feel the weight of thick metal belts lying across my chest restricting my movement.

The sterile walls are lined with familiar equipment and tools. I am in some sort of MedLab. I wiggle my toes under the tight sheets and let out a sigh of relief when I see the little peaks and valleys move under the covers. I bend my elbows, trying to yank my arms up from under the sheets but I can't seem to tear the restraints off through sheer force alone. Not at this angle. There's a belt over my chest, across my hips and arms, over my knees, and two around my wrists.

I'm trapped.

Was everything in Helix a façade designed to deceive? Like these bedsheets, at first glance offering a sense of security but masking something far more malevolent lurking beyond the surface? Was Reed also held in this room? Maybe there's a chance he's still in Helix? I need to find him and make sense of things.

Run. That's what Sio mouthed. And for all my lack of trust in her, I do appreciate the simplicity of the order. It echoes my instinct.

I struggle again to shift my arms; they can't venture more than a couple of centimeters away from my hips. I'm relieved to feel a slightly larger gap between my wrists and their cuffs. I can work with that. Using all the strength that I can channel into one wrist, I push against the metal cuff which groans as it bends. Not by much, but it's widened just enough to allow my entire hand to slip through.

With the additional leverage I'm able to push up on the metal belt restraining my hips and forearm. Sliding my arm through I quickly feel around for a latch, or some kind of buckle to release the belts. But I find none.

The glass slide, do I still have it?

I'm so preoccupied with finding my only potential weapon, I don't see the door handle turn. In walk two strangers in the standard Keeper uniforms of Level 23.

I yank my hands back down to the mattress, although I'm sure they can't see through the bed sheet.

"Hello, Subject," says the thin female in front.

"I see the paralytic has worn off," notes the younger brazen-faced male Keeper behind her. The glint in his eye as he says this gives me the impression he enjoys incapacitating others.

"Where am I? What's going on?"

The woman eyes me from head to toe with a wide smile. "You are a very special girl, and in great request. We are fortunate to have you here."

"When do I join the Saviors?" I demand. "When do I go outside?"

"You have received all medical clearances, so it won't be long."

Did they do something to me while I was unconscious?

"There are precautions that must first be taken," the man says, unsmiling.

"What kind of precautions?" I ask, fighting back the rising panic.

"Stay calm sweetie," the woman says, placing a soft hand on my shoulders. "You mustn't stress yourself before initiation."

Weighing my options, I reluctantly comply, sinking my head down into the pillow realizing how much tension had built up in my neck.

"What is initiation?"

"It's the final step before the Surface," she says plainly.

"We were never told about a final step."

The male Keeper abruptly yanks my legs, straightening them under the covers and proceeds to rewrap and tuck the barely disheveled blankets.

"Of course you weren't, it isn't exactly a pleasant experience, but it's imperative for a successful transfer."

"What is?" I swallow hard.

"Relax, sweetheart." The woman passes a hand across my forehead, applying the slightest amount of pressure, pushing me deeper into the pillow.

"When... when is the initiation?"

"In the morning. Don't worry we'll take good care of you," she says calmly as she shines a light in both my eyes. She then holds my eyelids open and shoots a puff of air into each with the same tool, following it up with another quick burst of light.

Satisfied with her observations, they both retreat towards the door.

"See you soon," the male cackles, which provokes an unamused scowl from the female Keeper.

"What will happen in the morning?"

But they're already out the door, and it locks behind them.

I slide my hand up, finding the glass slide still snug in my waistband. It hadn't been detected. Good. I reach for the furthest end of the metal belt over my hips. If there's no latch, I'll have to pull it loose if that's what it takes. I pull so hard I'm certain the veins in my neck are about to burst. On the third try, it gives. I pry it off, then yank away my other wrist cuff, and finally pull off the belt across my chest. I slink towards the door, trying to keep out of sight of the tiny window at the top. I press up against the frame and only catch the last few fragments of their conversation before they move on.

"Understaffed... At least we get to stay here... Ocular graft, 900 hours."

Confused, I peer through the little window and see a stark white hallway, each side lined with doors just like mine. I watch the Keepers walk away, their backs to me as the woman peers into a retinal scanner and opens the door to the room directly across from mine. Before the door closes, I see a dark-haired boy lying on a bed, strapped in just like I was.

He's unmistakable. It's Reed.

CHAPTER 31
ROSIO

As I load the DNA samples into the wells, the gel electrophoresis machine abruptly shuts down, lights flicker, and the lab is plunged into darkness. I'm caught off guard by the suddenness of the blackout. In all my years here, we have never experienced a power outage before. It's concerning.

The silence in the lab is oppressive, like being sealed inside a tomb. That's exactly how I've felt since the night of the gala – suffocated. Trapped. The gala was 11 months ago, making it almost two years since I first stepped foot inside the Helix. And in that time, I've lost myself, I've become something I despise. I am a monster. The lies I tell the Subjects have been fully woven into their lives. I let them dream of a day when they believe they'll save the Earth. But the reality is we are all trapped in a twisted nightmare of my own making.

My heart breaks daily. I see my Rune, but I can't reach out and hold her. I can't tell her how much I love her, how much I care, or that I've done all of this for her. And that I would do it again, despite everything.

She can't know, it's safer that way. On the night of the gala, Edric made it clear he could take my daughter and sell her off at any moment, at any sign of dissension. He proved it when he paraded her on stage, later showing me the countless bids he received for her. Unlike the other Copies which were bespoke orders, Edric would readily auction her off to the most compatible and highest sum.

Axe and I agreed it would be best to let the tensions die down before attempting another escape. All I could do was ensure she had someone close to protect her. Months later and I'm still too afraid to make a move. Too afraid to risk her life which is nothing but a commodity to Edric. As long as I play by the rules, she can be happy here. She can have a semblance of a life. She can stay safe.

As I watched Edric interacting with his family and expressing disgust for his own consumer base, I had a glimmer of hope that maybe, just maybe, he was starting to see the wrong in what he was doing, and that he would soon put an end to it. But things continued, business as usual, and it seems Edric's brief moment of introspection and self-reflection was nothing but a passing phase. He has no intention of changing his ways. He is willing to do whatever it takes to maintain his power and wealth.

The lab is pitch black. I can't see my own hand in front of my face. I reach out cautiously, my fingers searching for the gel to carefully extract it from the machine, preventing it from drying out and damaging the DNA.

What if this isn't just a power outage? What if something worse is happening? Reports from outside are worsening, citing scorched crops, increases in heat strokes, and humidity levels so high it's difficult to breathe. It's unbelievable how quickly things have deteriorated in mere months, this doesn't feel like a natural progression. Perhaps Edric was right. I am lucky to be sheltered inside the Helix.

I bring up my Bright-i in hopes of an explanation for what is happening, and I am greeted by a new comms message:

MEMORANDUM NO. 1078
From: Helix Security Service
Subject: Enhanced Security Notification

Conditions are escalating. We have received reports from the Surface confirming the validity of the rumored threat. It is still unknown where or when contact will be made, but we can assure you, any and all diversion measures are currently underway. As long as we remain within the walls of the Helix, we are all safe.

The power flickers back on, flooding the room with light. As I shield my eyes from the sudden glare of the bioreactor, I turn and my heart skips a beat. Edric is standing behind me, arms crossed and leaning casually against the wall. How long he has been watching me compile DNA orders?

"What's going on?" I ask, trying to keep my composure.

"Grid tampering," he says, removing an invisible piece of lint from his suit.

"And the memo?" I press.

"Haven't you heard? The world is ending." A hint of dry amusement plays at his lips. "And as we speak there are hordes of people attempting to sabotage our power supply and infiltrate our facility to escape the fires."

The horror and confusion must be written all over my face because he continues, "The heat storms have breached the city limits. Faster than I had imagined, but I prepared for this. Rest assured, we're safe here. This place was built to endure. We're self-sustaining, with all the resources we need to survive. So, in the interest of prioritizing our preservation I've initiated a liquidation sale."

I can't believe what I'm hearing.

"And, of course, orders are through the roof. Clients want to redeem their harvests now. They want to reign in the new world as their best selves," he sneers.

A knot develops in my throat as my worst fears come to fruition. "You're selling off all inventory?"

"The board believes we need to switch our attention towards accommodations for our clients."

"You'd be killing all the Subjects. Full harvests all at once is just murder. You're the Chairman of the board. Can't you persuade them otherwise?"

"It's what the Subjects were meant for," he states with chilling detachment.

"Let me get this straight, you're only offering refuge to the elite who've invested in your products. You're favoring the survival of the most self-indulgent, self-absorbed individuals just because they're your customers? I'm... absolutely disgusted."

He stares at me a moment, then flashes a wicked grin, lifting both hands in the air in mock surrender. "You got me," he laughs, the sound chilling and hollow. "Of course I can't save them," he pauses, his smile fading. "You made sure of that with your added DNA modifications."

My heart sinks. He knows.

"Don't look so shocked. I counted on your hatred of the Elite to drive you to sabotage their products. You despise them as much as I do." There's a glimmer of satisfaction, a sense of twisted pride in his voice. I had played right into his hands.

"Honestly, it was starting to get tiresome covering up the deaths of the earliest harvesters. And I wasn't entirely sure which Subjects you began inserting the sequence into. It's why I waited so long before harvesting my own. I had to be certain it was clean." He turns his hand over with sinister fascination.

I am speechless, trying to process the enormity of what he is saying. "My goal has always been to eradicate the elites."

"But they're your family. Your people. You're one of them," I say incredulously. If he could turn on his own, what did that mean for the rest of us?

"No!" he exploded. "Those creatures are primitive, driven only by vanity and the basest of animal desires. Caring solely for their own comfort and pleasure. No empathy." He pauses, rage simmering. "My mother was a saint, the most kind and generous soul you could ever meet, and when she died, my father's mask of concern was grotesque in its insincerity. He hired a procession of servants to fill the void of her absence, as if luxury could replace love, as if her very essence was just another replaceable commodity in his gilded world. In that moment, I realized the cold truth: to them, people are just accessories to their opulence. Even in death, we are minor inconveniences to be smoothed over and forgotten."

He shakes his head. "No, I am not one of them, they are merely callous creatures masquerading in human form."

He looks back down at his hands. "I, however, am pure," he says with a sudden chilling smile, flexing his fingers.

I shudder, realizing the true reason why he lived without an Adornment his entire life. It was to differentiate himself, to be seen as better than the rest.

"But don't get me wrong, I'm not completely devoid of sentiment. It's not like I'm letting them perish, never to see my family again. They'll continue to exist right here. Their Copies will call Helix home and thrive in the new world, under the rule of their beloved Chairman."

His words send a shiver down my spine. He is a madman, a dictator in the making, with an army of brainwashed super soldiers at his disposal to squash any dissenters who get in his way.

I have run out of time. I need to find a way to protect Rune and stop this nightmare he has engineered from coming true.

CHAPTER 32
ROSIO

As I stand on the platform, I can't shake the terror that grips me. Security swells at the edges of the room, masks hanging ominously from their necks – poised for what? It takes everything in me to act normal. We are safe for the moment, but what about everyone else? I hand Edric the slides. They are blank as usual, phony tokens for a phony ceremony. But this time is different – I have no idea who he will choose. Edric plans to use the Subjects to annihilate the elites and leave everyone else out to perish. Could I live with myself if I did nothing to prevent it? The ends do not justify the means, and I can't stand by as he wields tyrannical control over the lives of others.

Edric looks over the blank slides. He reads off the first name and the child rises eagerly to the stage. But when he draws out the second slide, his eyes flicker to mine as he coldly announces her number. My little one.

My jaw drops to the floor, disbelief and confusion flooding my mind. I had followed every rule, every protocol. How could he do this? We had an agreement; she was off limits. This has to be some kind of twisted joke.

I must have blacked out from the shock because the next thing I know, she is stepping into the Tube. I have to stop her, warn her. I yell out, desperation clawing at my throat. But before I can reach her, a guard grabs me, dragging me away from the platform. The world around me slows as she rises. Gas hisses into the air, and my eyes fix on Edric's, hatred for him boiling inside me. I struggle against the guard, my fingers itching to claw the smug smile off Edric's face as he mouths the words, "Don't worry, we'll make you a new one."

I am forcibly removed from the room. But as soon as we enter the hall, I'm abruptly released, and I collapse to the ground coughing violently. My lungs burning. The guard removes his mask; it's Axe.

"She's being taken to 17. I can buy you some time," he says hurriedly. "There's a rebel group on the Surface, the Sentinels. Find them. They will shelter you both."

I shake my head in disbelief. "What about you?"

"I'll make my way out. He doesn't suspect me."

My eyes well up with tears as I wrap my arms tightly around him, unable to contain my gratitude.

"Once she's safe. I'll come back," I tell him. "I have to stop him."

"I know," he says, urgency coloring his voice. "But right now, you need to go. Stop her harvest." He hands me a gun, his eyes imploring. "Take this."

I want to kiss him, to thank him in some way, a gesture of my long-suppressed love but I'm frozen in place. In that fleeting moment, our eyes lock, a silent conversation of might-have-been.

"Go."

Then with a heavy heart, I turn and run, glancing back at Axe just as the guards burst through the door of the Grand Hall, their weapons drawn. He raises his hands in compliance, then briskly elbows one of them in the jaw and attacks another. He lands several blows before he's hit with a baton. Blood erupts from his mouth.

"Go!" he shouts at me.

And I do.

CHAPTER 33
EVER

Corneal graft. That's what they said. Were they talking about me? Am I losing my eyes in the morning? That can't be it, what purpose would that serve the Saviors?

It's late, the lights have been out for hours, but I'm consumed by a single thought, one mission: I must get to Reed.

Maybe he can help me understand what's happening and find out the truth before... before whatever *"initiation"* is happening tomorrow. Has he undergone his own initiation already? If so, why is he still here? And are the other rooms filled with Subjects too?

There are too many questions.

The halls are silent, so I stand up, feeling my way around dimly lit obstacles toward the door. I try my luck at just turning the door handle, but of course it doesn't budge. That's when I notice a retinal scanner on the inside of the door. Holding my breath, I raise my face to the sensor. It blinks red, denying access.

I press myself against the door and let Reed's name trail off my lips. I'm not sure what I expect to happen, there's no way he heard that. I could barely hear it myself.

With confidence I try again, and I lace my whisper with more power, hoping he'll hear me and confirm I'm not alone.

"Reed."

Nothing.

"Reed!" I say again, louder, no longer a whisper. "Are you there? Reed, is that you?"

I strain my ears, anticipating any sign of movement from the room across from me, or even the approach of boots in the hallway, but neither come. The oppressive silence persists. I'm alone in the darkness.

"Reed, please, if you're there, answer me!" I nearly shout.

Still, not a stir in the room across from me, or anywhere down the hallway.

"I need to know if you're okay. What's going on here?" My words hang in the air, a gnawing sense of doubt growing within me.

It all happened so quickly, maybe it wasn't Reed at all in that room. Maybe I'm seeing things that aren't there.

As I walk back to my bed, a sudden, frantic knock echoes through the room, startling me into colliding with a supply cart. I whirl back towards the door, and the knock sounds again. I rush to peer out the window slot, but there's no one there. The halls are as empty and unchanged as they were a few moments ago.

Then I hear it again. It's not coming from the hall at all, but from the wall to my right. I rush over and place my hand against the barrier between my room and the one next door.

"Reed?"

The knocking continues in a procession of slow and rhythmic ones and twos. I realize it's code. It's our code. The code Reed and I used to communicate in our capsules, the one we used to let each other know the coast was clear and we could begin our childhood mischief. I let out a sigh of relief. This means he's okay. They must have switched his room in the evening.

They're watching, the coded knocking drums out.

The Keepers? I knock back.

The next message confuses me. *They aren't who they say they are. It's not safe.*

My mouth goes dry, and I feel instantly lightheaded.

"What–what do you mean?"

They are using us.

How? To what end? I think to myself. There is a long pause, which I'm grateful for as I try to collect my thoughts.

You need to get out.

His knocking comes more rapidly now, I find my comprehension is a little rusty and I'm struggling to keep up.

The Subjects are being gathered for t–

I can't quite make out the last word.

"Reed, please, I – I don't understand," I whisper, my voice trembling with confusion.

If possible, the next message is more alarming than the last. *Forget about Reed. It's too late for him.*

This person is not Reed. How do they know our code?

I knock back this time. *Who are you?*

My question is ignored, followed by the last few words. *They will be coming for you. Don't let them inject you. You have 12 hours.*

Then the communication stops.

"Wait, I don't understand. Who are you? What's happened to Reed?"

I wait, seated on the floor with my hands pressed against the wall hoping for more clarity. But nothing else comes, no new message, no new revelation to help explain away my now fractured reality.

You have to get out.

This mystery person has left me with more problems than solutions.

Don't let them inject you. You have 12 hours.

When morning comes and that door unlocks, I will do everything in my power to fight them off. But what good will that do? They'll just send more Keepers and people in boots to sedate me.

Forget about Reed.

That's simply not going to happen. I need Reed, and it's clear he needs me, he's not safe.

* * *

Twelve hours come too quickly, and the door lock disengages.

I know what I must do now, but I'm going to need help. I just hope my mystery neighbor got the message. I hadn't heard so much as a pin drop after I tapped my plan through the wall and secured myself back in the bed.

"Good morning, Ever," says the female Keeper from yesterday.

I say nothing in return. The unpleasant male Keeper trails into the room behind her, offering me a forced smile.

"Today is a very important day," she continues as she pulls a small cart towards the bed. "A new beginning."

The second Keeper remains near the door, standing guard. What do they think I'm going to do? I'm restrained... for all they know.

I keep my arms flush to my sides, hoping they don't notice the bend in the metal belts or the glass slide under my thigh.

"You must be anxious to transition over. It has been a long journey. You're finally fulfilling your purpose and becoming what you were always meant to be."

From her coat pockets the female Keeper retrieves two small glass bottles, followed by two wrapped syringes from her chest pocket. She peels back the sterilized packaging and places them on the cart's tray.

"Don't worry, this is the easy part. You won't feel a thing," she says, sensing my apprehension. She shakes the small bottle with a red label on it. "This will make sure of that."

Then she picks up the second bottle with a white label and dangles it in the air. "This one will ensure the first one is flushed throughout your entire system and can take effect. It's going to be okay."

"What are you going to do to me?"

"Trust us," the male Keeper decides to chime in. "You do not want to feel the procedure."

"What procedure? What is this *initiation*?"

The female keeper preps the syringes, inserting one of the needles into the rubber cap of the red labeled bottle.

"What are you going to do to me?" I repeat as she pulls the plunger out of the syringe, drawing the bottle's contents into its tube. She's working on formulating a response when a loud crash sounds from across the room.

My message was received.

A series of smaller but just as startling crashes follow the first.

"Not again," mutters the male Keeper. "Hasn't he learned his lesson by now?"

The female Keeper lays the now-filled syringe on the tray next to its bottle. She takes one quick look at me, confident I'm not going anywhere.

"This won't take long," she says before standing to leave the room.

Scanning her eye at the door, they both exit to address the commotion next door.

I sit up, the unsecured metal belt falls away, and I reach for the cart. I take the empty syringe and plunge its needle into the clear bottle labeled, *Saline*, drawing the solution into the tube. Next, I swap the syringe positions, putting the saline-filled one next to the bottle labeled in red as *Vecuronium*, not exactly a benign sounding name. I place the syringe she prepped next to the saline bottle. I hope she's too preoccupied to notice that the saline has been prepped as well. I scoot back into my position on the bed and tuck the belt back under the mattress where it looks good as new.

As if on cue, the door clicks open and the female keeper returns, this time alone.

My mystery neighbor created just enough of a disturbance to require the second Keeper to stay back and tend to them. The female Keeper scoots closer to me, grabbing the needle next to the red bottle.

"Okay, let's get this over with," she exhales, visibly disturbed. She drives the syringe into my arm and pushes the plunger. I scream at the feeling of the needle burrowing through my muscle, but immediately a cool wave washes over my body, like a thirst being quenched. I exaggeratedly lay my head back and let my eyes droop. Satisfied with my reaction, she turns around to dispose of the needle.

As she does so, I jerk upright, the chest strap falling to my waist, and I swiftly wrap my arm around her neck, pressing my glass slide tightly against her flesh.

Her voice shatters into pure terror. "No, no, please, don't do this!" Her eyes are wide with fear as her hands shoot up, trembling. "We can talk – just, please, put that down!"

"I'm done talking. You're going to get me out of here." I stand pushing the corner of the glass a little deeper.

"I can't do that. There's nowhere for you to go."

"What does that mean?"

She lowers her hands and places them on my arm. I'm doing all I can not to accidentally crush her windpipe or slice her neck open. I've never killed anyone before, and it's against our oath to harm our own kind. But that doesn't mean I won't.

"It means you're safest here."

Suddenly she throws her head back, striking my nose. Blindsided, I release my hold on her. She tries to run but I reach for the other syringe still on the tray and drive it into her neck.

She slumps in my arms, her muscles fully paralyzed, and I drag her onto the bed, pulling off her coat and pants. Her eyes run wildly as she watches me put on her uniform. She can't say or do anything to stop me.

I don't have much time, so I pull the syringe from the Keeper's arm, filling it with the remaining liquid in the red bottle, and slip it into my pocket.

I spend only the slightest moment to collect myself before I take the one thing that's preventing me from getting out of here.

I hope this works. I lean in close to the Keeper's face; her eyes are bulging, and her breaths are rapid. I press my palm down on her forehead and pull her eyelids apart with my index finger and thumb. I look closely at her eyeball, at the lining of her cornea to double check that she has the Bright-i implant.

I work up the nerve to touch her eye, hesitantly gliding my finger to the edges of the cornea and prodding the Bright-i lens to lift but it's attached to the tissue. I can feel her chest expanding and constricting underneath me. Her heaving breaths become shallower with each passing moment.

I step back and look into her frightened eyes. Her skin has paled, and a chill runs through me as I imagine myself in her place, lying in that bed trapped in my own unresponsive body. That was going to be me. How could the Keepers do this to us? If this is what our *initiation* looks like, then everything we've been told is called into question. It makes no sense, why would they deliberately harm us?

I look at the supply cart for something to help remove the corneal implant. I pull open its drawers filled with wipes, alcohol pads, empty containers, cuffs and gauze. But nothing that can help. I turn to the Keeper, her eyes dart frantically around the room, but her body is still, and her breaths have slowed. I need that Bright-i. My key out of this room. I notice her eyes aren't darting in random directions, but purposely aimed at something to the left. They are pointing. Specifically, to a machine with tangles of large tubes connecting to a mask. Nothing sharp.

Her lips have turned blue, and her chest barely moves. Her eyes gaze weakly off to the left once more. I don't understand what she's trying to tell me, nor do I have time to figure it out. The other Keeper could come back at any moment. Rummaging through a cabinet I finally find a scalpel. Gripping its cold metal firmly in my hand, I hold her eyelid open. She convulses at my touch, unable to scream.

I take a deep, hesitant breath. I know what I need to do. What I dreaded all along. Suddenly, a clatter rings out from the next room. It's now or never. With a careful touch, I stick my finger under her lid. My heart pounds in my ears as I close my eyes, feeling my way around, unable to watch my own actions. I scoop out her eyeball with its attached Bright-i and use the scalpel to sever the tissues and muscles keeping it affixed. The eye pops out, feeling like a small fluid filled sac in my hand, and I nearly drop it.

The Keeper's remaining eye is still and bores into mine. Her skin has paled and is blue-tinged like her lips. She doesn't move, which is the point of the paralytic, but something doesn't feel right. I lean in close; she isn't breathing. I reach for the side of her neck. Her skin is cold. I can't feel a pulse.

She's dead.

I yelp, and nearly fall backwards.

"I'm sorry, I'm so sorry." I stifle back tears. Did I just kill her?

I didn't mean to. Can removing an eye do that? Is this what was meant for me?

I rush towards the door, fighting back tears. I don't want to look at her. At what I've done.

Cupping the eyeball in both hands I hold it up to the sensor.

I glance through the window, the door across from me is shut, I can't see through its small window into the room from here, but I know in my bones it's Reed. I need to get to him. He might still be strapped to the bed, immobile like I was. Or even worse – already injected.

The light turns green.

The lock opens.

The door disengages.

I slide the severed eye into my coat pocket and step out into the hall.

CHAPTER 34
EVER

The door clicks shut, and I shudder at the sound. Someone had to have heard that.

Relax.

I stop myself from launching into a run, instead I stride over to the door across from mine with false confidence. I try to mimic the gait of the female Keeper and hope to simulate a routine checkup just in case anyone is watching. I lean towards the door sensor and lift my hand holding the concealed eye towards my cheek. It unlocks with the same resounding click.

No one seems to have noticed a thing. My room across the hall is silent, and the male Keeper must still be preoccupied with my mystery neighbor.

I step in and my breath escapes me. It's him. Reed's head lays limp on his pillow. A clear face mask covers his nose and mouth, with a tube penetrating down into his throat. His eyes are wide open, but there is no sense of recognition in them, no sense of presence at all. He doesn't even seem to have noticed the new visitor in his room.

Reed is lying in the bed in front of me, and yet he's not there.

His body is traversed by several smaller tubes feeding in and out of the machines by his bedside. And where his left arm should be is just a nub at the shoulder. His entire hand and arm are completely gone.

What have they done to you?

Then comes a realization that almost renders me too terrified to move. Reed's arm is not missing; I know exactly where it is.

The Chairman.

How could he do this?

"Reed." My voice shakes as I move towards him. He doesn't even blink. "Reed."

I shake him, but he doesn't react. Dread seeps through me. Was the mystery neighbor right? Am I too late for him?

I look up and down his body at the tubes diving in and out of his flesh. One way or another I am going to get him out of here.

I reach for the facemask and tube stuck in his throat, but there's a hissing sound that I notice for the first time, occurring in rhythm with the rise of his chest.

It's breathing for him.

His body is paralyzed, just like the Keepers. With a growing sense of horror, I realize the paralysis must be total, including the muscles of the lungs. The Keeper was suffocating, and she was signaling to the breathing tubes and machine on the bedside. My ignorance killed her.

What else will it cost me?

I can't pull his breathing tubes while he's still immobilized. I look at all the equipment which must be administering a continuous paralytic solution keeping him sedated.

There's no turning back now.

I tug on the ones at his legs slowly drawing them from the muscle. Long wiry needles slither out saturated with blood. Moving as quickly as I can, I stifle tears at the sight of him, pierced so brutally. The tubes appear to have shot out six-inch long needles extending throughout his body from the insertion sites. I carefully pull and slide another one out and drop it to the floor, silently willing his rapid healing ability to kick in.

A moment of sheer panic washes over me, as I notice no immediate response from Reed. I continue working, frantically removing the needles one after the other from his chest before moving on to the one arm he has left.

"Come on Reed, come back to me."

Goosebumps erupt across his chest, but there's still no sign of movement or reaction.

Anxiety gnaws at me as each second stretches into eternity. I reach for his neck and slowly pull. I can see the wires of needles slither up and outward through his veins. My heart races as the minutes tick past and Reed remains unresponsive.

I sprint to the door and peer out of the window at the still empty hall, but I know it won't stay that way for long. Any minute now the other Keeper will discover the body in my room.

Heart pounding, I rush back to Reed's side. "Come on, this is your chance to gloat. You were right," I whisper with a shaky, forced laugh.

Panic begins to take hold; the paralytic agent coursing through his system may not dissipate quickly enough, it's only a matter of time before I'm caught.

"Reed, please you have to wake up," my voice quivers with desperation. "I can't do this without you." I stifle a sob. "I need you."

I refuse to abandon him. I extract the final needle from his skin, unsure of what else to do, I rest my head on his chest, clinging to the hope that he'll come back to me.

Reed's body convulses with a sudden jolt. My heart races as he loudly coughs and gasps for air. His chest is heaving, and he grasps my arm tightly. Eyes wild, he pulls himself toward me. The recognition sets in, and his eyes water. I lift the mask off his mouth and nose as he continues to cough, sliding the tube out of his throat and tossing it on the floor. He pulls me forward to wrap me in a hug and pauses abruptly as he remembers his arm is missing.

There is so much to say, but no time for any of it.

"We need to go. Now."

He collects himself admirably, saving all the words that remain unspoken. I wrap his arm around my shoulders and lift him upwards. He slides his feet off the bed and stands wavering on numb legs. We labor towards the door, and I lean him against the wall next to it while I check that everything is still quiet outside the room.

Through the window, the halls remain empty and still. Now that I have Reed by my side, my plan starts to feel impossibly naïve. The moment we leave this room, surveillance will see us, and it's only a matter of time before they come looking. My only hope is that we can get to the mystery neighbor, and they'll know a way out of here.

"You look good as a Keeper," Reed says hoarsely interrupting my hopeless thoughts.

I bite back a smile and stay focused on action. "The coast is clear, let's go."

I grab his arm and can already sense he is gaining more control over his body. As the seconds pass, he needs less assistance, the full effects of the drugs wearing off.

"We need to make one stop," I say, lifting the Keeper's eyeball out of my pocket and holding it to the door.

He tries to conceal his shock.

"You want to get out of here, don't you? This is our best chance."

We walk unsteadily out into the hallway; past the room I was held in and on to the next. We pause by the door, but I can't see inside. Something is blocking the window.

"Who's in there?" Reed asks as he looks down both ends of the hallway.

I feel around in my pocket for the stolen scalpel, syringe, and paralytic, our only defenses.

"Someone who helped me escape. It's time to return the favor." I hand him the scalpel and scan the eye against the door, then slowly open it.

The male Keeper is still in the room. He yanks me all the way in, sending me to the ground in the process. He pulls out a syringe from his pocket and jumps towards me.

"Now how did you get out?" he asks without caring for an answer.

He pulls back ready to plunge the needle into my leg when Reed jerks him backward, wrapping his arm tightly around the Keeper's neck. I kick the needle out of his hand, sending it skidding across the floor.

The Keeper struggles against Reed's increasingly tight grip like a noose around his neck, as I retrieve my needle. I stab it into his chest and push down on the plunger. He immediately slumps and Reed loosens his hold on the Keeper's neck, letting him slide to the floor. He would be dead soon, my second murder. There was no time for guilt now, only action.

"Reed quick, take his clothes." But Reed doesn't move, he is pallid staring at the bed, the bulge of his Adam's apple traveling down his neck as he tries to swallow. I immediately jump to my feet and follow his gaze.

My jaw nearly hits the ground. I am halted by the sight of him, too petrified to move. My mystery neighbor, our savior, is Ira.

His spirals of brown hair have been shaved and his warm dark eyes have lost their light, but it's him. Or what's left of him.

They have taken him apart like a toy. Both of his legs are gone, his lower torso ending in a stump. I can see a mass of his neck had been removed, and where once rested an enviable button nose now extends a landscape of dull gray skin.

He is looking directly at me, holding my eyes in his, piercing me to my very core. I didn't realize tears had sprung to my eyes, and I can't stop them from rolling down my face.

He never made it to the Surface.

A slight movement of his arm causes the loosened buckle of his chest strap to knock against his bed railing. He twitches again, knocking several more times.

Hi Ev, I told you we'd meet again.

CHAPTER 35
EVER

I absentmindedly ran my fingers through his hair, silky chestnut waves lapping against the shores of my knuckles. I wondered if I could ever feel happier than I did in that moment, and I feared that my heart would burst.

Ira tilted his head towards me, his eyes consuming mine until there was nothing left of me, no stones unturned. My secrets were his to hold. I realized I loved him then, with our backs on the ground as we counted the stars in the sky. There were exactly thirteen hundred and eighty-two. I let my hand slip to his ear and traced down to his earlobe where I caressed it between my fingers. The sensation made him smile and his eyelids droop, interrupting his penetrating gaze. In that moment I was whole.

The exposed electrical circuitry of the Utility Room ceiling illuminated the room just as brightly as always, neon dots scattered throughout bundles of wiring. Even the rhythmic breeze of machine cooling fans was comforting. I didn't know it yet, but these were details I would never forget.

"Do you ever think if you just fought hard enough you could shift the world's course?" he murmured, his voice almost a whisper.

I knew where he was going with that question, but I didn't want to think about it, not then. I didn't want the moment to end.

"I know I can, and I know I will," he declared. His resolve both inspired and frightened me.

I pulled away from him. "And you can't be distracted by me to do so."

Relationships between Subjects are forbidden exactly for that reason. We were shaped with one singular purpose in mind. Sensing my withdrawal, he brushed his lips against mine and softly, slowly, the whole world turned upside down. He always knew how to put me at ease.

The next day, he was selected to ascend.

I'm ashamed of my inaction now, at not knowing what to do to comfort him. I finally take his hand into mine, embracing the frail skin-covered bones, and hoping he can't sense my fear of looking anywhere else but his eyes.

After a moment Ira parts his lips, they are dry and cracked with exhaustion, and a pained hiss escapes them.

"Get to the Tube."

The words are so strained; I can tell he has used all his available energy to give me this directive, a lifeline. The next sound he makes is so fleeting I have to concentrate on reading his lips but the message is received.

That's when the levee breaks, my tears overflow and I sob. I throw myself against him. I can't do what he has asked of me. I am not strong enough. I bury my face in his chest, shaking my head as my tears trickling down his ribs.

"No. I'm sorry. I'm so sorry," I cry.

I'm still shaking when he knocks his hand against the railing. *Please.*

"I can't."

Saying goodbye to him on Level 23 was the toughest thing I ever had to do, I can't do it again. Not when it's final.

I lay my head in the hollow of his sternum, unable to move, the drum of his heartbeat begging me to save him from this place. I am filled with self-loathing. I can't grant him this wish. I don't have it in me.

Whether it's out of fear or selfishness I don't know, but in the end it all amounts to weakness. That's when I feel Reed's reassuring hand on my shoulder, I had almost forgotten he was here. He squeezes lightly and gives me a faint nod. Despite our genetics, he truly is stronger than me, and always has been. He's brave enough to do what I can't, and at that moment I am grateful for his mercy. He moves to the head of the bed, analyzing the array of IV bags connecting to Ira's body. "He won't feel any pain." Reed assures, then increases the flow rate on one of the drips.

I turn my gaze back to Ira, his eyes brimming with tears yet fiercely brave. I lock his eyes in mine and hope that in them he can see the lifetime of memories that could have been. I hope that my dreams can give him peace.

"I love you," I whisper as I gently stroke his ear.

Ira smiles and nods slowly, his eyes never leaving mine. I lift his hand and kiss it as Reed injects the syringe filled with air into Ira's veins.

He drifts away from us in silence.

"May the light guide your way."

The minutes pass but I don't let go, feeling the blood slowly stop pulsing through his body, his heat dissipating.

"Ever," Reed whispers.

I know we need to go. I wipe away my tears and turn to see Reed donning the Keeper's coat. I guess this is the nature of war, no time to mourn.

An instant later we are in the hallway on the other side of the door, in a world I don't recognize, in a life I never could have imagined.

CHAPTER 36
ROSIO

I take a deep breath, hoping it will inflate me with the courage I need for what comes next. It's time for action. Edric has gone rogue, and I know I have to do everything in my power to rescue Rune. She is all that matters.

I remove the metallic band holding my bun in place and drop my chin to my chest, letting a dark curtain of hair obscure my face.

With my back pressed against the cold titanium wall, an attempt to both steady my shaking knees and remain in the blind spot of the camera mounted above, I clench the gun Axe gave me. I have to believe he is okay. They wouldn't harm him, would they? He's the farmer, they need him.

I slide my finger from the barrel and rest it on the trigger before rounding the corner.

You can do this. Breathe.

Then I pull.

The explosive sound of the bullet leaving the chamber rings through the hall, followed by the muffled thud of the Shift Operator's body hitting the ground. I hadn't begun the day intending to hurt anyone, but it was always going to come to this. Nothing and no one would stand in my way. I failed her once; I would not fail her again.

Across the hall, the Control Room is clear. In his haste after receiving the system-wide security alert, the operator left the door open, and it is now slowly hissing to a close. The hall remains eerily quiet in both directions, a sign that all personnel are likely following the alert's purge instructions. With determination I point my gun at the one camera facing the control room door and fire. To my surprise the shot hits its small mark on the first attempt, adrenaline has sharpened my mind. The sounds of my gunfire are undeniably reckless, but a necessary risk.

Rushing across the hall, I spare a quick glance at the operator as blood streams from the wound in his abdomen. I don't recognize him, which makes it easier to ignore his sputtering pleas for help.

It will all be over soon. That's what I should tell him. But providing comfort is an obsolete skill in this place, and I am out of practice.

Inside the Control Room, a canvas of thin glass screens, each blaring a nauseating green light, illuminates the otherwise dark space. I'm alone so I secure the gun under my white coat. It takes me a moment to locate her. They found each other, and are on the move. The boy would protect my Ever. I had carefully fostered the relationship between them for this very reason. Early on I knew they would have a stronger chance of survival together.

Now all I have to do is buy them a little more time. They cautiously make their way down the hall. It'll only be a matter of time before they set off a projection alerting all nearby guards of their position. I scan the feeds of all the rooms for a diversion, and promptly strike the glass panel in front of me releasing one of the door locks on Level 17.

On the surveillance feed, a 12-year-old boy advances with hesitation towards his exit. Luckily, he hasn't been sedated yet due to the shortage of staff on duty. He is much too young to have been placed on Level 17. It goes against all protocol. But rules no longer matter when it's the beginning of the end.

"Hurry," I urge him under my breath. He needs to move quickly to draw attention away from the other two Subjects. The boy steps out of his room into the vivid florescent lights of the hallway, pausing to let his eyes adjust outside the door for just a moment too long. He stands exposed, in full view of the Keepers completing their rounds in that hall.

"Hey!" one shouts, his voice echoing through the corridor.

"You there. Stay where you are," orders the other Keeper, signaling security with a swipe of the air, setting off an alarm.

The boy freezes, rightfully panicked.

Patrolling guards immediately turn down the hall in his direction, abandoning the path that was sure to lead them to Ever.

"Listen, kid, everything is going to be okay. You just need to go back into your room."

I release one more lock a few yards away; the boy hears it and runs towards the door.

"We've got a runner!"

The Keepers and guards in the surrounding area follow.

He doesn't deserve this, none of them do. But my priority is one girl.

The boy stumbles into the unlocked dispensary and frantically searches for something to barricade himself inside. He rolls a drug cart up to the door. Knowing that it isn't enough he attempts to find a hiding spot. With his limber body, he crouches down and folds himself as tightly as possible, then squeezes into the cabinet of a medication cart. I lock the door behind him, but it's only a matter of time before they open it. As the guards reach the other side of his door, I turn away.

That is enough on my part. At least now Ever has a chance. I will find them on the next level.

I exhale slowly, releasing the lingering pang of guilt in what remains of my heart. On the screens ahead I can see them all – all the children who remain, and all those in transition.

Those who lie eagerly awake in their rooms filled with hope, and those who now knew better. They are there because of me. This horror is because of me. To save one life, I sacrificed dozens of children. I am the monster Edric made me. Despite the haunting regret, I know deep down that I would make the same agonizing choices again.

Suddenly a flicker of light, a glitch, overtakes my view. Text blinks on, extending from one corner of my vision to the other and hangs in the air in front of me.

MEMORANDUM NO. 1094
From: Helix Security Service
Subject: Protocol 74 Launch

We have received verification from the Surface that the threat is near. Devastation is unavoidable. An emergency issuance of Protocol 74 is now in effect. Conclude purge procedures immediately. Prepare all lower levels for crisis shelter relocation services. Further instructions to come.

As I read the memo, a heavy sense of resignation washes over me. There is a sinking feeling in the pit of my stomach, the words confirm what I already know deep down: we are truly helpless, the climate conditions on the Surface have deteriorated to a nightmarish extent.

At terrifying speeds that seem almost unnatural, temperatures have skyrocketed to unbearable levels, making it nearly impossible for anyone to survive outside for long, even during the sun-safe hours. According to the reports, relentless heatwaves have turned our lands into tinderboxes, the uncontrollable fires are devouring everything in their path, making the air nearly unbreathable.

Desperation has driven people to extreme measures. Outside forces are already plotting attacks to breach the Helix defenses. It's inevitable as the Surface conditions continue to deteriorate. And in the past few months alone, more and more people have gradually sold their souls to work in the Subject Regeneration program to secure themselves a place within the walls of this fortress when the time came. Now, they are called on to commit murder. All the innocent Subjects that Edric has no use for. He will divert all available resources towards preparing the Helix to sustain life through years to come.

I can't change what's coming, the climate conditions that we created. My focus must remain on how Ever and I will face it together. There really is no safe place for us on the outside, but we can't stay here.

I wipe the memo away from my view, my eyes fixed on the screens ahead searching for any sign that they found their way off Level 17, when a click sounds to my right.

"Well, this is quite a disappointment," hisses a voice from the shadows, its venomous tone is followed by the sound of a bullet sliding into a chamber.

I stand perfectly still, not wanting to startle Vada into pulling the trigger. My own gun rests heavily in my pocket. I don't want to use it on her, but she has a calm resolve in her eyes that chills me to the bone. She would have no qualms in killing me.

"You know," she says, with the gun leveled at my chest, "I never did like you."

"I gathered as much." I silently wince at my words. Don't provoke her. She is barely more than a child herself.

"I couldn't quite put my finger on it until now." She relishes finally having the power in our dynamic. I allow her to continue. "You're ungrateful," she scoffs.

I have to keep reminding myself that she is not my enemy, just a mere obstacle.

"I've done my research on you. The *real* you."

I try to mask the confusion on my face, but she catches the slight twitch in my brows. Her lips curl into a sneer. "He confides in me. The Chairman trusts me implicitly. He knows my unwavering loyalty." She presses on. "You were in an accident.

You lost your kid. The Chairman gave you a life, made you relevant. We're the same in that way, you and me. He brought us back to life, he gave us a reason to exist. A purpose."

"Yes, that's true," I try to decrease the tension.

She smiles now, her voice dripping with disdain. "But you, you take that chance and try to undermine what he's building here. You go behind his back, you violate protocols. You are selfish. You know nothing of loyalty."

I attempt to interject, "I don't know what you think is going on here but the Chairman–"

"It's pretty clear, given the bleeding guard lying on the floor outside. This is an inside job," she snaps, her suspicions intensifying.

I shake my head.

"Who are you working for? How much are they paying you?"

I cautiously lower my hands, trying to convey sincerity. "I'm not working for anyone Vada. I just want out."

She cocks her head; I hit a nerve.

"If you try to leave here – if you open those doors, we'll be overrun," she warns.

I take a slow step toward her, hoping to deescalate her emotions. But she shakes the gun at me, and I stay in place.

"I'm just trying to help them. We don't need to continue with the program. We can just give them a chance."

"A chance at what? They are not meant for more, and we need their resources for others who deserve it."

"Like you?" I press. "I selected you. Was I wrong in doing so?"

"It was the *Chairman* who gave me a life worth living. He's focused on progress, the future. While you're fixated on something that isn't even real. She's not your daughter. I pity you." Vada makes her decision and cocks her gun. "Without Helix Colony, I have nothing, nowhere to go. I can't let you risk all our lives."

My time has run out. I rush at her.

In the ensuing struggle her gun goes off.

Vada stumbles back, grasping at her chest. Her face contorted with shock as she realizes what I have done. She collapses to the ground, struggling to breathe as blood seeps through her fingers.

Trembling, I drop her gun. "I didn't mean to – I didn't want to –" I stammer.

She coughs, blood spilling out of her mouth.

Desperation wells up inside me and I sob, "I need to protect my daughter." I kneel beside Vada and stroke her hair in a futile attempt to provide comfort. This life, her brainwashing, is my doing. I chose this path for her.

"Shhhhh, it's okay," I whisper. She holds my gaze as the darkness creeps in. It wasn't the ending I had imagined for her, but certain choices have grave consequences.

A sudden clatter echoes through the room. Startled, I look up to doorway, my gaze falling upon the figure of a large guard looming over me. My heart seizes as he advances, I look for Vada's gun but before I can reach it an iron grip closes around my arm. In one swift motion I am hoisted up and dragged away.

"The doctor has been secured," his voice crackles into his comms.

CHAPTER 37
EVER

We look down both ends of the hallway, the sterile bright lights burning into my already strained eyes, and the full gravity of our situation hits me. How are we going to escape? And where are we escaping to?

The expansive hallway extends as far as I can see, flanked by identical doors on each side like mirrors reflecting each other indefinitely.

"Which way?" I ask Reed, hoping he has a better sense for the layout of this place. Ira told us to get to the Tube, that's where we need to go.

"We don't have many options." He considers a direction, then slants his head towards the left. I guess it's as good a choice as any.

We try to maintain a calm pace walking down the hall and keep our heads down. We pass door after door, each with a window revealing rooms identical to the ones we were both held in. Identical to the one Ira was held in.

Was. The word weighs heavily on me. I force the thought away.

Most of the rooms are empty, but as we proceed, we soon reach several occupied by kids disfigured beyond recognition. Kids just like us, former Subjects subdued by medical tubing, integral blocks of their bodies removed. It disturbingly reminds me of the stacking game Reed and I used to play in the Utility Room. If we pulled the wrong building block out the entire tower would crumble.

What kind of monsters would do this to us? Was this our *purpose*? I have the urge to run in and help them somehow, but Reed holds me back. They're too far gone to be helped; they look like they've been here as long as Ira, if not longer. The Saviors never made it to the Surface.

A concentrated heat ignites in the pit of my stomach. Rage. Uncontrollable fury.

Is the Chairman behind this? Did Sio know?

We quicken our pace down the hall. The more I see, the harder it is to continue moving forward, the harder it is to overcome the thought of leaving them behind.

We near a cross section in the middle of the long hallway nearly hidden from view in all the symmetry. That's when I sense a blurring in the periphery of my Bright-i. Neon lines blink on and off incoherently. Something's wrong.

As Reed moves forward, a holo-projection comes to life on the left wall just ahead of us. We must have set off its motion activation.

"Hold your position. The following area is restricted," says the enlarged face of the Chairman.

Reed visibly tenses, the flicker in his eyes revealing a blend of anger and fear.

"It's just a recording," I urge him to continue moving.

"Failure to comply, will result in detainment," the Chairman persists.

Reed spits at the wall. A few more feet and we're past the projection. We are closing in on the cross section ahead now and I get the sinking feeling that one wrong turn could be our last. Where are we headed? Even if we do manage to make it to the Tube, where do we go from there? Are the Forms really out there, closing in on us? Everything we've been told is a lie. Our supposed purpose, the promise of a life outside the Helix, the true intent of our very own home – all fabrications. I don't know what to believe anymore.

Another projection springs up, this time between the walls,

in the middle of our path. A shiver runs down my spine. The enlarged face of the Chairman seems to be looking directly at me, as if he can see me. It's not possible, I know.

"You will not be warned again."

We continue forward. As we advance the projection moves backwards, eventually halting completely.

"0123XY and 1123XX, you are in violation of Protocol 1574. Return to your rooms immediately for processing."

Targeted messaging now. The projection is accessing the information in our Bright-i trackers, but we can't afford to pause. Instead, we charge forward, straight through it, the projection glitching in the air before dissipating.

Reed abruptly stops at the corner of the intersection, and I nearly crash into him. I hastily pull back and paste myself against the wall, my heart pounding. Reed cautiously peers around the corner, down the hallway then swiftly retreats.

"Crap," he mutters under his breath.

"What is it?" But I can already hear the inevitable, the faint sounds of boots in the distance, heading in our direction.

Reed takes a few deep breaths contemplating our next move then darts another quick glance around the corner.

"They're just strolling along, it looks like they might be on a routine patrol," he informs me.

I hope he's right. Reed takes the slightest of moments to compose himself, then stands away from the wall.

"Follow my lead."

I comply. I straighten up, trying to relax my shoulders and match Reed's body language. Casual.

"Now just keep your eyes on me."

I nod and dip my hand into my pocket, thumbing the syringe and paralytic that is still in there. We emerge from around the corner and walk down the hall. I keep my eyes on Reed, he smiles down at me and moves his lips. We are seemingly engaged in conversation as we move down the hall at a steady pace.

I can see Reed's eyes sweeping the periphery, and I instinctively do the same. The Boots are 20 meters behind us, also engaged in a light chatter.

"Why are we still here?" one of them voices, a hint of impatience in their tone. "Everyone else is heading to the shelters. My wife is already there."

"You know why. We're maintaining the order."

"What order, this about to be a graveyard."

"It's the job. Who knows, these might end up being our new digs."

After a brief pause, the first one muses, "Do you think we could use our discount for enhancements?"

There's a door up ahead on Reed's side of the hallway and he gestures to it. We slow down and approach the door, relaxed, careful not to draw any attention to ourselves. After all, we look like two Keepers behaving as two Keepers would.

One more step and the edges of my vision blur again.

"Wait," I try to tell Reed but he's already one step ahead.

A projection springs to life against the wall, larger than the previous two. This time rather than a face, large red block lettering pulsates in the air, followed by three sharp chimes.

UNAUTHORIZED PERSONNEL

"Hey!" one of the Boots yells from behind us.

Reed lunges for the door but it won't budge. It remains deactivated and locked.

"You two, stop right there!" shouts the other. They pick up their pace and are gaining on us.

We break into a full sprint, but this hallway seems too long to outrun them. For all we know, our next turn could lead straight into a dead end. The holo projection follows us down the walls, the red lettering intensifies, and the alarm chimes grow louder with each advancement.

The Boots have pulled out long black rods from their waistbands, directing them towards us. They aren't batons, they have a hollow tip.

They are going to shoot us.

I yank Reed towards the next door we reach on my side, zig zagging in our movements as one of the Boots unloads his gun. A long electric probe collides with the door we stood in front of just seconds before.

Non-lethals.

A new alarm goes off but on the other end of the hallway, startling the Boots just long enough for me to hold up the Keeper's eye to the door on my right, unlocking it. We tumble inside just as the second electric probe is unloaded inches from Reed's head. We slam the door shut; Reed pushes the full weight of his body against it as I search the room for something to barricade ourselves in with. This room is larger than the others and contains two metal tubs against the back wall, each surrounded by a curtain hanging from ceiling rods.

I pull some of the medical equipment from the perimeter of the room, but none of the pieces are big enough or heavy enough to hold the door shut.

With a beep, the door lock disengages, and a force pushes into Reed from the other side.

"Ev hurry!"

I frantically survey the room before running back towards the door, empty handed.

"What are we going to do?" Reed asks.

"On the count of three step back, got it?"

He nods still pressing against the door. I reach around the tall shelving anchored to the wall beside us, and ram my shoulder into it, pushing.

"One!" I shout.

The shelving unit starts to tear away from the wall, with the sound of contorting and creaking metal.

"Two!"

It shifts in place, teetering sideways.

"Three!"

Reed lets go and dodges the collapsing shelving. It crashes in front of the door, nearly obstructing its full height. I hear the Boots still pushing from the other side, but the door won't budge. We're safe.

For now.

Reed and I watch for a few more moments before breaking the silence.

"What now?" Reed asks.

I dig into my pocket for the scalpel. It's gone, it must have slipped out while we were running. I look around the room for a medical cart.

"We need something sharp."

"What for?"

"We need to remove our Bright-i trackers," I answer, rummaging through a drawer. "I think it's how they're targeting us. Help me find something to cut it out with."

Reed joins me in trashing the room, searching for a tiny instrument to extract our trackers with. The next drawer I open houses a small Index. I pull it out, my touch immediately activating it. Whoever used this last must have been in a hurry as they didn't bother to lock it. The Index projects the last data accessed, which appears to be some sort of inventory for blood count, all of which appear to be O negative.

I look over at Reed, remembering his warning. "It's our blood."

Reed retrieves a scalpel and walks towards me.

CHAPTER 38
EVER

"Did you know?"

My eyes dart to the scalpel clenched between Reed's fingers. Despite everything we've just endured together, a flicker of distrust snakes through me.

He knew we all shared the universal blood type, that it was significant somehow. Did he know what was going on? Did he let it happen without trying to intervene? If I had known, if he had confided in me, maybe I could have taken some action, or at least had the chance to try. If I knew, maybe I could have found a way to save Ira, to prevent him from being ripped apart like he meant nothing. My heart aches and I swallow hard, forcing back the tears welling up at the mere thought of him.

"Reed, did you know this would happen?" I repeat.

He walks towards me, keeping his expression even. The Boots continue to pound on the door outside, my heart matching their rhythm as it hammers against the walls of my chest.

"I need you to tell me everything."

"I didn't – I don't know," he shakes his head. "She didn't prepare me for this."

"Who, Sio?"

He turns his gaze towards the door, a hint of uncertainty etched on his face. "At first, I believed she was on our side.

She warned me about the IV infusions and the effects they had on our thinking. She told me that if I stopped taking them, I'd start to see things more clearly. But my body just rebelled, went into withdrawal and I felt like I was losing my grip on reality. Or maybe, that's what it feels like to truly grasp it. I don't know."

He looks exhausted, worn down, torn between conflicting thoughts. In that moment I know he's as much in the dark as I am. His eyes reveal a deep pain. He shared what limited information he had in an attempt to protect me. My best friend. Isolated, for who knows how long, with the knowledge that we were being deceived.

But did he place his trust in the wrong person? Sio failed to shield him from the Selection. From being brutally butchered. We have no idea what we're up against. She left us completely vulnerable and defenseless. We can't rely on her. All we have is each other.

The relentless pounding outside has stopped but the Boots' voices are still audible: "They're not going anywhere. Let's just get the other one," they grumble before their voices fade away.

Reed, still fixated on the barricade, speaks in a hushed tone. "The doors lock on both sides."

"What?"

"Why do you think that is Ev?" His voice remains steady and low. "I used to think we were kept down on Level 23 for our own safety, that the Tube, the security measures, all the precautions were to keep the threat from getting in. To protect us from a breach by the Forms, to keep them on the outside."

I nod, I know the stories well.

"I don't think there ever was a resistance," he breathes. "Or any Saviors at all. I think we lost a long time ago. The Keepers – they're not trying to keep the Forms out. They've been keeping *us* in."

He walks past me towards a reflective glass partition at the other end of the room. Doubt clouds my mind. If the Keepers could deceive us about our present, they could have easily manipulated our entire understanding of the past. Reed could be right. My head swirls with a cascade of questions, leaving me feeling overwhelmed and nauseated.

"We've been tagged and monitored." He looks at the space where his arm should be. "And mutilated, like some sort of experiments. They never intended to let us leave."

He gazes at his own reflection, taking in the haggard contours of his face. His expression is lifeless, cold and devoid of emotion.

"What if the bad guys already won?" he asks, lifting the scalpel and pausing at his neck.

"Reed, wait!" I'm afraid of what he might do next. "We can't just give up."

He leans into the glass, eyes wide. "If the Forms have already taken the Surface, there's no real escape."

"Please, you don't know that for certain. We have to try. For Ira. For all the other Subjects who never had a chance." I'm standing next to him now. "We need to make it out of here and uncover the truth for ourselves."

He takes a deep breath and raises the scalpel to his eye. He makes a small slice on the circumference of his Bright-i. Despite the bead of blood that trickles down his cheek, he shows no sign of discomfort. He lifts the clear layer of tech, releasing delicate bloodied tendrils that wave as they exit his eye before settling themselves inside the lens. Handing it to me, he then moves on to the next one.

"Wait," I hold his arm back, "are you able to see without it?"

I hadn't considered the possibility of blindness.

Reed blinks a few times, trying to clear the blood from his eyes.

"Yes," he confirms, wiping his face. "I once helped with a damaged Bright-i extraction in the MedLab. The fibers release an accelerated healing solution on exit to close the wound."

I nod, and slowly release his arm.

He extracts the next lens with ease.

After a moment I tentatively break the silence. "Our blood, O negative–"

"I think it's the reason we're kept alive," he cuts in. "It makes us the perfect donors."

His words hang in the air, it dawns on me that our very existence, the nightmare we were destined for, hinges on this unique blood type.

Abruptly, a rumbling cough erupts from behind us. I whip my head toward the sound, my hand instinctively reaching for the needle concealed in my pocket.

It's coming from one of the curtains encircling a tub against the back wall. How could we have been so stupid to not look behind there? I assumed we were alone.

Another strained cough is followed by a disturbing gurgle.

Reed and I stare at each other, thinking the same thing. I pull the syringe from my pocket and we both slowly approach the curtain. We stop a moment just in front, trying to make out the silhouette behind, but it reveals nothing. I nod to Reed, and he yanks the curtain back.

We look on confused at the metal tub in front of us, it's filled with water and ice and seemingly nothing else. Where did the sound come from?

In an instant, bare flesh breaks the surface of the water, and a naked body emerges with a sharp, gasp of air, shivering and trembling violently. Reed and I stumble backwards.

"Farrah?"

She lifts her upper body over the edge of the tub, grasping at the rim, choking on air.

"Quick! Grab something to warm her up with!"

Her pale frame is hueing towards blue and her usual lean musculature is blanketed in wrinkled pruned skin. How long had she been in there? How did she even *get* there?

Reed rips the over-hanging curtain from its rings. I wrap it around Farrah, and we drag her out of the tub, laying her shaking body on the floor. She is frigid.

She mutters something and I lean in closer feeling her icy breath against my ear.

"Skye," she exhales. Her head tilts towards the second tub.

I rush to the other curtain, whipping it away. And there is Skye, her small frame floating on the bed of ice, too light to sink. Her eyes are closed, skin pale, lips purple.

"Skye!"

I plunge my arms into the ice water, and wrap them under her body, pulling her out. Reed rips the second curtain down and drapes it over her. I gently place her on the floor next to Farrah.

Skye's eyes remain closed. I wrap her in my arms, shaking her gently, trying to give her some of my warmth.

"How could they do this to her? She's just a child," I murmur, my voice tinged with desperation. "Look at her, she's freezing, they nearly killed her..."

"That's been their intent all along. We've lost, Ev," Reed says, his voice sympathetic yet firm with conviction.

Some of the color has returned to Farrah's face, and she slowly sits up.

"I don't believe you two," she glares at Reed.

"What do you mean?"

She coughs once more, gathering her strength. "Lost? Please. This is what we trained for. Did you honestly think they would just send us up to the Surface fresh from Selection? This is just another hurdle, all part of the grand plan. It makes sense they would put us through additional trials. We need to prove ourselves."

I look down at Skye in my arms. How could this be a trial? They're picking us apart, nearly killing us. Farrah hasn't seen the horrors we've seen.

"You mean to tell me *this* is a test?!" Reed growls, startling us both. He points at the nub at his shoulder where an arm should be.

Skye stirs at the sudden noise.

"You were already Flawed," Farrah mutters. "What's one more imperfection?" With some difficulty, she leans back against the tub.

"I've been *dismembered*," Reed seethes, eyes bulging. For a moment, it seems like he might lose control and lash out at Farrah.

"It's a measure of your true strength; how well can you perform with a handicap?"

"If that were remotely true," Reed counters, frustration lacing his words, "don't you think I'd need my arm to be an effective soldier, to fight alongside the Saviors, at full capacity?"

Skye begins to cough up water. I puff a relieved breath.

"Who's to say you won't get it back?" Farrah offers.

Reed turns to me, his face marred by disbelief. "This is how they get us. She's so deep in the lie, she can't see the truth standing right in front of her."

I'm not entirely sure what to believe. Part of me wants to cling to the hope that we are just being tested, that we'll make it out of here to our rightful places on the Surface. But hope is what got us here, into this nightmare. Hope killed Ira. I don't know who the true enemy is, or what their end game is. But we need to get out of here before it's realized.

"It's the infusions, I'm telling you, if–" Reed reasons.

"I haven't had any since the Selection," Farrah retorts, nose in the air. "So according to your little theory I overheard, my mind is clear. Your truth is not my truth. I don't trust the word of a delusional Flawed. I trust only in my training."

"How did you get here?" I interrupt them. We're all in this together now, and we have better things to do than bicker. "What were you doing in the ice?"

"I was brought here right after the white room. She was already here," Farrah says glancing at Skye. "We were being prepared for an initiation. Some sort of transport, I don't know where."

"Listen, Farrah, you haven't seen what we've–"

Skye stirs in my arms, cutting me off, a hint of color returning to her lips.

Farrah rises, tugging the curtain tightly around her body. "Think about it – if you buy into what Reed's saying..." She rolls her eyes dismissively. "If we've already lost, then that would mean that the Forms won, wouldn't it? So, are they running this place? Why would they give us a home, a shelter to grow up in, feed us, or train us at all? And wouldn't they be after us right now if they thought we were trying to escape?"

I try to interject but she continues: "Listen. Do you hear anyone out there?"

"They're probably rounding up reinforcements. They'll be back," Reed warns. "We should leave now."

"Ever," Skye whispers. She's awake.

"There's no one coming for us, don't you get it?" Farrah scoffs. "This is a test, we just need to pass to the next level."

"And what exactly are we supposed to prove?" Reed asks.

I help Skye to her feet, draping my lab coat over her shoulders.

"Our dedication to the cause. This is just some sort of exercise, like the simulations. We need to assess the situation at hand and strategize a solution."

Reed shakes his head but decides not to engage her anymore. Speaking directly to me, he says, "We don't have much time. If they're coming, we need to remove their Bright-i lenses."

"Skye, can you stand on your own?" I'm reluctant to leave her side, but she slowly nods.

"Please," she whispers, petrified. "I don't want to die. I don't want to end up like the others. I saw them. In their rooms."

"I won't let that happen to you. Do you trust me?"

She nods.

Reed holds up the scalpel. "This will only sting for a second, then it's over."

"Easy for you to say," Farrah scoffs. "You feel no pain."

"I'll go first; you'll see it's okay." I walk to the reflective glass. With a steady hand, I bring the scalpel to my face and carefully scrape the blade across my cornea. A jolt of pain rips through my body, but I clamp my mouth shut, determined not to frighten Skye. Reed is at my side in an instant.

"Hold this." He hands me the torn down curtain rod. "I'll extract it for you."

I take the rod he's offering and grasp it tightly, then nod that I'm ready.

"Look up."

He swiftly plucks the lens and pulls it out of my eye.

I squeeze the rod so tightly it's crushed in my palms as he removes the second lens. Blood trickles down my cheeks. A soothing coolness washes over my eye, and then the pain is gone.

"See? That wasn't so bad," I assure Skye. Fear flashes in her eyes.

I glance at Reed, who is watching Farrah as she struggles with her curtain wrap. Irritated, he reluctantly gives her his lab coat.

I wipe my eyes, and crouch down to Skye's eye level. "You can do this. Removing our lenses gives us a better chance of staying undetected."

She nods slowly, then bunches up the curtain from her body and shoves it into her mouth. She screams into it as I remove her lenses.

Once she's collected herself, I ask, "You saw others in the rooms in the hallway? Do you think you remember how you were brought here?"

Skye nods. "I was still conscious when they took me from the white room and dragged me here."

They allowed her to witness everything along her route? What could their motives have been for Skye?

"Do you think you'd recognize which direction you came from?" Reed asks softly.

"I tried to count the doors, count the Subjects I saw on the way here. There were 25."

Farrah struggles with the buttons on the lab coat, her fingers clearly still numb.

"Well, that's helpful," she says under her breath. "There are probably at least twice as many doors lining the halls in both directions."

Reed cuts his eyes at her. "If you plan to come with us, I'm going to need your tracker."

"You're not touching my eyes." She backs away from him, clutching the white coat.

"There's no other way Farrah, they are monitoring us," I say.

"It's not like we can stay hidden. There are cameras everywhere, what difference does it make if they find us using our Bright-i trackers or surveillance? This is all a test; they *should* be monitoring us."

Reed sneers.

"Look, you can choose to stay here on your own, that's fine, but we're getting out of here, and we're not risking that because you're too afraid to let Reed touch your eyes," I say.

The words have their intended effect. Farrah's spine stiffens. "I am *not* afraid. I am eager to serve."

She marches up to Reed, grabs his hand and lifts it to her face, giving me a look that says, *I'll show you.*

While Reed slices out Farrah's Bright-i, I turn to Skye. "Is there anything else you remember?"

"There was a door," she starts and bolts up right as if struck by inspiration. "It was smaller than the others, a tiny square in the wall, with a handle and light above it. It was on my right."

I cast a hopeful look at Reed.

"It was around a corner from the glass entrance to the white room."

"Okay, so all we need to do is find that door," I say with determination. "That will get us to the Tube."

I turn to Reed for reassurance.

"That seems simple enough right?"

"And try not get caught in the process," Reed adds.

"Then what? What's your big plan once we reach the Tube?" Farrah crosses her arms, eyes bleeding.

I look at the door, still barricaded. "Then we escape."

Farrah exhales in frustration. "I'm going to need some dry clothes." After several moments of rummaging through drawers, Farrah and Skye change into dry scrubs, while Reed and I slip back into our lab coats.

I heave the shelving unit aside, and Reed peers through the tiny window. "Okay, let's do this."

I pull the Keeper's eye from my pocket. Skye screams.

"Are you crazy?!" Farrah looks on in horror.

"Wh-where did you get that?" Skye stammers looking at the exposed organ in my hand.

"It's our only way out of here; the doors use a retinal scan lock on both sides," I explain.

"Why don't you just *wear* its Bright-i? You removed yours, just wear this one." Farrah suggests incredulously. "For His Mercy's sake, don't just walk around with human eyeball in your pocket," she continues.

I hadn't thought of that in all the hurry.

Reed passes me the scalpel and I peel back the Keeper's lens and drop the eyeball into a nearby canister on a counter. I balance the Bright-i on my fingertip, tilt my head back and try not to watch the hungry tendrils extend and burrow into my eye. Grunting I massage the lens over my cornea letting it settle in. A blue light flickers in my right eye.

"I think it's working." I see letters and digits scroll past as the lens calibrates to a new user. I frantically swipe the air, maybe there's a map, or some sort of layout of the Helix that can help us navigate out of here. But the letters, numbers, and symbols keep scrolling past, pixelating perhaps sensing the foreign user.

"What is it?" Reed's voice is urgent and brimming with concern.

"I thought I could find a map, but the lens keeps glitching."

"The data could be user-locked. There's no time for a reboot, and we'd risk losing any clearances it has," he says.

I swallow hard, a knot forming in my throat. "Let's just hope this still works on the retinal scanner."

I open my eye in front of the sensor and exhale a brief sigh of relief as a green light blinks, the lock disengages, and then the four of us are out in the hallway, completely exposed.

"This is the direction the Boots came from," Reed says pointing to the right. "They must have come from the Tube."

We all charge into a sprint down the long corridor. The halls are disorienting in their symmetry, stark white walls with identical doors branching off into seemingly endless intersections.

I glance over at Skye whose eyes grow with uncertainty as we press forward.

"Where do we turn?" I ask her, desperation seeping into my voice.

"I-I don't know, everything looks the same."

"That's because it *is* all the same," Farrah snarls in frustration.

"This place is a maze." My panic rises as I scan the hallways that lead to more hallways with more doors.

"Of course it is," Farrah interjects coolly. "It's designed to confuse the Forms in the event of a breech."

"Or to trap us," Reed shoots back.

As we dart past, I force myself to peer into the rooms. With each glimpse, I clench my fists to control my revulsion and rage as we pass room after room of dismembered Subjects, lying helplessly in their beds.

Farrah freezes for several seconds outside the door of an unrecognizable Subject whose features have been so ruthlessly carved away she no longer has a face. With a heavy heart, I hope for her sake that she dies quickly.

"Keep moving," Reed snarls. Farrah glances down the hall bewildered, wavering a moment outside another room before I jerk her forward. I can feel her growing horror radiating through every trembling step as we continue to run through the corridor.

"Look!" I exclaim, spotting something in the distance. "Transporter bikes!" Two discarded bikes lie abandoned at the next junction, possibly left by the Keepers or the Boots patrolling earlier. My heart races as I sprint towards them – they could be our fastest way out of here, their GPS feature could take us directly to the Tube.

The others quickly catch up. "Come on, Skye, you're with me," I urge.

"Hold on, how do we start them?" Reed asks.

I glance at the retinal scanner on the handlebars, and a knot forms in my stomach. How could I forget – the bikes needed a Bright-i lens to activate.

"See, it was a mistake to ditch our lenses," Farrah mutters.

"Ever can still get them going," Skye interjects, her voice hopeful. She's right – I can use the Keeper's lens. With a heavy dose of apprehension at the possibility of triggering another tracker, I raise my eye to the scanner. The bike remains silent, the display flashing a stark *System Lockdown* message.

"The bikes are locked." I let out a sigh of dismay. As we stand at the intersection, uncertainty mounting, I scan the area, desperate for another option.

"That's it!" Skye announces, pointing at the small door in the distance, past where my eyes can see. "That's where I turned!"

We charge forward and a red square comes into view around the bend on the left. We turn with Skye, skidding towards a familiar glass walkway. On the other side I can see the white room.

"Let's go." Reed pushes forward. As we step onto the glass floor, I'm tempted to crawl on my hands and knees, the sudden prospect of plunging into the darkness below sends my head spinning. Beyond the glass walls of the hallway, which previously revealed nothing but black as far as the eye could see, now show capsule rooms in the distance, abandoned, lights flickering.

Something doesn't feel right. Where is everyone?

We emerge on the other side into the blindingly white room. The Tube terminal is exposed on the other side. It's empty.

As soon as we're all in the room, the walls shift, closing off the hall we just came from.

"No!" I shout. We're trapped again. Of course, this was their plan all along. Why waste resources coming after us when they could just corner us?

Reed peers down the Tube shaft. "Where is it?"

Farrah and Skye lean against the opposite wall. Skye is crouched down, her head tucked between her knees. She makes no sound, but the repetitive rising in her back lets me know she's crying.

I pace the room, trying to think of our next move.

"What do we do now?" Skye croaks.

I glance at the empty terminal, still no Tube in sight. I peer in and along the side wall I see a glint of metal, a series of lines extending upwards and downwards.

"We climb up," I say, hoping I sound confident.

Farrah stares straight ahead, eyes glazed over, I'm not sure that she registers what I said.

"We're not prepared. There's no way of knowing what's up there," says Reed. "Everything we've been told is a lie. What if there's nothing left? Maybe–"

"We can't stay here," I say.

"It's a test," Farrah whispers, with waning conviction, the horrors within the rooms we've run past weighing on her.

Skye has now stopped crying, she looks up and over at Farrah, hopeful.

Farrah abruptly sits up. Feigned confidence masking palpable uncertainty.

"It has to be. I mean, this can't be real. They're testing us, our reactions to the extreme horrors of war. It's a simulation." She pushes herself up shakily. "Ever is right, we climb, we demonstrate our fearlessness, and the strongest will ascend."

"Farrah!" Reed fumes. "This *isn't* a *test*. They dissected me! They cut into me; took a piece of me!"

"This isn't getting us anywhere," I say. "Whether it's a test or not, we have to keep moving."

"Can we just go back?" Skye asks. Her eyes balancing tears on her lower lash line. "I want to go back to my capsule. Can we just go back to 23? I'm scared."

"She's not a believer in the cause," Farrah sniffs. "She'll never make it."

"Farrah, shut up." I crouch down against the wall next to Skye.

"I'm sorry Skye, but we can't go back there; I saw them releasing gas to sedate the remaining Subjects."

Reed paces the room, frenetic and impatient, his hand gliding across the walls. He slips into a slight indent, activating a transition in the wall and revealing an access pad. We all look up. A small, green light blinks and a rush of air escapes the shaft.

"It's coming," he says.

Mercifully, a Tube docks in the terminal and slides open its door. "Where will it take us?" Skye asks.

There's a small keypad inside with only four stark buttons. The numbers 16, 15, 14, 13.

"We're going up," I say firmly.

As we all step inside, I cast a weary glance back at the wall across the room, half expecting to see Keepers and armed Boots barge in, but no one comes. The unknown stretches out before us, but with each level we climb, we edge closer to the truth.

Taking a deep breath, I press the button for Level 13. The glass doors glide shut, and we ascend.

CHAPTER 39
ROSIO

The hall outside Edric's office is flanked with armed Subjects. Subjects, I note, and not guards. They are just kids, the very same who had been subdued with gas at the last Selection. I wonder what lies he told them to convince them that acting as his security is for the greater good. I can't help but feel a sense of deep sadness and revulsion. He has created his own little army. And I helped him do it.

The guard's grip on my wrists is firm, almost biting, as he pushes me down the hall. I can still feel my own gun pressed discreetly against my skin, hidden deep in the waistband under my lab coat. The guard failed to search me in his haste, assuming the gun discarded by Vada's body was the only one. I hold my secret close, choosing my moment to act carefully.

"Subjects," I acknowledge with a nod, directing it at the youngest ones lining the hall. They instantly straighten, a reflexive response to my presence. Despite the fact that I'm restrained, the authority I once wielded over them remains ingrained.

"You're on the wrong side of this," I say to them as we pass.

The nearest Subject steps forward, perhaps their self-appointed leader. His face is a mask of subservience.

"We are at the command of the Chairman," he intones, his voice flat and devoid of emotion, each word carrying the weight of his indoctrination. "Our primary obligation is to safeguard the Chairman, not the Surface."

I can feel my blood boiling at his words. These children, brainwashed and manipulated, are nothing more than tools in Edric's twisted game of power and control. A game I played right into. I would never be able to absolve myself of the guilt for the atrocities I'm responsible for. But I could do something about it now.

"There may come a time when you'll have to choose who truly deserves your protection," I say, my voice steady despite the seething anger I feel. "And when that happens, I hope you'll see beyond your blind loyalty to the Chairman."

The Subjects shift nervously, but their leader remains stoic, his face set. "Our mission is clear," he declares with a steady voice.

"We are eager to serve," the row of Subjects recites.

"At ease," the guard tells them.

We halt in front of Edric's chambers, my heart pounding in my chest.

I take a deep breath and brace myself. I'm pushed into the room and find Edric facing the wall, his attention focused solely on the security feeds playing on screen before him. He is flanked on each side by two Subjects, who keep their eyes trained on me as I enter. The guard releases me and stands back by the door. I massage my sore wrists, unsure what to expect of my capture, prepared to reach for the gun tucked behind me.

"It's a shame what you've done to Vada," he speaks up, breaking the tense silence that settled over the room. "Her unwavering loyalty is quite a loss. She would have sacrificed anything for me."

I cringe at his words, disgust curling my lip.

He finally turns to face me. "Loyalty is not just a virtue, it's essential for success. Without it, one can never truly achieve greatness."

"That's what you're after? Greatness? Proving your daddy wrong?"

He ignores my questions. "With the Subjects it was easy enough, raising them from infancy believing in the cause, in me – they've known nothing else."

I glance over at the expressionless faces of those in his guard.

"They understand the real stakes," he presses on. "We must save humanity. Eradicate the plague that is the Forms living beyond these walls."

"Those were just stories we made up to prevent valuable property from trying to leave the facility. It was all lies."

"But, my dear, the best lies are rooted in truth," he says, a sly smile playing on his lips. "This has always been the mission."

Though my face twists with revulsion, he continues, "I had been following your career long before we met, watching you closely. I recognized your potential… Some people just need a little push."

My heart rate spikes as I listen. Where is he going with this?

"I made it my responsibility to propel you beyond your own limits. I created the circumstances and gave you the resources to achieve more than you could ever imagine – the ability to improve upon humanity."

I clench my fists at my sides and force myself to keep a calm exterior, even as his words send chills down my spine. "Why are you telling me what I already know? I'm disgusted with myself for helping you get what you wanted, but I won't help you gain any more power."

His expression is unreadable. "Power is just a means to an end," he says, his voice mild with an underlying menace in it. "I'm not interested in ruling the world or accumulating wealth. I'm interested in saving our humanity. And sometimes sacrifices must be made for the greater good."

I shake my head, overcome. "You're a monster," I murmur, my words barely above a whisper.

He shrugs, as if my words are of no consequence. "I've heard it all before," he says as he approaches closer. "You know that I'm right – that I've given you everything you've ever wanted. And you know that deep down, you're just like me."

I clench my fists tighter, feeling my anger boiling over. "I'll never be like you," my voice is low and dangerous. "I don't care about control like you; I just want my daughter. Call off your guards and allow us clear passage to the Surface."

"I can't do that. I won't risk a breech. If she reaches the top, she'll be met with lethal force to prevent that from happening."

I step towards him and the Subjects flanking him instinctively raise their weapons.

"You will not take her away from me," I declare, my voice steel.

"I can. I've done it before," he says with an unsettling calm.

Shock chills my veins as the pieces fall into place. "It... it was *you*?" My mind reels, grappling with the horrifying extent of his twisted agenda. "*You* orchestrated the accident?" I seethe. "*You* killed my daughter?" My knuckles are turning white. "Did you cause the explosion too? To keep me here?"

His expression is cold. "Like I said, there has always been more at stake – the fate of mankind."

My jaw drops in disbelief, a bitter laugh escaping. "The fate of mankind..." I spit out the words. "And you thought that gave you the right to play God with my daughter's life?"

He lifts both hands. "Look around you. What is a God if not a creator? Am I not that? Am I not worshipped? I have the power to rebuild and shape the world as I see fit. I am the divine ruler here."

In an instant, I pull the gun from my waistband and fire, determined to prove his mortality. But the bullet is plucked out of the air before it has a chance to reach him. One of the Subjects moves with such lightning speed that she predicted my move before even I did.

I barely manage to react when another Subject descends on me, their grip on my wrists like an iron vice, threatening to snap them in two.

Edric strides forward, towering over me, imposing dominance. "Take her down," his voice slices through the air. "We can't have her posing a threat to herself or others. But leave her unharmed. We'll need her for the next phase of Project Chimera." He pauses, his gaze piercing. "Put her next to the one undergoing mutation, so she can see what the future holds for her."

"I won't let you do this!" With a surge of fury, I violently swing my enhanced leg, striking Edric's knee. There is a gratifying crunch, and he stumbles, his façade of invincibility crumbling. But a Subject is on me in an instant, delivering a precise punch to the back of my knee, causing my legs give out, at almost the same moment she delivers a blow to my gut. She glances over at Edric apologetically. "Forgive me Chairman, I needed to subdue her."

I can't help but savor the sight of Edric clutching his now surely shattered leg. It is a stark reminder to him that even gods are not immune to human frailty, even if only temporarily, as he will inevitably harvest a replacement.

I am marched past the other Subjects lining the hall. Their eyes drill into me, observing with cold curiosity as I'm dragged away. I struggle against the Subject's grip, but it's no use. The more I fight, the tighter her hold becomes. Another Subject follows closely behind, ready to reinforce her hold.

As we round the corner, a glimmer of hope appears. The terminal for the Tube is open, but the vessel hasn't arrived yet.

In a desperate surge of adrenalin, I knock my head back into the face of the Subject restraining me, breaking their nose. I wrench myself free from their grasp and make a break for the terminal. The other Subject is caught off guard for a moment, but quickly gives chase.

My heart pounds in my chest as I leap into the shaft, my body tumbling out into the open air. For a moment, it feels like I am suspended, weightless and free. But then gravity takes hold, and I hurtle towards the darkness below.

I land on the roof of an ascending Tube, hard. It is taking me back up. I quickly scramble to the side and swing myself over to the wall of the shaft itself, grasping the emergency ladder. I climb down as fast as I can, away from the growing group of Subjects above me, poised with tranquilizers

Directly below, a trickle of light emanates from a terminal opening. I jump, hurling myself through to another level of the facility, landing heavily on my feet. The corridor is empty, but I know it won't be for long. I run.

CHAPTER 40
EVER

The darkness covers us as we rise through the Helix. It is so absolute, so unchanging that I question whether we are moving at all. Gliding silently along magnetic tracks, it feels like floating. The only indication of movement is the occasional blur of light reflecting off smooth, unyielding walls as we continue our ascent.

We glide past various chambers, one lined with endless filing cabinets, another a server room, alive with the pulsing light show of blinking data streams.

Skye's voice cuts through the quiet. "Back in the room, you said..." She pauses, shaking her head slightly. "Do you really believe the Forms won?"

Reed gives a resigned nod.

"That would mean we aren't safe anywhere," she whispers, more to herself than the rest of us. We exchange uneasy glances, unsure how to respond.

The Tube slows down. We creak into a terminal illuminated by red light. We brace ourselves, backs pressed against the glass of the Tube. Reed stands in front of us protectively, scalpel extended. Then the doors slide open to an eerie silence.

"Why did we stop?" Farrah asks.

"This is as far as the Tube goes. Level 13," I say, taking in the scene in front of us.

"There's got to be another Tube that will take us all the way up," Reed says, hopeful.

Unlike the white room from before, this one is filled with equipment, supplies, and data charts along every inch of wall, all flanking a single door at the opposite end.

Reed tentatively steps out of the Tube and assesses all corners of the room.

"There's no one here, I think we're clear."

Farrah and I follow him out. "Of course, there's no one here," she says. "No one is after us, this is some sort of puzzle we need to solve."

"I'm scared," Skye's voice trembles from the back of the Tube.

"It's okay, come on. See? It's just us here," I assure her, gesturing around the room as I turn.

Reed approaches the solid door, a red siren light flickers above it, casting the room in a red glow. Farrah analyzes the equipment and data dancing across the walls.

"This has to be our way out," Reed whispers. He reaches for the door handle, testing it. It's locked.

"Let me try." I peer into the pad with the eye that holds the Keeper's lens, and with a resounding click the door disengages.

"Okay." Reed nods. "Let's do this."

Before he can open the door, an agonizing scream rips through the room.

Skye collapses to the ground just outside of the Tube, gripping her arm in pain. My eyes widen in horror as the smooth flesh of her arm starts to ripple and contort. The veins in her neck bulge as guttural cries escape her.

"Skye!" I cry out, terror gripping me.

We rush towards her, but her erratic movements propel her backwards into the Tube. In an instant the Tube jerks and Skye tumbles further inside, just beyond the reach of my outstretched hands. She wails in excruciating pain as the door slides shut nearly taking my arm with it.

"No!"

She drags herself towards the glass, crying. I punch at it with all my strength, willing it to break. But it's reinforced. Farrah claws at the door, trying to slide it open.

"Move!" Reed launches a drawer from one of the nearby cabinets at the glass. It bounces right back.

"Help me!" Skye cries out as the Tube begins to descend. I frantically scan my eye across the wall trying to find a panel, but the Tube continues to move. We all watch helplessly as Skye shoots downward and out of view.

"I'll find you!" I scream, but she's gone. Frustration and desperation course through me, and I punch the wall next to the terminal.

"We have to go after her! We can't just leave her behind." I hurriedly search for a panel along the wall. "We need to call it back."

There must be a concealed keypad somewhere. I need to find her, help her – she's so small, so vulnerable. I could have sworn I saw something protruding from her arm. I need to protect her, but with increasing dread I realize I have no idea how to.

I finally locate an indentation and push, but the Tube doesn't return. I push again with more force. And again. And again. Despite my efforts there's no vessel in sight.

A gentle hand rests on my shoulder, and I'm surprised to find that it's Farrah.

"She'll be okay. Maybe this was supposed to happen all along, her path is different from ours."

I want to slap her.

"We'll find her I promise," Reed says firmly. "But we can't do it from here." He points to the door. "This may be our only way out."

I know he's right, though I can't help feeling like I'm abandoning Skye. I reluctantly search the room, looking for anything large we could use to defend ourselves, should the need arise. I make a silent promise to myself: we'll find a way to escape, find safety, and I'll return for Skye.

Reed gives us a single decisive nod, then takes a deep breath and cautiously cracks the door open. "What the–"

We are engulfed by a crimson glow as we step into a vast room extending far into the horizon. Rows of enormous glass cylinders filled with red liquid dominate the room, interrupted by the occasional centrifuge machines and towering racks of red vials. We slowly walk down the rows fixated by the enormity of the containers.

"This must be where it all goes." Reed whispers. That's when I understand what the cylinders are filled with.

Blood. There must be oceans of blood stored in this space.

The cylinders loom at least nine feet high and perhaps another six feet in diameter. Inscriptions on their bases confirm what I assumed – they are all O negative.

"I'll take the perimeter, look for another Tube terminal," Reed declares before darting behind a cluster of tanks.

Farrah watches as he disappears from sight, "I'll check the back," she announces, her voice steady. With a nod she sets off, her footsteps brisk and determined.

I slowly advance, weaving through several rows towards the center. I come to a halt in front of one of the cylinders, startled by my contorted reflection. Lab coat slumped over my shoulders, dark circles under my eyes and disheveled hair. I'm a shadow of my former self, unrecognizable. I lift a hand to brush the hair behind my ears.

But the reflection does not follow my movement. Instead, it lifts something and aims it directly at me.

There is someone else here.

A crack explodes and echoes through the air. The cylinder shatters and gallons of blood spill forward. I slip backward onto the ground, drenched in red and try to steady myself on crunching shards of glass.

"Ev!" Reed cries out.

The person on the other side of the glass jumps through the shattered cylinder, landing on top of me, holding his gun straight in my face. He is dressed like a Keeper, with scraggly hair that I mistook for my own. His eyes are wild.

"You're not supposed to be here," he hisses, pressing the gun into my forehead. The heat of the metal against my skin is surprisingly intense. "No one is supposed to be here." He contorts his face, he looks crazed. "Don't you understand?"

"Ever! Where are you?" Reed shouts again, his voice filled with desperation. I can hear him running, his footsteps echoing. But I'm frozen with shock and I can't speak.

The Keeper presses his knee into my chest. His sleeves ride up his arms and I see that his skin is littered with puncture holes, old and fresh. The weight of his body is crushing my lungs. But I can't just push him off, I might startle him into pulling the trigger.

"I said I wanted to be left alone, I wanted to end things on my own terms."

A shuffle to the left of us catches his attention, and as he cranes his neck, I catch the glint of metal under his collar. The chrome plating encircles his neck, and a chilling realization crosses my mind: Is this what we were warned about? He looks so human, but could he be one of the Forms? He's here, inside the Helix, dressed as a Keeper. Was Reed right? Have the Forms already won? The questions keep multiplying in my mind. Have they been controlling us all along? How many more of them are among us?

The rabid, bloody Keeper shoots at the cylinder next to us, and it shatters releasing another avalanche of blood that sweeps over my body. It washes over my face, choking me.

Reed charges from the opposite direction, tackling the Keeper. They collide on the floor nearby and struggle against each other. With the sudden release of pressure, I inhale, gasping for air. The Keeper's weapon slides a few feet away. I reach for it on hands and knees, coughing, but the blood sends me slipping out of control.

Two feet halt in front of the gun, and it is slowly picked up. Farrah examines it in her hands then raises it in our direction.

I fall back on my elbows, "Farrah–"

There's a hollow look her eyes. "This is all just a test. We need to prove how far we are willing to go," she insists, but her trembling hand betrays her uncertainty.

She aims the gun at the Keeper, now further disheveled, his shirt torn revealing the chrome plating extending into a metallic torso. His neck is fastened under Reed's arm.

"Farrah, wait!" I shout. "He can give us information, tell us how to get out of here, and where to find Skye."

She points it at his head.

"This is our way out. It's what we've been training for. Annihilate all Forms. Do whatever it takes to survive."

"Please! Tell us how to get out of here," I beg the Keeper my voice filled with desperation.

He makes an unsettling squirting sound. He's laughing. Under the weight of Reeds arm he manages to say, "This is all that's left."

Farrah's face is uncomprehending as she flicks her eyes between us.

"What do you mean?" I ask.

He laughs again and meets Farrah's gaze head on with a previously unseen clarity.

"Do it."

Farrah cocks her weapon.

"Wait!"

But she has already pulled the trigger, lodging a tiny piece of metal between his eyes.

Reed jerks back, immediately releasing. A dribble of blood travels down the Keeper's face, mixing with the canvas of blood that stains his body.

We stand there, stunned, expecting something to happen. Anything. For the first time, I hope maybe Farrah was right after all.

But nothing does.

Farrah breaks the silence, echoing my thoughts. "We did it, we passed. Shouldn't – shouldn't something happen now?"

Reed and I remain silent.

"I did it!" Farrah screams to the room, looking up at the ceiling wildly. "I did what I was supposed to do!"

No one answers.

"We passed!" she continues to shout. "We're done!"

I place a hand on her shoulder, then gently rest another on the weapon, taking it from her. She looks at me, imploring.

"Maybe this was just the first trial?" Her voice is small, less sure.

"There's another door," Reed says. "It could be an exit. We should keep moving."

With no other options, we trail behind him further into the unknown.

CHAPTER 41
EVER

A Tube is waiting for us at a new terminal. I secretly hoped to find Skye inside crouched in the corner, scared but unharmed, back in the safety of our company.

We look back at the chamber of blood one last time, at the horror concealed within, and pile into the Tube. The keypad here unveils another set of four numbers. Reaching the Surface won't be straightforward; the Helix's layout is more complex and terrifying than I could have ever envisioned, lacking any apparent direct route to the top. We'll have to keep searching for the correct terminal that will continue our ascent.

I select the highest available, Level 9. The door closes and up we go, uncertain of our destination but hopeful that each move brings us a step closer to the Surface, to the truth.

"Why didn't they come for me?" Farrah slumps against the glass, leaving a streak of blood on its surface. The thick, red fluid that had cascaded from the cylinder drenched us completely, leaving us looking as though we had emerged from a battlefield. We are the subjects of nightmares, caked in blood. Wild, rabid looking. Inhuman.

"We were never meant to succeed," Reed utters softly.

We say nothing more to each other as the Tube climbs.

This is all that's left.

That woeful laugh teetering on cracked lips would haunt me endlessly. The Keeper – no, the Form – was so deeply disturbed that they wanted to end their own life. What were they so afraid of? What did they mean by their final words? One thing is certain, we are completely unprepared for whatever awaits us at the top. I clutch the gun to my side, silently vowing to wield its destructive power against whatever harm comes next.

Through the glass we watch the blur of other levels, fleeting shadows as we ascend. With each passing moment I draw a mental map of the Tubes we've encountered so far in our desperate climb. The first only operated on Levels 17 through 13, so that's likely where Skye was deposited. That's where I will need to return. I shudder at the thought of what might happen to her, but I try to push the fear aside; she's smart. She'll find a place to hide and wait until we come back for her. Rescuing her now without a strategy, without a secure exit, would be reckless.

A now-familiar hush of air pierces the silence, and we dock on another level. The door slides open onto a room bathed in blue light.

The room itself is devoid of any furnishings or equipment. But the walls... the walls are *alive*. Swaying back and forth, rippling like waves.

I realize it's an illusion made from light reflecting off the ceiling. High above us, separated only by a thick sheet of glass is a pool of water larger than anything I have ever seen. The sight of it fills me with an immediate suffocating sensation.

Farrah steps out first, mesmerized. "It's beautiful."

"Let's just get out of here," I say, my breaths shallow.

Reed hops out and slowly makes his way to a single door across the room, much like the previous level.

I hesitate. The minute my foot leaves the Tube, it slides shut and descends. The wall shifts over the terminal, closing off its entrance. The temperature drops immediately, and we exchange wary glances, our breaths hanging in the air.

"We're closer to the Surface, so it's colder. It could be – what do they call it?" Reed grasps for the right word.

"Winter," Farrah offers.

I try not to look up, feeling more trapped with every passing second.

"We're under water, maybe it's the ocean?" I venture. I'm reminded of the videos of *Outpost Zero-Five-One*, the last remaining Surface city surrounded by waves of water. But was that just another lie?

I scan my eye and the door slides open. Dense frosted air escapes, engulfing Reed as Farrah and I follow behind him.

Once we're inside, the fog dissipates revealing the ongoing presence of the looming ceiling of water in what appears to be a massive refrigeration warehouse. It reminds me of the unit behind the Refectory. Reed and I once snuck back there after hours to try some of the Keeper's food bricks. Suffice it to say, we much preferred to stick to our IV infusion diets after that.

Rows and rows of drawers are stacked above each other, towering over us as they approach the ceiling. They cover the entire perimeter of the massive room. In the center hangs a large screen, displaying a chart filled with letters and numbers. Underneath it is a console, a touch screen reflecting the codes on the screen above. The codes are a series of Xs and Ys preceded by 4-digit numbers.

"They're Subject IDs," I realize, and I point to the screen. Code after code after code. The list appears to be some sort of inventory.

"I don't understand," Farrah says. "Why is my code up there?" Farrah selects her number on the screen pad. A drawer unhinges nearby and opens, illuminated by a light. From it, emerges a narrow sliding table encased in frost.

Inside, lies a body.

Farrah screams. Standing closest to the cold chamber, she has seen what we haven't. I approach for a better look. Lying on the table, in a cold yet restful sleep, is Farrah.

"What is this? What's going on?" she cries out in confusion.

Reed and I stand there utterly stunned, unable to formulate a response.

"This isn't real, that's not me! How can it be me?" She stumbles backward. The body looks exactly like her, perfectly maintained, save for longer red hair lying at her shoulders.

"Okay, Okay." Farrah paces rapidly, shaking her head vigorously. "This *has* to be some sort of test, clearly, right? Or maybe I'm just dreaming. I'm still in the ice bath after Selections." Her voice trembles with rising with panic. "That's why I feel so cold. It makes perfect sense. This is all a simulation, or a hallucination?"

Farrah has finally cracked.

I unglue myself from my position by her frozen body and move back to the control panel reading the numbers.

"It's almost every Subject," I tell Reed. I try to access their vital signs on the display, but they don't seem to have any cellular activity.

"They don't look alive," Reed says from a nearby cold chamber. "It's like they're being preserved."

"Did they... make *Copies* of us?" my voice cuts through the room. I search for my number, but it's not listed. Neither is Reed's.

I look around at the dizzying number of drawers throughout the room. *Skye.* I punch in her code. A drawer opens to the left, and I rush towards it, expecting to see her small frozen body. But it's empty.

"I know what this is." Farrah's breath on my ear is startling, making me stumble backwards. "We need to eliminate the bodies, sever ties to our old selves, prove that we only serve one united cause." Her tone is steady and resolute. And it frightens me to my very core.

"I'm sorry, Ever," she says as she jams her fist in my throat and yanks the gun from my pocket.

Farrah dashes toward the control panel and fires at the touch screen. Glass shards explode everywhere as I struggle to regain my breath.

"Don't you see?" she shouts hysterically, waving the gun in the air. "It doesn't matter! None of this is real!"

Reed charges from behind as she relentlessly shoots at the display, bullets ricocheting and cracking some of the cold chambers.

"Reed, don't!" I cry out, terrified she'll shoot him as well.

A deafening siren cuts through the room, and the massive screen in the center turns vivid red. The noise is so overwhelming, I have to cup my hands to my ears.

The blaring sounds have rendered Farrah momentarily immobile, and Reed disarms her easily. He tosses me the gun, and I tuck it under my shoulder.

The noise persists, and a voice echoes through the room, repeating the text displayed on the nearly shattered screen.

A THREAT HAS BEEN DETECTED.

FAIL SAFE PROCEDURES HAVE BEEN INITIATED.

LOCK DOWN WILL COMMENCE IN TEN... NINE... EIGHT...

"Come on!" Reed shouts, although I can barely hear him. "We have to move!"

I yank Farrah's arm and we run towards a door at the other end of the room, hoping it leads to another Tube terminal. The drawers behind us slide into the walls, lock shut.

SEVEN... SIX... FIVE...

We make it through the door, and to my horror the ceiling of glass persists, the level above must be entirely submerged, and the glass panel now begins to lower into the room.

FOUR...

The ceiling begins to retract.

THREE... TWO...

Water pours through the widening gap. The room floods quickly, and in no time, the water has risen to our knees, and we struggle towards the blank wall terminal where a Tube should be.

ONE.

The door clicks locked behind us, and the room continues to fill rapidly. We have nowhere to go.

A space in the wall retracts, and water gushes out through the opening, pulling us into a current hurtling towards the dark abyss below. I fight the pull, kicking against the flow with all my might.

Just before I feel panic taking hold, a Tube docks, and I could cry in relief. The door opens and we are sucked inside, knocking against the back wall as water flows in. The door struggles to close against the pressure. I feel myself rising to the top of the Tube with the water level. Before long, Reed, Farrah and I are rubbing noses with the ceiling.

"The door's jammed!" Reed splutters. "We need to push it shut."

I nod, and without direction I inhale a deep breath, plunge under the surface of the water and try to swim my way to the edge of the door frame, hoping my increased strength will overpower the water pressure keeping it open. Reed is on my tail, and with slippery hands we both push the door forward to slide, but it barely budges. We try again and find that it moves incrementally forward. Slowly, the flood of water begins to subside now that the Tube is nearly full. I lock eyes with Reed, he gives me a firm nod, and together we summon all our strength. My lungs scream in protest as we shove, finally managing to slide the door shut.

Relief washes over me as I kick my way to the top, past Farrah's floating feet, my lungs aching for a breath of air. Farrah comes down to meet me, shaking her head. I don't understand, but instinct pushes me upward. I have to take a breath. I have to ease the burning. That's when I realize, there's no air left, the Tube is entirely filled with water.

Farrah kicks the keypad below and the Tube travels upward. Our bodies float helplessly, suspended in the darkness.

This is it. This is how I die. In a watery tomb.

I never imagined when I was selected to ascend, that my new life would end so quickly. Yet, as I float here at the edge of darkness, I don't feel afraid, I don't feel pain. A sense of calm washes over me. I have no control, there is nothing I can do, so let it happen. I take Reed's hand as the fringes of my vision start to go black.

A glimmer catches my eye on the floor of the Tube. It's the gun. It was torn away in the rush of water and must have made its way back into the Tube like the rest of us. I vigorously kick towards the bottom.

I grab the gun and pull the trigger. A small crack spreads across the glass. I feel my last bit of strength waning, a throbbing headache nearly blinding me. I shoot again and the crack lengthens. I pull back and try to shoot the same spot, struggling to keep my hands from slipping from the trigger, but the gun jams. I'm out of bullets.

Our only hope for survival, gone.

Reed pulls the gun from me and slams the butt against the glass. My body convulses. He bangs it again, with everything he can muster. His eyes are bulging, and his mouth is wide open, screaming, choking on the water. Red fluid filters out of my nose. Farrah is kicking the glass, yanking the gun from Reed's weakening grip.

Kick. Bang. Kick. Bang.

The cracks give way and the wall of the Tube splinters, small streams of water escape. Farrah grabs me, and kicks to the top. My vision is almost entirely black. We touch our noses and mouths to the ceiling. I gasp for air in pain. Farrah dives back down and pulls Reed towards the gap of air.

Abruptly, the Tube stops and the door slides open. We rush out with the water, spilling onto the stone floor of a dimly lit room. Level 5.

CHAPTER 42
EVER

The floor is cold and rough, its texture a stark contrast to the sleek and sterile finishes of the other levels. The Surface must be close.

Once we've caught our breath, we scrape ourselves off the ground and glance around the cool, dark room. The walls are bare, made of stone. But there are three doors. Three potential exits.

"This is it," Reed exclaims. "We must be at the top."

We are sopping wet, holding ourselves up against the wall, panting. At least the water washed off all the blood.

"Let's get out of here." I motion towards the door on the left. It's as good a choice as any.

I lumber over to the scanner and pull the door open to reveal a vast, multilevel space segmented into separate cube-like sections. Not work rooms exactly; they appeared to be living quarters. The different levels and units are connected by intersecting bridges, walkways levitating and repositioning themselves. One rises from a floor below, turns clockwise, then stations itself in front of us, creating a pathway to the rooms across the way.

We inch towards the unprotected edge, careful not to slip. Below and across from us we see the chaotic movement of white coats.

"This is where the Keepers live," Farrah whispers in awe.

I flinch away, hoping we haven't been seen. Of course, I

266

had to choose the worse possible door to go through. We are exposed, vulnerable, and surrounded by the enemy.

"Let's go back, this way is too risky. We'll be spotted," I say, already turning towards the door. But Farrah pulls my arm, her grip firm.

"This is where we get our answers. This is where we get the truth." There is iron in her tone, but her eyes are filled with desperation. "I need to know."

"The truth is worth nothing if we're captured. We'll find another way." Reed motions towards the door.

"I can't do that. This is messing with my head, not knowing what's real and what's not. If this is a test, then this is the final battle. If it's not, then I have my answer. I'm sorry." Steeling herself, Farrah mounts the bridge in front of us.

"We need a plan," I insist.

"This is my exit strategy," she declares firmly. "One way or another, this will all be over."

I don't know what she means by that or if she even intends to survive once she has the answers she's looking for, but I'm helpless to stop her. Reed's face darkens with anger, both at Farrah for risking our lives, and at his own moral compass that won't allow him to leave her behind. Despite the chaos I can't help but admire his integrity.

Reed scans the tiered living quarters, wrestling with his thoughts. "If this truly is where they live, they must have a way in and out, right? And with multiple levels here, maybe this is our best chance?"

I hesitate briefly, then jump onto the platform before it moves away. Nodding in silent agreement, Reed follows suit.

The bridge approaches the opposite end of the pit, and we dismount. To my surprise no one seems to notice or pay us any mind. There's a spirit of frenzy all around, Keepers run through and past us without a second look. Glimpses of steel appendages peek out through flapping coats everywhere. They are completely exposed here.

I swallow hard, the knot in my throat tightening. We are surrounded by metallic body parts, the AI-controlled entities we've been warned about all our lives. Were the stories true then? But if they lied about everything else, Selections, Ascending, how can this be real? Or is there something else going on?

"Reed," I begin, my voice tinged with uncertainty, "I think you might right. Look at the Keepers; they are all Forms."

Farrah tenses, fear and anger rippling across her face.

One frantic-looking Keeper runs right into me, stumbles over, and continues off in the opposite direction, barely registering the soaking wet intruders on their premises. Keepers run left and right, leaving stations unmonitored, pods emptied and in disarray.

"What's going on?" Reed asks.

We pass a room with a series of screens, each surveilling a different section of Helix Colony. Perhaps one of them will reveal an exit. I immediately recognize the white never-ending hallways of the previous floors we were held on. So, they did see us. They were watching and yet no one came. Why?

A man sits in a seat in front of the monitors. We need to find a way out of here, and these surveillance feeds might be our ticket to freedom.

Farrah, fists clenched with anger, is poised to storm in. I quickly step in front of her, silently signaling her and Reed to watch the perimeter; a commotion is the last thing we need. I slip into the room without a sound, quickly wrapping my arm around the man's neck. I squeeze until he goes limp and crumples to the ground. Spotting a weapon on his hip I quickly seize it.

Farrah and Reed hold their positions at the door. No one on the outside has noticed. I frantically search the screens for any signs of an exit.

Light flickers in the red room, and another room is fully submerged underwater. I see the green room, the stone room, but no clear exit, or as I had hoped, a clue to Skye's location.

There's an empty series of capsules on one of the levels, completely evacuated. But not just any capsules, these are familiar. 23 flashes on the screen. Those are *our* dormitories. They are all empty, the halls are clear, Level 23 is abandoned.

"There's nothing left on 23," I say to the others, gesturing them to enter the room.

"What do you mean?" Farrah approaches the screen while Reed stands watch.

"There's no one down there."

Her eyes search the screen. "What about the other Subjects? Not everyone was selected. Not everyone passed. What about the Flaweds?"

I flinch at the way she emphasizes the last word.

"When are you going to finally get it through your head?" Reed hisses. "This isn't a test or some elaborately designed trial, or a dream. We are on our own. We've been held in captivity, lied to our entire lives, and now something *even worse* has everyone alarmed."

Farrah storms out of the surveillance room, muttering, "We need real answers." We scramble after her.

The next Keeper that crosses our path, Farrah slams against the nearest wall with ease. I raise my gun while Farrah pins her throat.

"You're going to tell me what's happening here, now, or I will not hesitate to hurt you. Got it?" Farrah growls.

The Keeper nods vigorously, eyes wide with fear, hands trembling at her sides.

"Where are the other Subjects?" Farrah asks inches from her face.

She says nothing,

"What are you?" Farrah presses her arm tighter against the Keeper's throat, her expression cold. The Keeper scratches at Farrah's arms with gloved hands, but she holds fast.

"She can't speak," Reed says from behind, but Farrah doesn't give.

"How do we get out?!"

"Farrah, she can't breathe," I warn, hesitantly lowering my weapon.

Her grip tightens.

"You're going to kill her!"

Farrah seems oblivious to our words, consumed by anger and despair.

I exchange a quick look with Reed before yanking Farrah back, trying to ease her grip before she strangles the Keeper, destroying our chances of finding out any key information about this place.

Farrah resists, pushing back against me. In the struggle, the Keeper manages to break free just enough to throw a frantic punch with her gloved hand, hitting me squarely in the ribs. With an audible crack, searing pain shoots through my body. As I'm doubled over in pain, Farrah's trance is broken and the Keeper runs away, glints of her metal hand peeking out of her sleeve as she flees.

"You should have let me kill her."

For the first time, I agree with her.

"Let's follow her." Reed steadies me, pulling me upright.

The Keeper leaps onto the bridge and sprints to the other side of the pit. We give chase, but the bridge is already moving. We reach the middle of the pathway but it's too late. The Keeper slides through an open door on the other side as we are whisked away in another direction.

"Hold it right there!" The command slices through the air, Sio's voice unmistakable.

CHAPTER 43
ROSIO

Our eyes lock over the barrel of Ever's gun. I'm holding my breath, adrenaline surging through my veins.

She hates me. She should.

She may kill me. That's okay too.

It should have been me who died in the first place. For all my ego and narcissism, at least I got to see her grow up. The girl standing before me is perfection. Smart, strong, caring. She's everything Rune would have been.

She tightly grips her weapon, aiming it at me, and we are locked in a standstill on the rotating bridge. Reed and Farrah close in behind her, poised to attack.

"Hands where I can see them," Ever says unflinchingly, her expression lethal, the corners of her mouth curling into a snarl.

I extend a hand, trying to connect with her just once without the mask of a Keeper. Her involuntary flinch stings, but I understand her apprehension. I draw my hand back, pressing my palms together over my lips in a silent plea. I knew it would be difficult for her to accept me. Taking a deep breath to steady myself, I hold back the tears welling in my eyes. I haven't been the mother I wanted to be, but I was the one I needed to be in this place. Now I can only hope I have the chance to make things right.

"Please, I'm not going to hurt you. I would never hurt you,"

I assure her, raising my hands in a gesture of peace. "Right now, you three need to come with me."

"We're not going anywhere with you," Reed spits, his voice dripping with scorn. I had failed to protect him too.

Despite the tension, I take a careful step forward.

"This is not a request, you need to follow me," I assert firmly, trying to maintain authority while keeping my voice calm. I take another cautious step.

"Stop!" Ever shouts, cocking her gun. "You've been lying to us our entire lives. That ends now, or I shoot you where you stand."

I don't doubt the determination in her eyes, and though my life hangs in the balance, my heart swells with pride at her tenacity. Against all odds, I know she will face every challenge with unshakable resolve. I'm overcome with admiration for the girl before me. At least I did something right.

I nod slowly signaling my compliance.

"I know you don't think you can trust me, but I'm trying to help you. That's all I've ever tried to do. Save you. I promise, I will explain everything, but we're losing time." It's only a matter of moments before Edric's guards find me. Find us.

Ever's glare remains icy and unyielding as the bridge halts, docking. I deliberately turn to lead them away from the chaos, but Reed rushes me and yanks me back. With a powerful jerk he forces me to my knees.

"You're staying right here. Like she said, start talking."

I had always planned for this moment. What I hadn't anticipated was just how quickly it would come. Their eyes bore into me. The anger, confusion, and fear, palpable enough to touch.

"What is this place?" Ever starts.

I fervently shake my head, trying to convey the urgency of the situation. "We're out of time. The Chairman has given orders to eliminate any assets that don't cooperate. It's not safe for you here. And it's not safe outside. Please, just come with me," I implore, hoping to convince her.

The bridge is switching position again. I don't see Edric's minions on any of the platforms yet, though I'm sure they'll come. Reed catches me scanning the area.

"No one is coming to help you."

"I'll ask you again, what is this place? Where are we?" Ever is seething now.

I shake my head knowing they won't understand. "Helix Colony is not a safe haven. Or a training facility. It's not even a real colony. It's a corporation. Helix Co."

"Corporation?"

I turn to Reed, imploring. "We don't have time. This is what I was trying to prepare you for. I'll explain once we go down."

This is not what Ever wants to hear; she knocks me in the head with the butt of the gun. With the shock of the impact, I collapse to the floor, my head floating over the edge of the bridge.

"We're not going back!" she shouts. There is something terrible in her face, a kind of anger so deep that I know for her this is the point of no return.

"I am trying to save you."

"Explain yourself!" Reed growls. He is now crouched down, hands squeezing my shoulders.

"This is an underground biomedical engineering facility, founded by Edric Easton, the Chairman." I see the confusion on their faces, they don't understand the information. I didn't prepare them for this world.

"Helix Co. sells biomedical and biotech products for profit." My voice is strained as my head hangs over the precipice.

"Products?" Ever demands, her voice sharp.

"Your ID numbers are stock keeping units, they mark you as property of Helix Co. You are highly-valued investments. Every minute of your day has been dedicated to making you the perfect product. Your kineti-training... IV infusions...

Psychological screenings and the inkblot tests in your simulations…" Each word is desperate effort. I kick my legs trying to inch my way back over the edge.

"Your blood donations confirm your vitals and provide unlimited transfusion sources for investors."

I can barely look Ever in the eyes, seeing her world crumble with every word I speak.

Farrah gasps. "Look, she's one of them!"

My leg Adornment is exposed under a raised pant leg. Reed backs away, examining the glimmer of metal.

"Show it to me!" Ever shouts.

I raise the pant leg higher to reveal where the Adornment connects with flesh at my knee.

"It's not what you thi–"

The gun goes off.

Ever looks as surprised as I feel.

A searing bolt of white-hot pain rips through my upper chest. Tearing agony engulfs the entire area, and I instinctively clutch the wet wound.

The bridge has docked again, Reed drags me onto the new platform, pushing me against the wall. "Enough with the lies! We deserve to know the truth!" He keeps me sitting on the ground and digs a finger into the fresh hole next to my shoulder. A torturous cry erupts from my throat, the pain so severe I nearly black out.

"I'm not li–"

"What about our gifts?" Farrah cuts in. "We were chosen for a larger purpose–" She narrows her eyes at me, searching for deception in my words.

Ever still aims her gun at me, although it's lost some of its intimidation power now that I've been shot. She doesn't look eager to pull the trigger again.

"Your gifts were *chosen* from a menu. Customers paid a premium for upgraded features. Each one a higher cost," I explain, starting to feel lightheaded.

"So, if I understand this correctly," Reed's voice trembles with anger, "you're selling us off to the highest bidder?"

"You were *created for* the highest bidder," I clarify, "in their likeness. You are the younger, unimpaired, thriving versions of the investors, offering them the chance to enhance themselves whenever they want."

Gritting my teeth against the pain, I address Farrah. "You were commissioned as a Copy for an elite swimmer. At 140 years old, she wanted to dominate in the water, and swim without coming up for air."

"And what about my arm?" Reed snarls.

I shake my head slowly, staring at Reed's shoulder, at the space where his arm should be. Ever's breath catches, her expression shifting with sudden realization.

"The Chairman," she murmurs.

There's no use in holding anything back now. Not when I can feel life seeping out of me, not when there is still so much they need to know. "Reed, you are the Copy of the Chairman."

"What?"

"You were replicated from his DNA. His body is in poor condition – severe nerve damage in his left arm and hand. He wanted to restore himself with original parts, so he created you."

This isn't how I wanted them to find out, but I have to make things clear, make them understand what they need to do to survive.

"Wait." Ever pauses, her voice trembling with disbelief. "So we're just Copies waiting around until the originals decide they want upgrades?"

"We've been raised to be... harvested for parts?" Reed asks incredulously.

"Organic parts are more viable... stronger when grown as a whole," I sputter, spraying specks of blood onto the ground. "So we created an environment for assets to flourish in. Social connection and interaction are essential to survival, so you were bred together with a purpose, a goal, to work towards."

"How many of us have there been?" Farrah's voice trembles. "How many Copies? I... I saw myself..." she falters, struggling with the words.

They had discovered the storage room.

"Because of sizable investment and resources used, we made back-up Copies to protect the project."

I can see Ever's head is spinning.

"I don't understand. Why put us through this? Why raise us all these years and give us hope? Why such cruelty?"

I swallow hard, trying to tamp down the guilt.

"This isn't what I wanted. My plan was to get you out of here and destroy the program and everyone who benefited from it. But there is nowhere safe anymore."

"You allowed this to go on for *sixteen years*?" Ever's voice is full of scorn and disgust.

"It may feel like a lifetime. Biologically you are sixteen, but chronologically... you're under two years old."

They look stricken, the weight of my words sinking in. Ever breaks the silence. "What about the Forms?"

"If we gave you something to fear on the outside, it would stop you from attempting to escape. I invented them to shield you from the real monsters within these walls... including myself. There are no Forms, just us."

"If there are no Forms, then what are you?" Farrah demands, her voice heavy with and betrayal.

"I'm human, just like you. We've been becoming increasingly artificial for centuries, first for vanity, then out of necessity to survive. When we became more artificial than human, a new trend emerged – being real." I cough up a little blood.

"They created us for themselves." Farrah's words are a sorrowful whisper.

A chill creeps over me now, I'm losing too much blood.

"You were created in a lab, yes. Subjects weren't rescued, they have no families, no parents. Except for one."

With each word I struggle to maintain my composure.

"One of the first Subjects was not a Copy of a wealthy investor. She was just a little girl who deserved a second chance. One who I needed to see grow up, even if only from afar." I speak very slowly now. "I lost my daughter in an accident," I confess, my voice strained with emotion. "I made a vow that if I could bring her back, I would make her stronger, more resilient. immune to harm. I wanted her to be *everlasting*. And so, I gave her a new name. Ever."

I hold her gaze firmly.

"You are my daughter."

CHAPTER 44
EVER

Sio leans against the wall, blood trickling down from her gunshot wound. I abruptly shut my eyes, not wanting to see what I've done.

Her words ring in my ears on a loop. *You are my daughter.*

I don't know when I lowered my weapon. Or when I kneeled beside her.

"Please, listen to me," she pants in little shallow gasps. "All I've ever wanted is to keep you safe." She grabs my arm, eyes frantic. "Don't go outside. If you reach the lobby, the Chairman will have you killed."

"I'm not afraid of the Chairman." I grit my teeth feeling a wave of defiance; she pulls me close.

"It isn't safe anymore. Heat storms have breached the city limits, the air is virtually unbreathable. It's like the nightmares we created have come true."

I don't recognize this distraught woman before me. Always so stern and cold, devoid of warmth, now so utterly broken. I can't reconcile her words with the reality I've known. Can I trust her? She's a monster, she said so herself. I'm torn between wanting to believe this woman who claims to be my mother, and knowing with certainty that she has never been that to me.

Sio's expression softens as she raises her hand to cup my chin. Through teary eyes, she gazes at me for a moment, as if committing every detail to memory. "It wasn't supposed to be like this," she whispers, her lips trembling. "I just wanted more time."

I remain motionless, letting the sentiment wash over me.

"I love you, Rune."

At her words, a surge of unexpected anger rises within me, and I recoil. Where was this woman when I needed her? Where was this soft touch, this gentleness? Was it always meant for someone else?

"I can't," I murmur, pulling away. I can't just give in to her, I can't trust her so easily. The hatred I've held on to for so long... where does it go?

"I understand, it's okay," she says, her voice breaking, eyes heavy with regret. "Too much damage has been done, I can't take it back. You don't need to forgive me, just listen." Her eyes plead with mine. "You won't survive out there. Your only chance is within this facility. I can buy you time. Away from the Chairman, from harvesting." She forces the words out between labored breaths. "Reed knows the way down, the red shoot – there's an unfinished space from the facility's early construction. It's not under surveillance. There's food and water. You can survive there... That's where you need to go."

She shoves something into my hand and closes my palm.

"Take this," she sputters. "You'll understand. I gave you full access."

Reed looks at me, uncertainty clouding his eyes.

"I'm sorry," Sio whispers, she holds my gaze as her breathing slows.

That's when I notice the amount of blood that has pooled on the ground beneath her. Too much.

"No!" Fear grips me as I realize what is happening. "Why didn't you tell me?!" With trembling hands, I crouch down and grasp her shoulders, shaking them in desperation.

She doesn't respond.

I shake her more violently, but each moment passes in silence.

"I needed you!" I cry.

Reed finally pulls me away from her. "Ev, let's go."

Tears stream down my face and I don't know if they are from anger or remorse.

He helps me back to my feet. "Boots will be coming for us at any second." Picking up my gun, he heads toward one of the three doors we originally entered from. Then stops and turns to me.

"Where to?" He asks softly, his eyes tender, leaving the choice to me. I steel a quick glance at Farrah for a hint of guidance, but her face mirrors my own unease. They are looking to me to lead. Despite everything we've just heard, I can't allow myself to be controlled or manipulated any longer. And I don't want to just survive; I want to live. I've spent my entire life in the dark, and now I need to see the truth for myself. *May the light guide your way.* The irony of our contrived parting blessing hardens my resolve.

I meet their anxious eyes. "Let's go outside."

They nod in silent agreement, and Reed leads the charge, swinging open a door which hopefully leads to another terminal with a Tube to the Surface. Farrah's right behind him. Despite what Sio said, we're going to get out of here.

I turn to follow, but cast a lingering glance back at Sio, the mother I never knew. I open my hand to see a small container, its contents gleaming faintly. Her Bright-i lens. I tuck the last piece of her into my pocket.

Reed opens the door, and a few feet ahead a Tube arrives with a whisper. As Reed steps on, I stop and run back through the door to Sio.

"What are you doing?!"

I lean over her, close her eyes and lift her to my shoulder. "We can't just leave her here. I want to take her where it's quiet."

Farrah walks out to help me. She holds the door open until I safely lay Sio's body down against the wall of the terminal and whisper a silent goodbye. It's all that I can give her.

I straighten up and see four Boots approach the slowly closing door just behind Farrah.

A shot rings out. The bullet flies inches from my head as Farrah turns and tackles one of the Boots to the ground. She disarms him, takes his weapon, and shoots another in the knee cap. He crumples to the ground. She shoots the next in the chest.

"Get to the Surface!" she shouts at us. "I'm right behind you." With swift and eager movements, she dispatches the Boots, seizing the opportunity to unleash all the hurt, anger, and betrayal within her.

I hesitate, ready to jump in and help her but Reed calls me back. "Come one, we've got to go!"

Farrah shoots the last one in the chest and runs toward us when a deafening ring rips through the air. She halts mid step, and my heart sinks as a small red dot blooms on her forehead.

"Farrah!" I shout horrified, as she collapses to the floor. "No!"

"Run!" Reed fires his gun at the sprawled-out Boots.

I dart across the floor, sliding to the entrance of the Tube, bullets raining on the ground behind me, adrenaline ringing in my ears. I reach for the keypad, as Reed empties his clip. There's one destination: *Lobby*. It's the same word Sio used. That must be the top. I punch the button, and the doors shut, metal colliding with the reinforced glass in sparks.

We glare down at the men as we slowly rise. Then they're gone.

Reed speaks first. "Are you okay?"

I nod but clench my fists behind my back to hide their trembling. I can't fall apart now, not when we're so close.

It shouldn't have happened like that. Farrah deserved more. We all did.

"Are you sure you want to do this?" His question pulls me back to full attention. Sensing my confusion he adds, "Go outside? What if Sio was telling the truth?"

I think back to our relationship throughout the years. She was always so much tougher on me than was warranted. Always undermining me. Marking me down. Maybe it was her way of protecting me, but I can't know that for certain.

"There's only one way to find out."

I look up at the glass ceiling of the Tube; the light is approaching.

With a deep breath I gather the courage to ask the question that has been gnawing at me. "Do you think she loved me?"

Reed's expression is gentle. "I think love defies logic and reason. People will go to crazy lengths to protect the ones they care about, even if it means pushing them away."

He holds my eyes in his, and I realize he's not just talking about Sio. For the first time, I notice a flicker in his gaze, the way the grays seem to swirl with emotion. He leans in, unspoken words lingering on his parted lips.

The Tube slows.

"This is it," I whisper.

Before I know it, his lips are on mine. An unexpected warm sensation rises in the deepest part of me. Growing, and spreading like a wildfire, engulfing me.

Our lips part.

"I don't want to live with any more regrets." His breath is hot as it brushes over my skin, gently forcing the corners of my mouth into a smile. "Whatever we find up there, we'll face it together," he reassures me. "It's still you and me against the world, like always."

The Tube comes to a gentle stop. I look back up, ready for the sunlight to warm my skin. I'm afraid to look directly into it, but I don't want to miss it. That's when I see the bulbs.

"Reed." My voice cracks. "We're still inside."

The doors open.

Boots are waiting, weapons aimed.

Reed spins in front of me just as they pull their triggers.

My blood-curdling scream pierces the air as Reed crashes into me, shielding me against the side glass of the Tube, away from the direct line of fire.

I feel nothing. I am numb, hands frantically groping for the warm blood, searching for the hole in my flesh. But I find nothing, my shirt intact.

Reed's eyes are locked on mine, filled with concern. Time has stopped; the Boots are frozen in place, as am I. Relief floods Reed's face as he realizes I'm okay. A slow smile spreads across his lips but is soon followed by a thin stream of blood trickling from his mouth. Reed's eyebrows knit together in confusion at my horrified expression. Instinctively, I run my hand along his back, and it returns soaked in blood. Reed drops to one knee.

"No!" I hear my screams this time from outside myself. I drag him deeper into the Tube, pushing him against the glass and holding onto him for dear life, my mouth pressed to his head. "Please Reed, stay with me, I can't lose you!"

Boots approach.

"Stay back!"

"Look at me," Reed whispers.

But I don't want to hear his goodbye, I can't.

"Look at me, Ev," he says, harsher now.

I tilt my head downward, tears streaming and falling onto his face.

"I love you Ever, I always have."

The words barely leave his lips when the Boots march in and pull me from him.

"No!"

I'm dragged out of the Tube, thrashing and kicking wildly like something feral. Yanking one of the Boots' weapons from their side in a frenzy, I aim it at the lights above us, sending sparks everywhere, flames dancing in the now darkness.

I swing at the man holding me, sending him crashing clear across the room, landing hard enough to crack bone.

In a blur of motion, I shoot at each of the others, shoulders, arms, legs, debilitating them, the closest unarmed man backs away hands raised. With his own gun, I strike him unconscious for good measure and sprint back to Reed. Mercifully, he's still breathing but losing a lot of blood. I lift him up, his back is littered with bullet holes. His healing ability likely saved his life, but such severe injuries wouldn't heal quickly. I wrap his arm over my shoulders; he manages to get to his feet and moves his legs along with mine.

We make it down a dark tunnel across from the Tube and I veer sharply left into what I pray is salvation.

My stomach drops as we're confronted with a dark wall straight ahead. A dead end.

I desperately scan the hall, trying to blink away the white spots in the center of my vision. After several attempts, one spot remains, and I realize it's light filtering through the wall. It's a door. We hurry towards it and Reed groans as we burst through. I am immediately blinded by the brightness. The door shuts behind us with a click, and its edges immediately vanish and seal, blending seamlessly into the wall.

I lift my hand to shade my eyes, the bright light painful after the darkness. Through my fingers I catch sight of the most beautiful view I have ever seen. A city unfolds ahead through breathtaking panoramic windows. A vision more vivid than I could have ever imagined, surpassing my wildest dreams. The skies are a brilliant blue as far as the eye can see. Tall glass structures pierce the skyline, their reflective facades shimmering vibrant shades of azure. Distant mountains provide an awe-inspiring backdrop, while streets weave through the landscape like ribbons, bustling with life and colorful activity.

"Reed, we made it!"

Something tight in my chest eases. I shake my head, stunned, the sight mending some jagged piece of my soul. None of it was true. The Chairman's lies about the earth being ravaged by the Forms, Sio's warnings about it being on fire – this view was proof. Out there, outside Helix Colony, the world was thriving. Just a few more feet, through the massive picture window doors, and we would be out of this nightmare. We made it.

"Reed–" I didn't realize he had left my side. Then I take in our surroundings for the first time, the large vacant space with impeccably polished floors. A desk sits off center with the emblem Helix Co. etched into its surface. The chair behind it is still rotating slightly, clearly recently vacated. I grip the gun I just seized, ready for the person who occupied it.

But we appear to be alone. Reed stares at small flickering projections along the opposite walls of the room, displaying haggard looking men and women with metallic body parts speaking directly at us. The projections must be glitching because there's no sound. But I don't need to hear what they're saying to understand the message. The images quickly shift to the same men and women with youthful skin, bright smiles and, most importantly, real body parts.

What's more, I recognize each one of them, they are images of past Saviors.

There's a larger screen suspended from the ceiling behind the desk. There's no sound coming from it either, and what I see leaves me utterly baffled. There is a man on the screen, appearing unnerved as he speaks. Sitting behind a large table he wears a dark uniform, papers in his hands, and an image projected behind him of paved roads with large structures lining them.

The signal cuts to crowds of people standing in long lines. Then switches to images of large, deserted edifices, rows of long shelves in disarray within, metal carts toppled over, empty boxes strewn about. Next, the scene shifts to a place packed with protruding metal frameworks, engulfed in flames.

I look back to the window, the view still serene. Reed is behind me now, watching the screen in horror. "I don't understand."

I couldn't believe it, was this some last-ditch effort at fear-mongering? The doors were right there, we could see outside.

"It's another scare tactic. We made it Reed, we just need to walk through those doors."

He looks at me with uncertainty, then takes a deep breath, his piercing gaze softening as he says, "Okay. I'll follow you anywhere."

The weight of his words hangs in the air, and I feel a lump forming in my throat. I reach out and grasp his hand, his unwavering trust and loyalty igniting a warmth in my chest. I squeeze gently, and a smile tugs at my lips.

"Then let's go."

Reed advances to the doors as I take one last look at the screen, at the final, horrific attempt at brainwashing. Whatever this place was, the evils it carried out, I would never understand it.

As I turn, I catch sight of a glass sign adjacent to the desk with the words: *You Are Here* next to *Level 1: Lobby*.

For a moment I take in the place we called home. This hell, this maze, this *corporation*, as Sio called it, the mystery finally uncovered. Each level is identified: *Research and Development, Marketing, Sales, Records, Pharmacy, Human Resources*. Further down the list I recognize the nightmarish floors we've just escaped: *Blood Bank, Surgical Ward, Hydroponics, Cryostorage* and finally, *Level 23: The Orchard*.

The irony of it all almost makes me chuckle. The images and projections we've been shown our entire lives – the idyllic, lush orchards, laden with colorful blossoms and ripe fruit – were simply a mirror. A reflection of our real purpose. The truth was right in front of us the entire time. We were grown and raised for harvesting.

A glint of light on the glass catches my eye, and my stomach clenches. It's a gun. Before I can react, before I can even move, it fires. Agonizing pain tears through my back and pierces my abdomen. The sign in front of me shatters and I collapse to my knees, turning just in time to see two Boots pull a needle from Reed's neck and drag him backwards in the direction of the seamless door. With his last conscious breath Reed croaks, "Go!"

With every effort, I rise, lifting my gun and shooting at the Boots. But they're too fast and I'm hit again, this time in the shoulder and I stumble back colliding with the windows. There has to be someone outside who has seen us. Someone who will come help.

"Asset secured," one of the Boots reports into a comms system.

"Initiate lockdown."

An echoing groan reverberates through the lobby as a solid titanium panel begins to descend over the wall. I stagger towards them, body screaming in pain, firing at will as they slide through the door and out of sight. I continue to shoot, but the bullets just ricochet, and then I'm out. The wall is now sealed shut, stretching across the length of the lobby.

"Reed!" I cry out, despair taking hold. We were so close, we're at the top. I stare at the wall, the weight of our journey crashing down on me. I promise to come back for him, for Skye, for all our fallen friends. I'll get help on the outside, and I'll come back.

I turn toward the window, and to my horror it's an entirely different view. Now a vast forest with a canopy of trees whose branches intertwine and tangle with one another. I approach slowly, dumbfounded, my eyes fixed on a tiny glittering speck.

As I reach the window, the familiar light refraction of a glitch comes into focus. I shake my head, broken, trying to refute the reality of what's in front of me. I slam my fist into the window. The view abruptly shifts to a beach. Rage floods through me and I punch again, knuckles aching. The scene changes to snowy mountaintops.

It was never a window, just another projection. I'm still trapped inside. And now completely alone.

I strike the projection once more, pain shooting through my hand as it transitions to a new cityscape. The tears that had been welling up inside me finally fall, and I sag to the ground. I'm going to bleed out and die here, never having seen the sun.

I place a bloody hand on the exit wound in my abdomen. I'm surprised to feel only a dull pain. Even the throbbing in my shoulder has subsided. I lift my shirt to see a brown scar where the bullet had torn through muscle. Did I have hidden healing abilities? Abilities that had never been tested? How could they when I've never truly been hurt before? Realization dawns on me – something Sio had said. She made me everlasting. Was this part of it?

I had survived too much. I couldn't give up now. I had to get up, for Ira, for all the Saviors who never had the chance. My fight isn't over. Liberation is on the other side of those doors.

There's a retinal display next to the exit, I scan my eye.

It won't open. Did the Keeper not have clearance? Panic rises in my chest.

I try again, still nothing.

This can't be all there is. It's not over. I slam the butt of the gun on the doors, the image flickering with each impact. I pound relentlessly, channeling all my strength. A small splinter appears, and I don't stop, heaving with each blow, the scenery cycling through landscapes.

A crack begins to spider out and the image flashes to a hazy gray across the panoramic window projection. I pause briefly, the adrenaline pulsing in my ears so loudly I almost miss the drumming on the other side. I press my ear to the fracture and hear a droning, grating noise that grows louder. There's something outside the door. Something big. The glass shudders violently, and I jump out of the way just as an enormous transporter bursts through, shattering it to pieces and crashing into the reinforced titanium wall across the lobby.

I've never seen anything like it, but I have no time to process the shock as bodies, dozens of them, rush in scrambling over each other through the crumbling entrance.

I am frozen in place; the horde pushes forward – metal body parts colliding, faces contorted in desperate fear and rage. They are running for their lives. *In*to the Helix

I'm sent sprawling and from the ground, I catch sight of a blazing light filtering through the jumble of bodies. I scurry toward it, toward a small gap in the mass of steel and flesh Forms.

Once through, I collapse onto my hands and knees, breathless and trembling. Heat sears my skin and smoke assaults my lungs, but there's something else. Soft, textured blades that tickle my fingers. Grass.

I am on the Surface.

Air gushes from my lungs, and I almost cry. I'm free.

I lift my head to stand but instead of relief, a wave of panic and dread crashes over me. Aside from the small patch of yellowing green I landed on, the rest of the world appears to be an endless gray. I look to the sky, desperate for just one glimpse of what I'd hoped for my entire life. In the distance, through the ashen air, I can just make out the silhouettes of jagged, skeletal skyscrapers. Hissing curls of smoke writhe all around them, and I realize… I have clawed my way out from the darkness of Helix, only to find there is no sun here. It remains concealed beyond a fuming haze.

The wave of bodies continues to surge forward like an unstoppable force, pummeling into me with no regard.

"What's going on?!" My voice comes out strangled as I stumble, pushing against the current of the wild-eyed mob.

"We have to get inside! We're going to die!" a man shouts as he shoves past me.

"What? What happened?" But he is swept up in the crowd advancing through the hole before I can get an answer.

I push forward through the throng, distancing myself from the Helix, every step feeling heavier than the last, weighed down with uncertainty.

"What happened here?" I shout, coughing through the charred air, hoping someone will answer me amidst the chaos.

A frantic older woman collides into me, a child clutched in her arms, his bare metallic foot glinting under her elbow.

"Please," I beg. "Can you tell me what happened? Why is everything in ruins?"

She stares at me in disbelief, a chain around her neck bearing a symbol I don't understand. "We're being punished."

"Punished? By who?"

"The wrath of Mother Nature," she replies, her voice trembling. "We're no match for her fury."

I look around helplessly, my surroundings a war zone.

The woman's eyes soften with a moment of compassion. "Come with us child, at least you'll have a chance."

My mind races, have I made a grave mistake? Did I just escape one nightmare and step into another? These Forms – no, these *people* – are desperately fleeing the Surface. Sio was right.

But I can't go back, I know what waits for me down there.

I shake my head, my decision resolute.

Suddenly an explosion rocks the far right side of the Helix. The façade collapses into rubble, sending dust and debris into the air. The woman runs past me, panic flashing in her eyes, risking everything to get inside before the opening caves in. There are already people trapped under the wreckage. My heart pounds in my chest.

Not thirty seconds later, another blast detonates, this one closer. The walls crumble, concrete chunks raining down. There's no safety here.

I need to move, and fast.

The ground shakes violently beneath me, accompanied by a blinding white light and a deafening bang that echoes in my ears. The force of the blast hurls me forward, my body slamming into the ground.

Pain reverberates through me. The screams of the injured and dying pierce the air, mixing with the smoke and dust. The Helix is completely buried in debris, impenetrable. Every instinct screams at me to flee, but where can I go?

I slowly roll onto my back, the movement agonizing. With a final, determined breath, I rise, driven by one primal urge. Survival at all costs.

I have made it out, and I will endure. Whatever awaits, I am free.

I begin to move, navigating through the debris, into the smoke and ash, towards the unknown.

ACKNOWLEDGMENTS

A big shout out to my kids for their impeccable timing: I completed my first draft on my first child's due date, the second draft on my second's, and the manuscript edit on my youngest's. Clearly, I work best with deadlines – especially theirs.

Jonathan Johnson, thank you for encouraging me to pursue this dream, for your steadfast support, and for your incessant "Are you done yet?"– This is only the beginning. You are the water to my roots, and because of you, this orchard bloomed. Your endless patience with my ramblings about plot twists and character arcs, and your confidence in me kept the keys clicking and clacking.

Amy Rivera, thank you for reading my roughhhhhhhh draft and showing the excitement that made me think I could do this. Also, thank you for flying back from vacation to babysit so I could go pitch The Final Orchard.

A colossal thank you to Gemma Creffield and the entire Angry Robot team. Gemma, your belief in me and your sharp editorial eye transformed a chaotic manuscript into something worthy of print. Your willingness to take a chance on me has meant the world, and I'm forever grateful for your faith in this book. A special thanks to Dan Hanks, your insightful feedback and advice played a crucial role in shaping the core of this book. My gratitude to Caroline Lambe and Amy Portsmouth for showcasing this book in its finest light for its debut. And to Desola Coker, for getting it across the line.

My thanks to John Baker for being so enthusiastic about my work and for expertly guiding me through the stages of publishing. Additionally, thank you to Bell Lomax Moreton for being an inspiring group I am delighted to be included in.

To my parents, who have always been my biggest fans. Your love and motivation sowed the seeds for this entire journey.

Thank you, Dalissa, for all your conspiracy theories and TV show recommendations that sparked new ideas. Thank you Lisa Zheng for Ever. And to all my family and friends, your enthusiasm and support have been invaluable.

Thank you to the incredible workshopping group of badass SFF female writers, affectionately named Bitches and Pitches, for your help in crafting a great query.

A heartfelt thank you to Ness Brown, Patricia Raybon, and Molly Crowe for the time you put into reading The Final Orchard. Your thoughtful words mean the world to me. Thank you.

And finally, to the readers who've taken a chance on this book. Your curiosity and imagination breathe life into these pages, and for that, I am eternally grateful.

ABOUT THE AUTHOR

CJ Rivera is an adult dystopian author exploring the depths of dark futures and stark realities. Before diving into speculative fiction, Rivera enjoyed a successful career as a Producer, creating captivating content for media giants such as NBC Universal, as well as producing for large-scale international events. She resides in Maryland with her family and a thriving hydroponic garden.